Bodies by Design

The 2nd Jasmine Frame novel

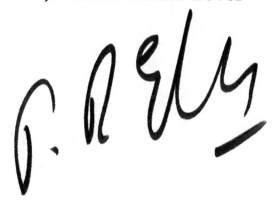

ALSO BY P R ELLIS

JASMINE FRAME

PAINTED LADIES

Bodies by Design

The 2nd Jasmine Frame novel

P R Ellis

Bodies by Design
First published in Great Britain by Ellifont, 2015

Ellifont, Woodside House, Bridge Street, Leominster HR6 8DZ
www.ellifont.wordpress.com

British Library Cataloguing in Publication Data.
A catalogue record for this book is available from the British Library.

ISBN 978-0-9933647-0-9 Print edition
ISBN 978-0-9933647-1-6 eBook edition

Printed and bound by CPI Group (UK) Ltd, Croydon, CR0 4YY

This book is a work of fiction. All names, characters, places and events are either a product of the author's fertile imagination or are used fictitiously. Any resemblance to actual events, places or people (living or dead) is purely coincidental.

to Lou – for everything

PROLOGUE

Be ready@3. The slim, dark-haired girl read the message on the screen of her smartphone. She had been expecting it and, brief as it was, it told her all she needed to know. It was two-thirty now, so she had half an hour to get ready – plenty of time.

She slid off the king-size bed. It dominated the small studio flat and left no room for chairs, so it doubled as a place for relaxation as well as sleeping - and more. Now it had to be made ready for her guest. She pulled the duvet off, folded and rolled it as tight as possible, then stuffed it on top of the wardrobe, squashed against the sloping ceiling. The four pillows were stacked between her chest of drawers and the wardrobe. Then she stripped off the sheet, rolled it up tightly and pushed it between the pillows. The mattress was revealed with its smooth rubber cover sheet; the steel bars of the head and footboard looked menacingly like a cage.

She pulled open the bottom drawer of the chest and selected the items required. A pair of ankle restraints, two wrist cuffs and a ball gag. She clipped the ankle restraints around the vertical bars at the ends of the footboard and the handcuffs to the matching bars on the headboard. The gag was placed on the mattress ready for use.

The girl walked around the bed and looked out through the venetian blinds at the backyard of the building. As she expected, the gravelled car park area was empty at this time of day. She pulled on the cord to close the blinds. She didn't want anyone climbing the stairs to be able to see in. Only the dormer window at the front of the room let in light. She lit a candle and placed it on the small drop-side dining table beside three bottles of spirits - she or her guests occasionally enjoyed a drink. The candle added a bit of atmosphere and gave off a sweet flowery smell that she hoped her guest would like. She stepped into the small inner hallway, turned the front door knob and pressed the button to *keep the latch open. Now her guest would be able to enter unhindered.*

The girl returned to the main room, leaving the internal door open, and stood by the bed. She glanced at the time on her phone. 14.45. Still time to wait. She sat on the edge of the mattress, knees together, back straight. Her heart was beating faster than usual and she felt nervous. It was always the same before one of her guests arrived, but today there was an extra degree of anticipation. There was something important she had to say and she wasn't sure how her news would be received. Still, it had to be said.

14.50. Time to get ready. She didn't want the anxiety of not being prepared. She stood up and pulled her t-shirt over her head and dropped her skirt to the floor. Reaching behind her back she unclipped her bra. The cups loosened and fell from her breasts. She tugged on her knickers, pulled them down her smooth legs and stepped out of them. Naked, she gathered up her clothes and stuffed them in the wardrobe.

The rubber sheet was cool against her skin. She shuffled across so her bottom was right in the middle of the mattress, stretched her left leg out and leaned forward to fasten the leather cuff around her ankle. It snapped shut, grasping her ankle tightly. She stretched her right leg to the other corner of the bed and fastened that ankle in the same way. Her legs made a wide V. In the long mirror on the wall at the end of the bed she could see the image of herself through the bars of the footboard. Her nakedness and the restraints gave her a familiar thrill. She lay back, stretching out her left hand to the headboard and grasped the wrist cuff. Twisting, she reached with her right hand to complete the fastening around her left wrist. It locked with a sharp click.

She lay back and slipped her right hand into its cuff but did not press it against the mattress to lock it. Three limbs were immobile, spread wide, exposed and vulnerable. Her guest would want her fully restrained, but she was reluctant to make the final commitment and lock her one spare hand, just in case they failed to arrive. With one hand free she could release herself. With both

2

wrists locked she was trapped. Her guest would expect her to be gagged too, but the ball gag remained by her side unused. Today, she needed to be able to speak.

Closing her eyes, she waited, her heart still thumping. Perhaps this would be the last time she did this - offering herself as if as a sacrifice for another's pleasure. She hoped she wouldn't have to do it again despite the thrill and arousal it gave her. She wanted to get on with her life, to actually be someone.

The resounding clank of leather-soled shoes on steel announced the arrival of a visitor, presumably the one she expected, on the stairs. The footsteps approached, then stopped. The visitor was on the landing outside the front door. The door creaked softly as it was opened...

1

WEDNESDAY

Stakeouts weren't her favourite job. When she had been a police officer, Jasmine had always preferred the excitement of interviewing witnesses and suspects or poring over forensic reports. It was, therefore, ironic that her new job as a private eye involved sitting in her car for hours and hours on surveillance. She arched her back and shuffled her bottom on the driver's seat, but nothing could ease the stiffness and soreness of sitting still for such a long time. That, and the nausea that had been coming and going for weeks now.

She had known what to expect when she took this job, of course, and dressed appropriately. It was summer, after all, so a pale blue vest top and short indigo cotton skirt with her little blue pumps should have been the most comfortable outfit. Actually, it had turned out wet. She had to keep turning the ignition of her old Fiesta on to let the wipers sweep the raindrops from the windscreen. Was she draining the battery? Getting stuck here would be embarrassing as well as inconvenient, but she needed a clear view for shots with her camera with its long lens.

Her head itched and she scratched underneath the edge of the dark brown wig. It was stupid wearing a wig in this warm, humid weather, but she needed the disguise. Her short blonde bob was too much of a giveaway, her face too familiar from appearances in the newspapers, on TV and on internet news sites. It was all DCI Sloane's fault, bloody man. If he hadn't hailed Jasmine a heroine for getting the "tranny killer" caught, she wouldn't have been outed as "The Transsexual Private Eye".

For two or three weeks there had been reporters and cameras every time she went out of her flat, until other stories pushed her off the front pages. At least the fame and the praise of the Kintbridge police had helped her get some jobs, like this one, for the Fraud Investigation Service working for the Department of Work and Pensions but she still had to wear the long wig to prevent herself being identified by passers-by.

She glanced at her watch. It was gone five; she wished she could give up, but she couldn't, not yet. A movement at the edge of her vision jolted her back to her task. Damn, her concentration had gone again. It was a wonder the subject hadn't come out, got in his car and driven off while she was letting her thoughts wander. Thankfully that hadn't happened. There he was in the road beside his car, a big four-by-four, one of the cheaper ones, but she'd missed him coming out of the terraced house. He had his crutch. Was he limping? He was just standing there, his hand fiddling in a pocket, pulling out a key, opening the car door.

Jasmine sank down while raising the camera to her eye. She peered through the viewfinder, choosing her shot. Would the picture show whether he was relying on the crutch for support? Did he need it? Was he the benefits cheat the FIS suspected? Was he going to get in and drive off? Jasmine clicked off a few shots.

The subject, a middle-aged man with greying brown hair wearing old jeans and a battered sweatshirt, reached inside the car and withdrew a package. He closed the door. He began to move with difficulty around the bonnet back towards the pavement. Good, he wasn't going to drive off, not yet anyway. Jasmine took a few more pictures. He paused, looked up the road. Jasmine wondered whether he had noticed her but he was staring, not at her but at something on the pavement opposite. He began to walk quickly, almost breaking into a run, his crutch not performing any role at all

High pitched cries finally penetrated Jasmine's consciousness.

'Fire! Help!'

Jasmine looked out of her side window. Standing on the kerb opposite was a young woman with wavy brown hair wearing denim micro shorts and a cut-off vest. She was shouting.

Jasmine dropped the camera onto the passenger seat, grabbed her shoulder bag and opened the car door.

'What's the matter?' she called, getting out.

'There's a fire! Upstairs!' The girl ran towards her just as Jasmine's subject arrived puffing and leaning on his crutch. The girl pointed to the top floor of one of the Edwardian terraced houses. 'I heard the alarm going off,' she added.

Jasmine looked up. Thin wisps of dark smoke rose into the sky from a small dormer window.

'Is there anyone up there?'

'Xristal. Oh my God, I think she might be trapped!' The girl shivered.

'Show me the way!' Jasmine's training took over and she spoke firmly. She urged the girl back towards the house, hurrying her along. The subject followed more slowly.

There were two doors in the front porch. The right one was open. The girl led Jasmine into a dark hallway, through a small kitchen and out into a gravelled backyard. A steel staircase rose to the upper floors. The smoke alarm's whine was clearly audible.

'Do you have a phone?' Jasmine asked the girl.

'Yes.'

'Well, dial 999 and get the fire service here as quick as you can!' Jasmine ran up the staircase. Two short flights brought her to a narrow landing and a door to the first floor flat. Two more flights and she stood at the door to the top flat. The alarm was deafening.

Before her was an old wooden front door, half glazed with patterned translucent glass. Jasmine turned the handle. Locked. The door felt quite solid. It wasn't going to give with a slight shove. How could she get in? There was a window on her left, but it was shut. No smoke escaped. The blinds were closed so

7

she couldn't see anything inside. It would have to be the door. She worried that the fire would flare up if she smashed the glass and let in fresh air but Xristal was in there still. She would be unconscious. Just two lungfuls of smoke was enough to knock you out. A third killed you.

How could she break the glass in the door? Use an elbow? She had no sleeve to protect her. There was half a brick lying on the landing, probably used to prop the door open. She picked it up, took a firm grip and smashed it against the bottom left corner of the window.. The glass shattered. Most of the glass fell inwards but some fell at her feet and small shards flew passed her face. She'd forgotten to protect her eyes. At least it wasn't armoured or wired glass. She had access. The alarm sounded even louder. She used the brick to knock off a couple of jagged edges then, with care, reached through the hole. She felt for the handle of the lock, turned it, withdrew her hand and pushed the door open.

She found herself in a small hallway with closed doors to the right and the left. A few tendrils of smoke curled out of the top of the door on her left. Enough to set off the smoke alarm fixed to the middle of the ceiling. Jasmine grasped the handle of the door into the flat, and paused. This was it. What would happen when she opened it? A handful of tissues from her shoulder bag covering her mouth would have to do as a mask. She pulled the door open.

The smell hit her like a hammer in the face. Acrid, sharp, but also reminiscent of cooking - of overcooked, burnt fat. The air was warm and had a sticky feel, but it was not hot. The fire must have died. Nevertheless, the old adage held – where there was smoke there was or had been fire. Jasmine stepped into the room, cast her eyes quickly around it with practised skill, wary of flames. She took in the kitchen area with a sink and neatly-piled, clean crockery, a cooker alongside, on her right a small dining table with bottles on it, and two dining chairs. On the far side of the room there was a wardrobe and chest of drawers, but filling the entire centre of the room was a huge metal-framed bed. Its incongruity in such a small flat distracted her briefly, but the smoke wasn't thick enough to prevent her seeing what was on the bed.

It was meaningless for a moment, until her brain interpreted the image. It looked like there had been a bonfire in the middle of the mattress; a blackened heap of - something. Then, with mounting horror, she saw pale arms and legs, like the disconnected limbs of a mannequin, and recognised them for what they were – the unburnt limbs sticking out of the charred torso,. She moved closer to the bed and saw a head. Dark, scorched hair and a white face, eyes open - staring, unseeing.

The smell and the realisation of what she was looking at made Jasmine's stomach churn. She swallowed, tasted the acidic, fatty smoke in her mouth, gagged, swallowed again, recovered – for now. She dared not move any closer in case she lost the delicate control she had over her guts and vomited over the scene, but she forced herself to look to try to interpret what was before her eyes.

Jasmine presumed the body was that of the woman the girl in the ground floor flat had referred to. She'd called her Xristal. What had happened to her? Jasmine recalled pictures claiming to be of cases of spontaneous combustion. The scene before her seemed similar – bodies with the torso consumed by fire but the limbs and head almost unaffected. She had read something about the wick effect, the fat in the body melting to fuel the flames but the fire dying as the supply of fat ran out.

She heard a chorus of sirens adding a discordant harmony to the continued wail of the smoke alarm. Moments later came the rumble of a heavy vehicle manoeuvring below. Then, heavy boots clanged on the stairs. Jasmine turned to face the entrance. Two firefighters in full gear, helmets and masks over their faces, entered. One of them pulled the breathing apparatus from over his mouth.

'Who are you?' he shouted over the noise of the smoke alarm.

'Jasmine Frame, detective. I broke in to see if there was

anyone inside.'

'Police?'

'No.' Not anymore, she considered adding.

'You'd better leave. The fire appears to have died down but it could flare up again now we're letting in fresh air.'

'I think it was only the victim that was on fire,' Jasmine said pointing to the body on the bed. 'Try not to disturb anything. This could be a crime scene.'

'We understand, but now please leave so we can make sure it's safe.' The first firefighter pushed past her and moved around the bed while the other spoke into his radio. Jasmine backed into the hallway and out onto the top of the stairs. She took a deep breath and coughed, acrid smoke-flavoured phlegm filling her mouth. She spat it out over the railings. Another breath allowed fresh air to enter her lungs fully. The air tasted sweet and refreshing after the stench inside the flat. Jasmine felt light-headed and leaned against the metal safety barrier.

'Are you alright, miss?'

Jasmine looked up to see a young police constable at the top of the stairs. She took in another large gulp of air and stood up straight.

'Yes, thanks, I'm fine. There's a body in there, so you had better cordon off this area, get back-up and call out Soco.'

'My partner's doing that. Who are you?' The young police officer tried to look authoritative.

Jasmine dug in her bag for her private investigator's ID and flashed it at him.

'Jasmine Frame, Investigator. A girl from the ground floor flat said there might be someone up here, so I broke in and found the body. I'll have a statement to make to the investigating officer as the fire service may contaminate the incident scene.'

It took a few moments for the officer to take in all that Jasmine had said. Then his manner changed. He relaxed a little and looked at Jasmine with something like respect.

'I see. Was the fire an accident?'

'I don't know, but it's odd. Only the body has burned.'

His face turned pale. 'You mean, like spontaneous combustion?'

'It looks like that, but there's no such thing.' Jasmine was trying to make herself think rationally, while all the time her mind was filled with the stench and image of the burned body and the noise of the alarm. The smell she now realised was the result of the girl's body cooking in its own juices and the thought made her shudder. She retched and clamped her hand to her mouth, thankful that she hadn't eaten anything other than a couple of biscuits during her day of surveillance.

'Perhaps you should come downstairs, miss,' the young PC said, reaching out for her elbow. Jasmine nodded, afraid to move her hand from her mouth.

They descended slowly, the police officer holding Jasmine's arm to steady her. She was surprised how sick and faint she felt. It wasn't the first time she'd seen a body, not even a burned one. They paused at the first floor as three more firefighters bustled up the stairs, one a woman, Jasmine noted. At the bottom of the stairs was the girl who had raised the alarm. She looked anxiously at Jasmine.

'Is she OK? Xristal?'

'I don't think you should be here, miss," the police officer said. The girl gave him a fierce look then turned back to Jasmine.

'Is she?"

'Was Xristal a friend of yours?' Jasmine said, swallowing and making a determined effort to act as if she was in charge.

'Sort of. Hadn't known her long.'

'What's your name?'

'Tilly.'

'Well, Tilly, she's not OK. If it was Xristal who was in the flat, then I'm afraid to say she's dead.'

Tilly covered her face with both hands and began to cry. A firefighter came down the stairs.

'Move away please. This is the Incident Zone. Please move

back, away from the building.'

The police officer guided Jasmine and Tilly towards the lane that ran behind the row of houses. They edged past the two fire appliances that almost filled the width of the lane. Another police officer was cordoning off the area. A Ford Mondeo drew up and a tall, broad-shouldered man with black hair got out. He walked towards them.

'Tom!' Jasmine called out. DS Tom Shepherd stopped with a confused look on his face.

'Jasmine?'

'Yes, of course.'

'I didn't recognise you. The hair...'

Jasmine had forgotten her wig. She tugged it off and shook her blonde hair free.

'Sorry, I forgot I was wearing that thing.'

'Why...?'

'To stop people recognising me. Thanks to Sloane I'm still a bit of a celebrity. I couldn't work if people recognised me all the time.' She shoved the wig into her bag.

'No, I meant, why are you here?'

'Oh. By accident really. I was on a job out in the road.'

'A job?'

'Yes, you know. Watching someone.'

Tom looked her up and down.

'You don't dress up for work then?'

Jasmine looked down at herself, seeing her skimpy top and short skirt through Tom's police protocol eyes.

'I wore what I thought would be comfortable for sitting in a car all day.'

'Hmm. OK. Who's this?' He nodded at Tilly.

'This is Tilly. She raised the alarm. I went up to the top flat, broke in and found...and found...' The smell and taste returned sickeningly to her mouth.

'A body?' Tom offered.

'Yes.' Jasmine was about to add, a burned body, but recalled that Tilly was by her side.

'Do we know who it is?'

'It's probably a girl called Xristal ... uh,' she looked at Tilly for help.

'Xristal Newman,' Tilly said, stifling a sob. Tom had his pocket book out.

'How do you spell that?'

'She spelt it with an X; X-r-i-s-t-a-l,' Tilly said between sobs. Hearing the name spelt out made Jasmine doubt that it was the name she was born with. It sounded like an affectation.

DS Shepherd turned to the police officer. 'Call HQ and get the pathologist here a.s.a.p. Right, let's see what's happening.' He strode off towards the fire engines. Jasmine ran after him.

'You can't go back in there!' one of the police officers called out. Jasmine ignored him. She caught up with Tom and followed him into the car park and towards the stairs. The monotonous wail of the smoke alarm stopped suddenly. The relative silence felt like an absence.

'What are you doing, Jas?' Tom said, turning towards her.

'I'm going to examine the scene of the incident.'

'But you're not a police officer, Jas!'

'That's not something I can forget, Tom, but I was the first on the scene. I saw it before the fire service started trampling all over it. I can tell you if anything has been changed.' Jasmine watched various expressions pass across Tom's face. At last he came to a decision.

'OK, but don't touch anything.'

'Of course not.'

Tom led the way up the stairs, his heavy police shoes making the metal treads vibrate. They met a firefighter coming down.

'Is the fire out?' Tom asked, flashing his ID.

'Yes. Looks like it. We're keeping an eye on it but it looks safe now. It'll interest you guys.' He carried on downwards.

'Sounds exciting,' Tom said, continuing the climb. That wasn't quite how Jasmine viewed it. She wasn't sure she wanted to face that sight and smell again, but the thrill of being on an investigation outweighed the nausea she felt. A couple more firefighters emerged from the top floor flat and squeezed passed them. As Tom and Jasmine entered, the last two firefighters were standing in the hall, their breathing masks dangling from their helmets.

'Hi, I'm DS Shepherd. I'm in charge of the investigation, until further notice.' He waved his ID with practised authority.

'Well, it's certainly one for you,' one of the firefighters said.

'There's a body?'

'Just the one.'

'And the fire's out?'

'Yes, you can go in. We'll hang around to make sure and complete our investigation. There was only one site of the fire.' The firefighter led Tom and Jasmine into the main room. The smoke had cleared, but the smell was still almost as strong. Jasmine felt herself beginning to retch again. She clenched her jaw, determined not to be sick. Tom hesitated just inside the door.

'Not nice,' he muttered. Jasmine squeezed past him so she could look at the charred remains and the peculiar arrangement of limbs.

'Do you know the cause of the fire?' she asked.

'There's the stump of a candle beside the body,' the firefighter said, 'and there must have been an accelerant, probably alcohol. There's an empty bottle there.' He pointed to the table. One empty bottle stood apart from the fuller ones. Jasmine bent to see what it was – vodka.

'Why is the body so badly burned while the rest of the flat is practically untouched?' Tom asked, shaking his head at the sight before him.

'The burning alcohol burnt through the skin and melted the subcutaneous fat,' the firefighter explained, 'but there's barely anything flammable on the bed – the victim was naked, there are no bedclothes and it's a sprung mattress and steel frame so there was little else to fuel the flames. The body has probably been smouldering for some time, and with the door closed the smoke only just built up enough to set off the smoke alarm a short time ago.'

'Was the door closed, Jas?'

'Yes. When I broke in through the front door there was just a little smoke coming through the cracks.'

'So, the girl must have been asleep, unconscious or dead when the fire started.'

The firefighter shook his head. 'Not asleep. The initial shock of the burning alcohol would have woken her up.'

'Unless she was drugged?' Jasmine suggested.

'That's a possibility,' Tom agreed.

'She looks almost as if she's been laid out.' Jasmine indicated the star pattern of legs, arms and head.

'Do you mean, like in some kind of ritual?'

Jasmine stroked her cheek, unsure what she meant.

'I don't know, but it looks like a deliberate killing and not an accident or suicide.'

'Yeah, I can't see how she could have done this to herself,' the firefighter said, backing away. 'I'll leave you while I make my report.'

'Let's take a look around, Jas. I suppose we need a formal identification that the body is this Xristal girl. But take care. Soco will be here soon in all their gear.'

Tom remained staring at the body while Jasmine moved slowly and carefully around the bed to look on top of the chest of drawers. There was the usual clutter of bits and pieces – cosmetics, a few coins, tissues, a photograph.

The early evening light through the window illuminated the small photo that lay flat on the chest. Jasmine examined it. It showed two young women in bikinis, arm in arm on a sandy beach in summer sunshine. Both girls wore bikini tops that barely covered their firm breasts, although their bikini bottoms were more substantial. One was slim and dark-haired – Xristal? The other was a good eight inches taller and stockier with blonde hair piled high and spilling over her shoulder. She had huge breasts. To Jasmine she appeared top heavy, with her narrow waist and hips.

Jasmine rummaged in her bag for her smartphone, swiped it on and held it above the photo. She pressed a finger against the screen. There was the anachronistic click. She looked at the picture, then repeated the process.

'What are you doing?' Tom asked.

'There's a photo here, two girls, one of them Xristal, I think, but I don't want to pick it up. I've taken a few shots, – here, have a look.' She held up the phone to him. His glance flicked from the screen to the pale, waxy, smoke-smudged head with the singed dark hair on the bed.

'Yeah. Looks like her. Not good enough for a formal ID but something to be going on with.'

'I'll see if Tilly recognises her.' Jasmine started to move towards the door.

'Before you go, was there a phone or wallet or handbag over there?'

'No.'

'I can't see any of her personal stuff anywhere.'

'I suppose she could have kept everything in drawers or in the wardrobe?'

'Yeah, we'll have to wait for Soco to come and open everything up.'

'I'll ask Tilly what she knows about Xristal.'

'You do that.'

Jasmine stepped out onto the landing. It was drizzling. At least it was washing the smell of smoke from the air. She hurried down the stairs. The young police officer was standing at the bottom.

'Hi, where's the girl, Tilly?' Jasmine asked.

'In her flat,' he replied. 'The fire crew said it was safe to go back inside.'

'Thanks.' Jasmine ducked under the stairs and approached the back door of the ground floor flat. She tapped on the door and entered. Tilly was standing in the small kitchen watching a kettle start to boil.

She looked at Jasmine. 'Oh, it's you. You look different.

What's happening?' Jasmine recalled she hadn't put the brown wig back on. Too late now.

'The police are starting their investigations. We need to check that the body is Xristal's. Do you recognise her in this photo?' Jasmine handed over her phone.

Tilly stared at the picture and began to sob again.

'Yes, that's her.'

'The dark-haired girl?'

'Yes. Is she... is she the one upstairs?'

'Looks like it. Who's the other girl in the picture, the big blonde?'

'Oh, that's Honey.'

'Honey who?'

'Honey Potts. Silly name, isn't it?'

Jasmine nodded. Another assumed name, she thought.

'Xristal and Honey were close friends,' Tilly added.

'Where does Honey live?'

'I don't know. She used to have the middle flat here, but she moved out a couple of weeks ago, pretty suddenly.'

'So you were all friends here, were you?'

'Oh, no. I only moved in a month or so ago. I hardly knew Honey. Didn't really get to know Xristal much, certainly not at first. She and Honey were close. But in the last couple of weeks, I suppose Xristal and I had a bit more of a chat – but only when we bumped into each other.'

'What do you know about Xristal?'

'Why?'

'So we can build up a picture. Perhaps get an idea who might have done it.'

'Done it? You mean Xristal was murdered? It wasn't an accident?'

Damn, Jasmine thought, I must be out of practice, I didn't mean to give that away so easily.

'Perhaps,' she said, trying to backtrack, 'Look, any chance of a coffee?'

'Oh, yeah. I was making one myself.' Tilly collected mugs

and coffee. 'Milk? Sugar?'

'Just plain black please.'

Tilly poured the hot water and passed her a mug. Jasmine thought she might be offered a seat in the main room, but Tilly remained standing holding her mug with a pensive look on her face.

'So, what was Xristal like?'

'How do you mean?'

'Her manner – happy, sad, quiet, loud?'

'Oh, Honey was the loud one. Never stopped talking, telling jokes, leaping around. Xristal was sort of quiet, composed.'

'In control?'

'Nah, I'm not sure about that. She always did what Honey asked her to do. Ran round after her.'

'But Honey left suddenly?'

'Well, neither of them told me she was going. There one day, gone the next.'

'Didn't Xristal say anything afterwards?'

'Didn't mention her.'

'Had they had a bust up?'

'Dunno. They may have done. I heard them having a row, well, Honey having a row, a day or so before she left, but that wasn't unusual – she was always shouting.'

Jasmine remembered that she was supposed to be finding out about Xristal's handbag.

'Hmm. Did Xristal have a particular handbag?'

Tilly pondered. 'Yeah, she did carry a leather bag around with her - red, good quality but pretty old.'

'With a phone and a purse or wallet in it?'

'Don't know about that, but she definitely had an iPhone or something.'

Jasmine finished her coffee.

'Thanks. I'd better be getting back to Tom, uh, DS Shepherd. Thanks for the coffee.'

'Why are you asking all these questions? You're not a detective are you?'

Jasmine was about to bridle and insist that she was, until she remembered that she wasn't - officially.

'No, just helping DS Shepherd until the other police investigators arrive. Oh, by the way, do you have any contact details for family or friends of Xristal?'

'No, nothing. I didn't even have her as a contact on my phone.'

'Right. Well, hang around because I expect they'll want to speak to you again.'

'Oh. It's a bit inconvenient right now.'

'I know, but they'll need all the information they can get on Xristal - and Honey too.'

A worried frown passed across Tilly's face.

'I see. I'd better make some calls.' She ushered Jasmine towards the door, appearing a little flustered, as if she had just realised the effect that the police investigation would have on her life.

Jasmine returned to the dreary and damp backyard. A figure in blue overalls was approaching the stairs.

'Oh, hello. Jasmine Frame, isn't it?'

The voice of Dr Winslade, the pathologist, was familiar and Jasmine recognised her face, despite the hood pulled tightly to hold in her hair.

'Hi.'

'What are you doing here?'

'I discovered the body.'

'Oh, lucky you. Top floor isn't it?'

Jasmine nodded and followed her up the stairs. They found Tom standing in the hallway talking on his phone with his notebook open in his other hand. He nodded and beckoned the pathologist through. Jasmine followed her into the flat.

Dr Winslade stood by the bed and looked up and down the body, then bent and peered closer at the torso. She examined the crotch, then her examination moved up the fire-blackened chest.

'DS Shepherd told me when I was on my way that the body

was a woman called Xristal Newman.'

'That's right.'

'Well, she's a woman with a penis and testicles.'

'What?'

'They're somewhat charred but still largely intact. Oh, and she has breast enhancements. They're made of silicone – it doesn't burn.'

'You mean she's pre-op trans?'

'Like you?'

'Um, yes.' Jasmine tried her best to forget that she still had her male organs, but they were always there to remind her she wasn't yet who she wanted to be.

'Sorry, I didn't mean to embarrass you, but it appears that although Xristal seems to have been living as a woman she was still technically male.'

'But with enlarged breasts?'

'Yes. You haven't had that done?'

'No.' The thought of having her chest slit open to squeeze in bags of silicone chilled Jasmine. 'I'm hoping the hormones I'm taking will make mine grow.'

'Good luck. It appears Xristal wasn't as patient.'

Jasmine thought about Xristal's bigger-busted friend, Honey. Were her boobs fake too?

Four more overalled figures arrived, filling up the room. Jasmine backed out to join Tom in the hallway.

'Xristal's TS,' she said in a quiet voice.

'What?'

Jasmine took a deep breath and explained, 'Xristal Newman was a transsexual woman, like me.'

'Oh. Well, that's an interesting titbit for Sloane when he arrives.'

'He's coming here?'

'Yes, just to check we're doing everything right. So you had better get out of the way.'

'But I've got to find out what happened to her! What if it was because she was trans? It could be a transphobic murderer.'

'What, like the last ones? I don't think so, Jas. This seems different.'

'Yes, but it could be important. And I discovered her. Sloane is bound to want my statement,'

'Yes, I'm sure he will, but he won't want to find you in the middle of the crime scene.'

Tom was right. A confrontation with DCI Sloane here in Xristal's flat was possibly not the best way for Jasmine to ensure that she was kept connected to the investigation. She was reluctant to leave, but her presence would not be welcomed.

'OK. I'll go, but you will keep in touch, won't you Tom?'

'I suppose so. You'll pester me if I don't. Now get out of here before he sees you.'

Jasmine hurried down the steps. The uniformed police officer stood on guard at the bottom as the scene of crime officers in their blue hooded coveralls moved back and forth carrying pieces of equipment. Jasmine debated whether to knock on Tilly's door again and leave by the front of the building. She decided instead to explore the rear access, as that was probably the direction that Xristal's killer took. The lane was clogged with the one fire appliance that remained, Tom's car and other police cars and vans. Jasmine walked past them until she came to the road. She turned right and a few metres further on came to the road on which she was parked. A large Volvo turned into the side road and she caught a glimpse of the grey-haired, grey-suited DCI Sloane in the passenger seat.

Jasmine crossed the road to her car and saw with relief that her camera was still lying on the passenger seat. At least no opportunist thief had decided to nick it, because she couldn't afford to replace it. The engine spluttered into life and she lurched off in first gear.

The evening rush hour was easing, so it took just five minutes for Jasmine to drive back to her flat. She pulled into the car park and sat still for a moment. A day that had promised little but bum-numbing boredom had turned out far more dramatic than she could possibly want. The smell and taste of the smoke from burnt flesh was still in her nose and her mouth. Her skin felt sticky, as if it was coated in Xristal's fat. The image of the burned body filled her mind. The body of a girl like her. Well, someone who had the appearance of being a girl, but actually still had the physical form of a man. Did Tilly know that Xristal was TS? Damn, she should have knocked on her door and asked. What about Honey? The photo suggested that she was too. The two of them looked so happy in that photo, although Jasmine was sure she herself wouldn't appear so relaxed in such skimpy beachwear.

She pushed the car door open and hauled herself out, feeling weary after the long day. It was just a short walk to the steps leading to her flat. A man was leaning into the back of an Audi estate car. Jasmine thought it was a somewhat smarter car than those that usually graced the car park of the flats. The man straightened up with a cardboard box in his arms, turned and almost bumped into her.

'Oh, sorry, bab,' he said with a Birmingham accent. He had olive skin and short wiry hair. Jasmine reckoned he looked just a little older than her – early thirties perhaps?

'No, my fault. Your car caught my eye. It's not familiar. Are you moving in?'

'Yeah, temporarily until I get a house sorted. Managed to find an affordable place to rent here for the time being.'

Jasmine found the Midlands lilt with a hint of Caribbean friendly and likeable.

'Well, they're certainly cheap for this area.' Jasmine noticed he was looking at her closely.

'Hey, bab. Aren't you the detective who caught the knife killer a couple of months back? The transsexual?'

Jasmine felt a weight drop into her stomach. When was she going to get her anonymity back? Why did people still recall the pictures of her? OK, they'd been on the front pages of all the dailies and on TV and the internet, but that was weeks ago now. And why did people always remember that she was trans?

'Yes, that's me,' she muttered, turning away and hurrying to the door of her ground floor flat.

'Sorry. I didn't mean to embarrass you!' the man called out.

She closed the door behind her, gratefully closing out the rest of the world. There was some post on the mat: some junk mail and a white envelope. She picked them up and dumped the junk mail with her bag and camera on the sofa. The envelope she tore open. The A4 sheet inside carried the NHS logo. Her eyes scanned the page and picked out the news she was anticipating, news that she was both hoping and dreading. There was a date - next Monday; a place - a London hospital; and confirmation that she was booked as a day case for a biorchidectomy.

Jasmine stood rooted to the spot, the letter grasped in her hand, a cold sweat making her shiver. The medical term could not disguise the treatment she was booked to receive; - she knew what it meant. Her testicles would be removed and the source of the testosterone that was fighting the oestrogen that she was taking to feminise her body would finally be gone. It was what she wanted - but the thought of the scalpel slicing into her flesh made her shudder.

Jasmine dropped the letter and reached into her bag for her phone. She had to speak to someone, but who? Angela was the obvious person. Despite being divorced for what was it now - three months - Angela was the person who had supported and guided her towards her transition. They were still close, although they hadn't been in touch for a few weeks. She pressed the contact, but after just a couple of rings the call went to voicemail. Jasmine hung up. She wanted to talk to Angela, not recite her news. It didn't feel right just broadcasting it. Tapping out a text didn't seem right either. Who else could she speak to? There was one other person, her GP, Dr Jilly Gould. The young doctor had shown genuine concern and had given Jasmine her direct work number. It was in her contacts list. Jasmine found it. It was gone seven now. Would Jilly still be at work? The phone was answered.

'Hello, Dr Gould, Jilly?'

'Who's speaking?'

'Jasmine Frame.'

'Jasmine! Are you alright?'

'Oh, Jilly, I'm so glad you answered. I'm sorry to bother you.' Jasmine felt herself fluttering.

'No bother. I was just doing some paperwork. What's the problem?'

'There's no problem, not really, it's just that I've had the letter and I needed to tell someone – you.'

'Letter? Oh, you mean about your biorchidectomy?'

'Yes. I have an appointment for next Monday in London.'

'Oh good. Is it OK for you?'

'It's very soon.'

'They must have had a cancellation or something and you were next on the list. You are happy about it, aren't you?'

'Yes, well, except for the operation itself. You know what I'm like with knives.'

'You won't feel or see a thing.'

'I know but... It's all happened quicker than I expected.'

'Well, unlike the full gender reassignment, this is just a minor op. A quick snip, whoops, sorry. What I mean is, it will be over and done with in no time. You'll be able to finish taking those anti-androgen tablets and the oestrogen can get on with doing its job. That should put a stop to most of the unpleasant side effects.'

'That's what I wanted to hear.'

'Don't forget you'll need someone to pick you up afterwards. You'll be pretty sore and groggy, but the hospital will discharge you after a couple of hours.'

'Oh, yes.' Jasmine hadn't arranged who would collect her after the operation. Since Dr Gould and the consultants at the gender clinic had suggested she could have this "minor" procedure she hadn't given it much thought. Now she had just five days to sort something out – but who could she ask?

'I don't suppose you are available?'

'Sorry, Jasmine. A few of the partners are away next week and I'm left minding the shop. But drop in some time and we'll have a chat about everything. How's business?'

Jasmine was about to blurt out about finding Xristal, but stopped herself. No point burdening Jilly Gould with it; she did enough already keeping her balanced and sane.

'Oh fine. I've just got involved in a new case. I'll tell you about it sometime. I'd better go now. Thanks for the chat.'

'Oh, right. Well as I said, come and see me before you go up to London.'

'Yes, I will. Thanks.' Jasmine ended the call and sighed. She wasn't sure how she would have managed without Dr Gould keeping an eye on her. She had taken up her case with enthusiasm and found out all there was to know about gender reassignment. She encouraged and reassured Jasmine whenever she felt the process was taking too long. Excitement filled Jasmine which her long-standing fear of cutting couldn't dampen. It was a relief to think that the nausea, flushes, loss of concentration and lethargy would be a thing of the past, to say nothing of the possible damage the anti-androgens were doing to her liver. Taking the gender-altering drugs had been an important step - but this was a bigger one. Losing her testicles was irreversible and she would never again have the sexual response of a man. The longing to be fully female obsessed her, but that day was a long way off thanks to the bottleneck that was the National Health Service.

She headed for the shower with renewed vitality, dropping her smoky clothes into the laundry basket. Soon she felt clean again, and once she was dressed in bra, knickers and a loose cotton dress thought about something to eat. As usual there was little in her fridge; it would have to be toast again. She took two slices, dropped them into the toaster and went into the living room. Picking up her camera, she scrolled through the pictures she had taken of her benefit fraud suspect – were there any that provided evidence for the FIS? Photo after photo showed the man standing leaning on his crutches. No evidence there. She hadn't taken any when he had started to run in response to the call of "Fire!" That was a missed opportunity and meant she would be back on surveillance duty tomorrow.

The strident whine of the smoke alarm informed her the toast was overdue. She rushed into the kitchen to see smoke curling up from the toaster and the smell of burning in the air. She stabbed at the stop button on the toaster cursing the old machine and the drugs that contributed to her loss of concentration. Jasmine opened the window as the smell got to her. The scene in Xristal's flat flashed through her mind. Why was she lying on that unmade bed? Who had set fire to her? Tears filled Jasmine's eyes, partly caused by the acidic smoke and partly from the memory of Xristal's burned body.

The doorbell rang. Jasmine hurried to open it, wiping the tears from her cheeks. The man she had met in the car park stood there holding a bottle of wine. The smoke alarm fell silent.

'Hi.' He paused, 'Look, I wanted to apologise. I'm sure you're fed up of people recognising you like that. It was rude of me.'

Jasmine held the door, wondering how to respond. He looked at her closely.

'Hey, are you OK? You've been crying.'

'Well, I'm tired and hungry, I found a body this afternoon and I've just burned my supper.'

His eyes widened, but he quickly recovered.

'Well, I brought this bottle as an apology. You and I could share it and I'll try to cheer you up. I haven't eaten yet either, so perhaps we can order a takeaway?'

Jasmine's first instinct was to thank him and close the door. She was wary of strangers and slow to form new friendships. She had to be sure that people accepted her and weren't going to react badly to her transsexualism. But this guy seemed different. He knew who and what she was, but had taken the trouble to apologise for blurting it out when they had met. The wine was an attraction too - she needed something to get rid of the smoky taste in her mouth. The promise of a takeaway was the clincher. She opened the door wider and summoned up a cheerful voice.

'That sounds like a good offer. Come in.'

She stepped back into the room and he followed. Jasmine

stooped to remove papers and her bag from the small sofa.

'I'll see if I can find a corkscrew, uh, I'm sorry, I don't know your name.'

'It's Viv,' he said, smiling broadly, 'I brought a corkscrew, just in case, but perhaps you have a couple of glasses?'

'Oh, yes, um, Viv. I'll get some.' Jasmine hurried to the kitchen, grabbed a pair of wine glasses from the wall cupboard, her only two as it happened, and returned to the living room. Viv was still standing. There was a cheerful pop as the cork was pulled from the bottle. Jasmine held out the two glasses and Viv poured the dark red wine into each. He put the bottle down on the table and took the glass that she offered. Jasmine noted that he was about four inches taller than her.

'I'm sorry, another apology. While I recalled the reason why you were in the papers, I don't remember your name.'

'It's Jasmine, Jasmine Frame. Welcome to Kintbridge. At least, when you said you were just moving in I presumed you meant that you were new to the area?'

'That's right. I'm down from Brum as you can probably tell,' he clinked his glass against hers, 'Thanks.'

They each took a sip and Viv folded himself into Jasmine's battered old sofa. Jasmine sat on a dining chair and, ensuring her knees were together, leaned towards him.

'So, Viv ...?'

'Short for Vivian. Vivian Jackson. My parents, or rather my father, named me after his great hero.'

'Hero?'

'Viv Richards, the cricketer.'

'Um, yes. I'm not sure....' Cricket wasn't top of Jasmine's favourite pastimes.

'My father was born in Jamaica and came here with his parents in the Fifties. He's always supported the West Indies cricket team, even though now he's become more British than the British. Viv Richards is his all-time favourite player.'

'I can understand that.' Jasmine knew enough about cricket to be vaguely aware of the name.

'But that's why I was so annoyed that I had embarrassed you. I know what it's like to be different. My mum's white and even in the Eighties life for a mixed race family wasn't easy. So, I shouldn't have blurted out about you being transsexual.'

Hearing Viv say the word again made her wince. It was the truth and she'd known it for years, but she hated the label. She just wished to be seen and recognised as a woman. But she appreciated what Viv was saying.

'That's OK. It's just that it's happened so often since the story got into the media, I'm sick of it.'

'I'm sure you are. Look what about that takeaway? What do you suggest?'

Jasmine rarely ate out because of her need to save money, but she and Angela used to have meals delivered occasionally before they parted. The name of the restaurant was somewhere in her memory.

'Do you like Chinese? The, um, Peking Palace used to deliver and was pretty good. I don't have their number though.'

Viv had already pulled his phone from his pocket and was tapping the screen. 'Got it. What do you fancy?'

2

Thursday

Jasmine awoke to the beeping of the alarm on her phone. She lay still, thinking about the previous evening and wondering why her head wasn't aching after having shared the bottle of wine with Viv. Perhaps it was because they'd drunk the wine with food over a few hours. It hadn't seemed that much time had passed when Viv had got up to leave, but it had been nearly midnight. Viv's witty and humorous tales of his childhood in the Midlands had kept her interested. He hadn't pressed Jasmine to tell her story and she hadn't, but she felt that she might if they met again. He had made her happy by simply accepting her for who she was. The other people she occasionally socialised with had all known her before, in her past life as James. It was a new experience to chat casually with someone who only knew her as Jasmine, even if they did know she was trans.

She was about to put the pleasant thoughts to the back of her mind and make a start on the day, when the doorbell rang followed by a rap of knuckles on the door. Jasmine jumped out of bed and threw on her dressing gown, wondering who it could be. She stopped a few steps from the door and put a hand to her chin. She felt bristles. They would be blonde, but she hated being seen with a night's growth. Damn, who could possibly want to see her before she had had a chance to shave?

There was another rap on the door. Jasmine pulled the collar of her dressing gown up to her face and tugged her bobbed hair over her cheeks. It didn't really work, but she felt a little protected.

She pulled the door open a crack, covered her face with a

hand and peered out. The figure of Tom Shepherd filled the doorway. She dropped her hand from her face.

'Tom? What on earth are you banging the door down for?'

'Sorry, I thought you might still be asleep.'

'Well, I'm not. I do have a job to get up for, you know.'

'Do you? Oh, yes, your surveillance.'

Jasmine opened the door wider. 'You'd better come in. What's this all about?'

'Sloane wants you.'

'DCI Sloane wants me?'

'That's right. He wants to speak to you.'

'Well, he, or you, could have phoned. I was prepared to come into the station to make my statement. Why send you to hammer my door down?'

Tom stepped inside the door and looked down at her.

'He was in one of his moods this morning. Said we couldn't make progress on this case until he'd interviewed you.'

'Interviewed me?'

'Yes, and he wasn't prepared to wait for you to swan in at your own convenience. Those were his words.'

'Oh, I see,' Jasmine felt the familiar knot form in her stomach when DCI Sloane's manner wound her up. 'Are you going to give me time to get dressed properly?'

'Yes, of course. I'm not going to drag you to the station in your dressing gown.'

'Well, thanks for that. You'd better sit down while you wait. Better still, make us both a cup of coffee – you know where the kitchen is.'

Jasmine turned and huffed back to her bedroom, not caring whether Tom followed her instructions. What was Sloane up to, hauling her into the station for questioning? Did he think she knew something about Xristal's death? Of course, that was it - Xristal was trans too. Sloane would automatically assume that as they were both transsexuals they were bound to know each other.

She went into the bathroom, sat on the loo and had a brief

shower, but shaved carefully. Returning to her bedroom, she opened the wardrobe and contemplated what to wear. She enjoyed winding Sloane up, but that was probably not the best course of action today. She decided to dress modestly but as femininely as possible. A glance out of the window showed that it was a warm if somewhat dull morning, so she chose a plain white vest top, a blue Topshop skirt and a pair of flat sandals. She paid careful attention to her make-up and finally emerged into the living room to find Tom sitting at the dining table with an empty mug in front of him. He glanced at his watch.

'We'd better get moving.'

'I'll have my coffee first, if you don't mind, since you have deprived me of breakfast.' Jasmine reached for the full mug beside Tom's empty one.

'Look, I'm sorry about this, Jas, but you know what Sloane's like.'

Jasmine downed the lukewarm coffee and replaced the mug on the table.

'I know, and I don't want to get you into trouble, so let's go!' She picked up her bag from the floor and rummaged for her car keys. Tom watched her.

'I'll take you.'

'And bring me back?'

'Of course, unless Sloane bangs you up.' He added a chuckle.

'Don't joke. I wouldn't put it past Sloane to keep me hanging around all day.'

Tom led Jasmine through the reception area of Kintbridge Police Station and through the security doors into the corridor of interview rooms. Jasmine followed him, trying to look nonchalant. She nodded to the officer on the desk as they passed. He looked at her, his eyes registering recognition before lowering them to his book without a comment. She tried to act as if this happened every day, but although the entrance foyer was as familiar as ever after all her years in the force, she felt almost like a criminal being led through.

Tom opened the door of the interview room and ushered Jasmine in. She surveyed the familiar small room with its four plastic chairs either side of the Formica-topped table, next to the wall with the switches of the recording apparatus. She glanced up to the corner of the ceiling to see the camera angled towards the table.

'Take a seat, Jas. I'll tell Sloane you're here. I'm sure he won't be long.'

'I wouldn't bet on it. I don't suppose he gives a toss that I'm supposed to be observing a suspected benefits fraudster.'

'Yeah, probably not. Look, I'll take you back home as soon as you're done.' Tom pulled the door closed. Jasmine was almost waiting for the click of the lock, but it didn't come. She was still a free woman then. She walked around the small room, delaying sitting at the table, but, with little space and no windows, there was nothing to occupy her. She settled on a chair, smoothing the skirt under her thighs and dug in her bag for her phone. A quick check revealed no calls or messages.

The door was thrust open and the imposing figure of DCI Sloane entered. Despite his nondescript grey suit he dominated the room. Jasmine looked up at him but did not move from her seat.

'Ah, Frame. Glad you could come in.' Sloane sat down in the chair opposite her. She heard it groan as it took his weight. Jasmine looked at him expectantly, not gracing him with a response. He flicked a switch on the wall.

'About the death of this, um, person, in a fire. The Fire Officer's report states that you, Frame, were in the flat when the fire and rescue service arrived.'

'That's correct, Chief Inspector.'

'Could you tell me what you were doing there?'

Jasmine took a deep breath. 'The occupant of the ground floor flat, Tilly, said there was a fire in the top flat. I went up to investigate. The door was locked so I broke a window to get in and found the, uh, body, on the bed.' Despite her efforts to remain dispassionate, Jasmine found her voice wobbling a little as she recalled the smell and the scene that had confronted her.

'You were visiting this Tilly girl?'

'No. I was in the street outside the house.'

'Were you about to call on the victim?'

'No. I don't, didn't, know her.'

'So, what were you doing in Bredon Road?'

'I was collecting evidence.'

'Evidence of what?'

'Benefit fraud. Look, you can check with the Fraud Investigation Service. I am under contract to keep George Parfitt of 29 Bredon Road under surveillance for the purposes of determining whether he is eligible for disability benefits.'

They stared at each other, Jasmine trying not to blink before Sloane.

'So it was a coincidence that you were in Bredon Road while this person, Xristal Newman, was burning on the bed?'

'Yes. I'd been there all day, sitting in my car, waiting for Parfitt to come out. When he did, it just happened to be at the same time as Tilly appeared, panicking and shouting "Fire!"'

'I don't like coincidences. Are you saying you didn't know this Newman person even though she was, ah, transsexual like... like you?'

'That's right. I have never seen or heard of her before in my life. Now and again coincidences happen. This is one of them.'

Sloane sucked in his cheeks and smacked his lips together.

'I see,' he said at last.

'Do you really suspect me of having something to do with Xristal's death?' Jasmine said, struggling to control the anger that was building up inside her.

'Everyone connected with the deceased is a suspect until the evidence suggests otherwise. Your fingerprints are on the door handle.'

'Of course they are. I didn't carry gloves with me and I thought someone might be trapped inside. I didn't touch anything inside. Not when I saw...'

'That's correct. We haven't found any of your prints inside

the flat.'

'I realised that it was a crime scene not a rescue. I haven't forgotten my training, you know.'

'I'm pleased to hear it,' Sloane growled. 'Miss Jones, Tilly, confirms your story as does another witness, a Mr Parfitt...'

'Oh yes. He came along when Tilly shouted out.'

'He says he saw a woman get out of a car, an old Ford Fiesta, when the alarm was raised. He says the woman ran into the house with the Tilly girl. The woman had dark brown hair and your build. Your hair is fair.'

'I was wearing a wig.'

'So DS Shepherd reported. It appears therefore unlikely that you are the perpetrator.'

'Well, thank you.'

Sloane glared. 'But it was reasonable to think you may have been visiting this person as you are both...'

'Look. I don't know every trans person in Kintbridge. There are quite a lot if you count in all the transvestites and transsexuals together; dozens, possibly hundreds, even in a place this size.'

'Hmph. In that case your assistance will be even more valuable.' Sloane spoke calmly and without a trace of his previous belligerence.

'My assistance?'

'Yes. Since you have no connection with the deceased and as his transsexual nature may be a contributory factor in the murder, your knowledge of these matters will be of use to us.'

'Of course it will.'

'I am therefore offering you the temporary position of special advisor for transgender matters. You will liaise with DS Shepherd.'

'Oh, right. OK.' Jasmine was struggling to cope with Sloane's change of tone.

'We'll sort out the contract at a later date. Normal rates for advisors will apply.'

'Thanks.'

Sloane stood up and advanced towards the doorway.

'You can go. Shepherd will fill you in and note any information you may have.' He opened the door and was gone.

Jasmine remained seated, stunned. So Sloane had given her a job, a paid job with a title. OK, only temporary, but for the duration of the investigation. It meant that she was entitled to know how the search for Xristal's killer was progressing.

'What are you still sitting there for?'

Jasmine looked up to see Tom standing in the doorway.

'I was thinking about what Sloane has just asked me.'

'About being a special advisor?'

'Yes. Did you know he was going to do that?'

'We discussed it after this morning's briefing. He said not to mention it until he was sure that you weren't involved with Xristal.'

'Well, he certainly pushed me on that, but I had never heard of her before yesterday.'

'Sloane doesn't like coincidences.'

'So he said.'

'So, are you coming or do you want to stay sitting here all day? I've got work to do after I've been your taxi driver.'

'Oh, yes.' Jasmine jumped to her feet. She smoothed down her skirt.

Tom's car edged its way through the tail end of Kintbridge's morning rush hour traffic.

'What else can you tell, me, Tom?'

'Probably no more than you know already. We know the victim's name, Xristal Newman, but there was nothing in the flat to confirm her identity or tell us anything more about her. What there might have been was possibly in a bag, which seems to have been removed.'

'So we don't know much about her.'

'That's right. I think Sloane was hoping that you did know her.'

'What about how she died?'

'Don't know yet. It was late last night when Winslade had the body removed – that wasn't easy. I hope she'll have some more for us later today.'

'I spoke to Tilly. She didn't seem to know Xristal or her friend Honey very well.'

'Honey?'

'Honey Potts. The big blonde in the photo with Xristal. Tilly seemed to think they were pretty close until Honey disappeared a couple of weeks ago.'

'I don't know anything about this Honey.'

'I thought you'd spoken to Tilly? Sloane said she confirmed my story.'

'She did, but I don't think she was asked about anyone else.'

'What about the photo?'

'Which photo?'

'The one on Xristal's chest of drawers. The one I took a photo of myself on my phone.'

'Oh, that one. That's at the station. We're using it to check who recognises Xristal.'

'Well, find out what you can about Honey too. I think she's TS as well.'

'Why?'

'Haven't you looked? She's tall, broad-shouldered, with big tits that look too good to be real.'

'I hadn't noticed.'

'Call yourself a detective? Oh, by the way, Xristal had an old, red leather handbag.'

'How do you know?'

'Tilly told me.'

Tom sighed and turned the Mondeo into the car park of Jasmine's flat.

'It's good to have you back on board, Jas. We need you.'

'I'm glad Sloane thinks so too. I want to find out how Xristal ended up smouldering naked on her bare king size bed and whether it had anything to do with her being trans.'

'We all do. Here we are.'

'Thanks for bringing me back. I had better get back to Bredon Road and see if I can continue my surveillance without being recognised. That's going to be difficult since Parfitt saw me go in to investigate the fire.'

'Parfitt?'

'My suspected fraudster.'

'Oh yes.'

'Give me a call when you have some news.'

'Of course. Now do you mind getting out? I have to get back.'

Jasmine got out of the car.

'Thanks Tom,' she said, pushing the door closed. Tom drove off immediately.

Jasmine went into her flat. She realised that she was starving having only had a cup of coffee before being rushed off to the police station. She looked in a kitchen cupboard and found a lonely cereal bar. Munching on it, she hunted in her bedroom for another wig. She had bought two cheaply when she realised she needed a disguise for her surveillance operations. Now Parfitt had seen her with brown hair she needed a change, but where was the other one? She found it nestled at the bottom of the wardrobe like a black rabbit. A vigorous shake dislodged the dust from it and restored its shape. She decided to stay dressed as she was – it was different to what she'd been wearing yesterday.

Jasmine got into her car and pulled the black curly wig on to her head. A look at herself in the mirror confirmed her suspicions: she looked appalling, but it certainly made her look different. Perhaps it would fool Parfitt.

Jasmine turned into Bredon Road and realised that parking on the road was no longer possible. Parfitt had seen her, well he'd seen someone with brown hair and her figure, and he'd seen her car. He'd become suspicious if he saw the car again. She would have to park out of the line of sight of Parfitt's house. There was a short side road nearby and she was delighted to find a space near the junction. She did a quick turn and backed into the space facing towards Bredon Road. This was going to have to be a different type of stakeout. A matter of loitering in the street rather than a sitting in the car.

Jasmine stood on the corner trying to look as though she was waiting for someone. She glanced at her phone frequently, to give passers-by the impression that she was impatiently checking the time or text messages. In fact it was because she was bored, plus she needed the camera on her phone ready in case Parfitt appeared. She couldn't very well stand there with her big SLR camera.

Looking up the road she could see Parfitt's SUV parked outside his house, but there was no sign of him. Someone walked along the pavement and turned into the house which Tilly and Xristal occupied – a middle-aged man in a business suit. He disappeared from view, presumably invited in.

Jasmine decided to take a walk. She crossed to the other side of the street and sauntered slowly along, making sure she only took brief glances at Parfitt's house. A dozen more steps took her to another side street, where she stood discreetly out of sight for a while. Luckily there were few pedestrians and cars on Bredon Road, so she didn't feel conspicuous.

Over an hour later, the man emerged from Tilly's front door. He looked briefly in Jasmine's direction then walked off hurriedly the other way, back towards the town centre. Still no sign of Parfitt, though.

After a few minutes, Jasmine decided to retrace her steps to her first viewing site. As she crossed back over the road, another man walked up Bredon Road and turned into Tilly's entrance. Jasmine's curiosity was aroused, so instead of merely watching for Parfitt's appearance she kept a look out for the man's re-emergence.

Time dragged and her attention wandered. The operation she would undergo in five days' time worried her. She desperately wanted her male organs to be gone so as to be free from testosterone's masculinising effects. Nevertheless, her mind was filled with the dreadful image of a knife slicing through flesh. It was a silly phobia and it must not stop her from achieving what she wanted, but she worried that getting to the hospital next Monday would be a trial. She still had to find someone to accompany her or at least pick her up to bring her home. Who could she ask? Angela, Tom, someone else? Who else was she close enough to?

At last, the second man emerged from Tilly's flat and strode along the street. Jasmine stepped out of her hiding place just as he reached her. He almost jumped into the road in shock, and increased his pace back towards the bustle of the high street. His nervous behaviour aroused Jasmine's suspicions. She walked down the road, turned into Tilly's entrance and rang the doorbell.

The door opened a few inches and Tilly's blonde head appeared.

'Who are you?' she asked.

Jasmine stepped forward, placing her foot against the door - a risky thing to do not wearing standard police footwear, but she had to stop Tilly closing the door on her.

'Jasmine Frame. We met yesterday.'

'I don't know you!'

'Let me come in and I'll explain.'

'Why? I'm expecting someone – not you.'

'Another client? That will be three in a morning will it?'

'What do you mean? Have you been spying on me?'

'Let me in and we can discuss whether your landlord knows you are operating as a prostitute.'

'What!'

Jasmine gave the door a firm shove. Tilly didn't resist. Jasmine slipped into the narrow hallway and whipped off the black wig.

'Oh, it's you!' Tilly stepped back and raised a hand to her mouth. In the dim light of the corridor Jasmine was only just able to make out Tilly's appearance. Her hair was tied in bunches on each side of her head. She wore a white cotton shirt with the top three buttons undone revealing a cleavage unfettered by a bra. A school tie dangled loosely between her nipples protruding through the taut fabric of the shirt. The bottom buttons were also unfastened and gaped to reveal her flat stomach and the rolled up waist band of her grey twill skirt which barely reached mid-thigh. Completing the look was a pair of white ankle socks and little black pumps. Considerably shorter than Jasmine, she looked like a precocious fourteen year old.

'So you excite your clients with the schoolgirl routine, do you?' Jasmine said.

'I provide a service,' Tilly pouted, 'Anyway, I'm probably protecting under-age girls from some of them.'

'If you have evidence of that, then I'll march you down to the police station right now.'

Tilly recoiled. 'No, of course I haven't got evidence. I didn't mean it. I don't know anything about them except they are grateful and pay up.' She sniffed. 'Look if you're here to talk about Xristal, you'd better come in.' She led Jasmine into the studio room.

The curtains were open but there were heavy nets at the windows to prevent passers-by peering in. There was a small double bed and the usual bedroom furniture, but about a third of the room was laid out like a classroom. A blackboard sat on an easel in front of an antique school desk, and behind the desk was a chair on which rested a cane. A black gown and mortarboard hung behind the door.

Tilly pointed to a small armchair beside the bed. Jasmine took the hint and sat down. Tilly sat on the edge of the bed, her skirt riding even higher up her thighs.

'Does your landlord know how you pay the rent?' Jasmine asked.

'Mr Taylor? Perhaps. He's never mentioned it, but he's never been here. His wife has though; she collects the rent each month.'

'What about the other girls, Xristal and Honey, are they, were they, prostitutes too?'

'We never talked about what we did, but I used to hear people going up to Honey's flat. Occasionally, I saw people going up the stairs at the back, but they could have been going to see either Honey or Xristal.'

'Did you know Xristal was transsexual?'

'I guessed. She never discussed it but, well, her figure was a bit of a giveaway – narrow hips, broad shoulders and those perfect tits. She was so proud of them.'

'She admitted they were false?'

'Oh, yes. She went on about how many thousands it cost to get them done properly.'

'What about Honey?'

'There was no doubt about her. She was more like a man in drag – her clothes, mincing walk and her height. She was even taller than you.'

Jasmine realised that Tilly had seen through her too.

'Being tall doesn't mean anything.'

'Doesn't it? There are other giveaways though, aren't there? Things you can't quite put a finger on.' Tilly sucked her finger, innocently.

Jasmine knew only too well how right Tilly was. It took years and years to learn the subtle mannerisms that conveyed true femininity and she knew that even now, after transitioning, a close inspection of how she stood, walked, sat and spoke revealed her nature. There were so many things she had to learn, but completing gender reassignment would help her to feel like a real woman.

'Well, you'd better prepare yourself for your landlord finding out about how you earn your living. He could find himself on a charge of living on immoral earnings by operating a brothel if it's true that Xristal and Honey were prostitutes too.'

Tilly frowned.

'Do you mean I'd better get out of here?'

'Only if you want the police coming after you for Xristal's murder. If you are as helpful as you can be you might avoid being charged yourself, but be prepared for some embarrassing questions.'

'Oh!' Tilly held her face in her hands. 'What should I do?'

'Tell the police officers everything you've told me, and don't answer the door in the outfit you're wearing now. You'd better cancel your clients for a while.'

'Bugger. I need the money, but clients aren't going to want to come here if the police are all over the place. The two this morning were nervous.' Tilly stood up and stepped across the room to the dressing table. 'Here, you'd better have this.' She handed an envelope to Jasmine. 'The postman dropped it in this morning. He said he couldn't get upstairs because of the police tape.'

Jasmine glanced at the address and noticed the name Newman. Then she looked more closely and saw it was addressed to "Mr C."

'This was for Xristal?'

'I suppose so. There's no one else called Newman here.'

'Right. Thanks. I'll pass it on.' Jasmine stood up. 'I'd better get on. Take care of yourself and don't do anything stupid.' She headed towards the door with Tilly following.

'No. I won't. Look, I really hope you find out who killed Xristal.'

'So do I.' Jasmine tugged the black wig onto her head.

Back on Bredon Road, Jasmine contemplated whether to walk up and down again or loiter on the corner. Parfitt's car was still outside his house, so she hadn't missed him leaving while she was inside Tilly's flat. Her phone rang.

'Hi, Tom.'

'Jas. Winslade has rung through saying she's got some preliminary results from the autopsy on Xristal Newman. She thinks you might be interested.'

'I am. Shall I meet you at the hospital?'

'Yes. As you're an official advisor now, it'll be OK for you to come in. I'm on my way there.'

'I'll see you there.' Jasmine thumbed the off and dropped the phone into her bag while hurrying back to her car. What had Dr Winslade found? This was much more exciting than looking out for Parfitt all day – that could wait.

The smell of disinfectant, and other undefinable substances always made Jasmine's stomach turn when she entered the pathology lab. She and Tom were dressed in overalls and hair nets as they pushed through the rubber doors.

'Hi DS Shepherd, Jasmine,' Dr Winslade was standing by a table on which lay the remains of Xristal Newman. The blackened torso with its four white limbs and dark-haired head were recognisable only because they were arranged similarly to how they had been on the bed. Tom and Jasmine looked across the body at the masked pathologist.

'What have you got then?' Tom asked.

'Quite a lot actually,' Winslade replied. 'First of all, she was dead before she was set alight. There's no smoke in her lungs.'

'Someone else was definitely involved then.' Tom said.

'How was she killed?' Jasmine asked.

'I'd say she was smothered; probably with a pillow.'

'Wouldn't she have struggled?' Tom queried.

'Certainly, but she was fastened to the bed, spread-eagled. There are marks on her wrists and ankles.'

Jasmine looked at the pale limbs on the slab expecting to see the deep cuts of ropes made as the victim struggled. There were none.

'The marks are quite faint and broad,' Winslade went on. 'She wasn't tied up with rope. I'd say she was restrained hand and foot with cuffs. Good quality ones, designed not to leave marks while immobilising the subject.'

'Do you mean Xristal's death was the result of a BDSM scenario gone wrong?' Jasmine asked, wondering if that was the service Xristal provided. If indeed she was a prostitute like Tilly.

'There was evidently bondage involved, but the killing wasn't an accident. The killer would have had to hold the pillow down for a considerable time to cause death. Whoever did it must have been aware what they were doing.'

'There was no sign of bondage gear in the flat,' Tom said.

Jasmine had an idea. 'The killer must have removed it along with Xristal's handbag, phone and stuff.'

'We did wonder why the bottom drawer in the chest was empty,' Tom commented, 'It seemed strange to have a spare drawer when there was so little storage space.'

'The killer must have wanted to hide what had happened,' Jasmine said.

'That's probably why they set fire to the body after removing the bonds,' Winslade said, 'but they didn't do a very good job.'

'Why's that?' Tom asked.

'Well, there just wasn't enough flammable material near the body to get a good blaze going,' Winslade answered, 'No clothing or bedding, the mattress was interior sprung, the outer fabric contained flame retardant and the bed frame was steel. Part of the plastic sheet melted but didn't ignite. The killer must have been in a hurry once they had removed the bindings. They threw the vodka over the body and tossed the lit candle on it. The alcohol burned off pretty quickly, singeing the skin and melting the subcutaneous fat. That started a wick effect with the fat smouldering and melting more fat. It produced enough smoke to set off the alarm, eventually. But, well the victim didn't have a lot of fat on her and the heat wasn't sufficient to spread the fire to the arms and legs. It fizzled out.'

Tom and Jasmine stood looking at the body, silently taking in what the pathologist had said.

'Can you give a time of death?' Tom asked.

'Well, it's not easy. The fire masks the indicators. The fire service report says that they responded to the call at 5:20 p.m.'

'That's right,' Jasmine said, 'It was gone five when I broke into the flat.'

'The fire was probably out by then. I reckon it probably smouldered for one to two hours, perhaps a little longer, but not much.'

'So, it was started between three and four o'clock?' Jasmine calculated.

'That's right. I'd say she died before four.'

'So there was plenty of time for the killer to get away unnoticed?' Tom said.

'Presumably.' Winslade nodded.

'Is there anything else?' Jasmine asked.

'There are a few things of interest about the victim,' Winslade said. She pointed to the torso. 'I told you about the breast augmentation.'

'Yes,' Jasmine agreed.

'Well, she's also had cosmetic surgery on her nose, probably giving her a more feminine appearance; her whole body is hairless and she has had electrolysis on her upper lip and chin.'

Tom was confused. 'Electrolysis?'

'To remove hair and stop it growing.' Jasmine said.

'That's right. She's also had collagen injections to fill out her lips and she had a recent visit to a manicurist and pedicurist.'

'What?' Tom said.

'She's had her finger and toenails done professionally,' Jasmine explained.

'She really made herself look female then.' Tom said.

'Yes,' Jasmine said, totting up the cost of all the procedures, 'and she must have been earning enough to do it.'

'Oh, and I've got the preliminary results of blood tests,' Winslade added.

'And?' Tom's eyebrows rose.

'There's no evidence of any drugs.'

'So she wasn't an addict.' Tom nodded.

Jasmine thought Winslade meant something else. 'No drugs at all?' Winslade's smile showed even with her face covered by her mask.

'No drugs, Jasmine. No artificial oestrogens or anti-androgens. Her natural testosterone was at a normal level for a male.'

'Uh, what does that mean?' Tom asked.

Jasmine was ready with the answer. 'It means that, despite

45

appearances, Xristal was still fully male.'

'You mean, she could...'

'Yes. She could have erections, fuck, ejaculate, the works.' She now had a new mental image of Xristal, one in which they were not so similar after all.

'I don't get it. Why have the boob job but not the hormones?'

'Xristal was what is known as a she-male.' Jasmine surprised herself by feeling a bit disgusted and let-down.

'What does that mean?'

'She-males adopt the outward appearance of women, even to the extent of having breast implants and other cosmetic procedures, while retaining the ability to use their male genitals and have sex as a man.'

'So they're not transsexuals, then.'

'Depends how you define transsexual.' There was an anger in Jasmine as if her own identity was being questioned. 'On the one hand, they sit astride the boundary between male and female - but she-males don't really want to be women, they want to show off their great thrusting pricks and ejaculate and fuck like blokes.'

'They're not like you then,' Tom said with a smile.

'Definitely not!'

Tom looked at Winslade for help.

'Jasmine's right, Tom. Xristal Newman was a fully-functioning male despite her feminine appearance.'

'And a whore too, or rent-boy, whatever you want to call him,' Jasmine said.

'How do you know?'

'Well, the BDSM is one clue, but Tilly is a prostitute and she suspected Xristal was as well,'

'How do you know Tilly's a hooker?' Tom asked.

'I was with her before you rang. I observed two men enter her flat this morning and each spend about an hour with her. She role-plays being a precocious schoolgirl for them. She admitted it when I confronted her. She wouldn't say so, but I'm sure she thinks Xristal and Honey were also on the game.'

'All three of them?'

Jasmine added, 'I bet Honey Potts is a she-male too and that she and Xristal had a sexual relationship.' It was a wild leap of imagination, but it felt true. She could imagine two she-males sharing their sexual fantasies and urging each other on.

'This upsets you, doesn't it, Jasmine?' Dr Winslade said, pulling the mask down from her mouth.

Jasmine examined her emotions. She felt angry, upset, confused.

'Yes, it does.'

'Why?' Tom asked.

'I thought Xristal was like me; someone who thought she was female but had the wrong shaped body. I suspected that she might be working as a prostitute – many transsexuals do. It's often the only way that they can earn enough to pay for the gender reassignment. Now I realise that Xristal wasn't like me at all.'

'I'm not sure I get it,' Tom said warily, as if expecting another outburst from Jasmine.

Jasmine felt hot and knew her face was flushed.

'Because Xristal went to all this trouble to make it look as though she was female. She sort of designed her own body, but she still wanted a functioning cock and balls. I want to get rid of mine. I am getting rid of mine – next Monday.'

'What! You're having your sex-change next week?' Tom said.

'Not the full thing, just my testicles removed.'

'To stop the production of testosterone?' Dr Winslade said.

'Yes. So that I don't have to take the anti-androgen tablets which are making me feel crap.'

Jasmine could see Tom wincing as he took in the meaning of what she had said.

'So after you've had this operation, you won't get erections anymore?'

'That's right, and the feminising drugs, the oestrogens, should work better. I'll be a little closer to being what I want to be.'

'Won't you be out of action for a while? It must be a big op.' Tom said.

'No, Tom. It's just a little snip, according to my doctor. I'll be in the hospital for a few hours, sore for a couple of days and then I'll be fine.'

'Oh. Just a little snip?' Tom looked distinctly pale. Jasmine had an image of the knife and felt a little sick.

'That's wonderful for you, Jasmine,' Winslade said, 'and I can understand how you feel about Xristal.'

'So let me get this straight. I think I must be a bit naive.' Tom said. 'These she-male prostitutes have sex with men who like having sex with women with penises or men with tits? I don't know which they are.'

'Take your pick, but that's probably the case,' Jasmine replied. 'They can have normal sex with women too.'

Tom stroked his chin. 'At least it makes a few things clearer. We have some hints of a motive for killing her.'

'Like what?'

'A client taking against her perhaps?'

'Or a pimp?'

'Or perhaps a falling out with her friend Honey - or is it business partner?'

'It's quite a list.'

'It's frustrating that the killer apparently removed all the information on Xristal. We hardly know anything about her/him.' Tom said.

Jasmine remembered the envelope Tilly had given her. It had been stuffed in her bag with her phone when she had run to the car. She dug in the bag for it.

'There may be something in this.' She handed the envelope to Tom. He looked at it closely.

'Where did you get it?'

'Tilly gave it to me. The postman delivered it to her because he couldn't get to Xristal's letterbox.'

Tom carefully slit the envelope open and pulled out the sheet of folded paper. He looked at it.

'It's a bank statement for an account in the name of Mr C Newman. Jesus, there's a fair bit in it, and some recent transactions. This is a great lead if Mr C is Xristal.'

'No doubt. Xristal can't have transitioned fully.'

'We'd better get back and look into this,' Tom was still scanning the page, 'Thanks, Doctor. You've been a great help. Come on Jas. There are things to do.' He headed for the exit.

Jasmine paused, looking again at the sad remains of Xristal.

'How are you feeling, Jasmine?' Dr Winslade asked.

'I'm confused,' Jasmine replied, 'I thought Xristal and I were similar, so I was determined to find out why she had died. Now I know we weren't similar at all and I'm not sure how I feel.'

'Presumably Xristal was happier with her body after the changes she had made to it, like you will be happier when you've had your op next week?'

'I suppose so,' Jasmine said, not sure where Dr Winslade was leading.

'So you both need changes to your bodies to achieve what you want.'

'You mean we're similar because we both planned to change the design of our bodies?'

'That's right, Jasmine.'

Jasmine could see that Winslade was trying to restore her sympathy for Xristal, but she couldn't accept it.

'But I can't get over that she was happy having a penis. I'm not.'

'I understand, Jasmine, but I think you've got a long way to go to find out why Xristal was how she was and how she ended up like this.' Winslade nodded at the body in front of her.

'You're right,' Jasmine admitted, 'We need to find out more. Thanks for the encouragement.'

She left Dr Winslade to carry out further examinations on the body, and returned to her car in the hospital car park. Tom was long gone.

Jasmine sat in the driving seat wondering what to do next. She glanced at the time on her phone. It was gone two o'clock; past lunchtime and she felt hungry but had no food with her. What was she to do? She could return to the police station and join Tom and Sloane and the rest of the team, but she couldn't be involved in the regular police work. What else could she tell them about Xristal? She-males were an unknown quantity to her and she had no knowledge of how they led their lives. Perhaps she had just better go back to Bredon Road and continue with her surveillance of Parfitt until Tom had more for her to do. The black wig was still on the passenger seat where she had dumped it on arrival at the hospital. Decision made, she pulled it back onto her head and started the engine.

3

THURSDAY AFTERNOON

Damn, Parfitt's car was gone from its parking space. An opportunity to catch him walking without his crutches had been missed. She would just have to wait for him to return. Jasmine found a space to park and pulled the ghastly black wig off. It was just a short walk back to St Benedict's Street where there was a Tesco Express. She returned to the Fiesta and sat eating a cheese and pickle sandwich. It had turned out a warm day, so she couldn't bear to put the wig back on. If someone recognised her - tough.

She reflected on what Dr Winslade had said. Were she and Xristal similar? OK, so they were both prepared to have surgery to achieve the bodies they desired. She conceded that point. But the thought of using her male organs to have sex as Xristal must have done, and to earn money for it, disgusted her. What's more, Xristal apparently allowed herself to be restrained by someone, presumably her clients. What did she let them do to her? Jasmine could not imagine handing over control that way. How much had Xristal worried about entrusting herself to her clients? Was it simply to get money for her body modifications?

An hour had passed, with no sign of Parfitt returning, when her phone rang. It was Tom.

'Hey, Jas. Where are you? I thought you would follow me back to the station.'

'I'm doing my job; watching out for Parfitt in Bredon Road.'

'Is he there?'

'No.'

'Well, your other job needs you.'

'What job?'

'You're our transgender special advisor. Remember?'

'But I don't know anything about she-males.'

'You know more than Sloane or me or any of the other guys and gals on the team. Look, Sloane's very pleased with what you've given us already. We're following up that letter. I'm on my way to call on the landlords, the Taylors. I'd like you with me.'

'OK, but I'm not sure what I can do.'

'I'll pick you up in Bredon Road in five minutes.'

The call ended and Jasmine sat for a few moments just staring at her phone. Tom seemed very keen to see her, but surely he didn't need her to interview the Taylors about Xristal's flat. She shrugged and pulled the wig back over her head, then dropped the phone in her bag. She got out, locked the car and walked back along Bredon Road to the main road. It would be easier for Tom to turn around and head wherever they were going.

Jasmine stood on the corner watching the traffic move slowly along the narrow but busy road. It was more than five minutes before she recognised Tom's Mondeo inching towards her. He reached the junction and did a one eighty, which caused a couple of drivers to hit their horns. Jasmine opened the passenger door and got in. Tom re-joined the slow stream of cars and vans immediately.

'What's this all about then, Tom?' Jasmine asked, pulling the seat belt across her chest.

'We're going to visit Taylor, the landlord, out of town, on the Bristol Road.' Tom glanced at her, 'You're not wearing that wig, are you?'

Jasmine plucked at the curls with her fingers. She certainly hadn't forgotten she was wearing the hideous thing.

'I prefer not to be recognised when I'm interviewing someone.'

'Ok.' Tom shrugged.

'So why are we visiting Taylor?'

'We spoke to him briefly last night informing him of what was going on at his property, but this will be more interesting – we want to find out if he knows his flats are being used for prostitution.'

'We haven't got any proof, you know, that Xristal and Honey were on the game.'

'I know, but it looks pretty certain doesn't it?'

'Almost. But that's not the reason why you've picked me up, is it?'

'No. Sloane asked me to have a chat with you to discuss where we go next. We need some suspects.'

'I told you, I've never had anything to do with she-males. I have no idea who'd murder one.'

'But you will know better than us where to start. Look, the bank statement you picked up will give us some good leads about Xristal very soon. It makes interesting reading. Xristal was making pretty regular, sizeable deposits, hundreds of pounds at a time. That sounds like income from prostitution to me.'

'If she hasn't got a legitimate job.'

'We'll see. She also made some large transfers to another account recently. It will be interesting to find out what they were for.'

'Hmm, yes. Perhaps she was planning a holiday or some more cosmetic surgery?'

'Whatever. Anyway - suspects. Who are they likely to be?'

'You could do this guessing game as well as I could. People she knew – Tilly, Honey, Taylor, neighbours – and of course clients.'

'How do we find them?'

'Look Tom, you've dealt with prostitutes before.'

'Not men with tits and pouting lips.'

'No, but they work in the same way. Perhaps Xristal solicits on the street, or has cards in telephone boxes?'

'That's the old-fashioned way.'

'Of course, so you also need to trawl the internet – websites, social networks.'

'I knew you were going to say that – you can help point us in the right direction.'

'As if I go searching for she-male whores every day!'

'You know what I mean, Jas.'

'Hmph.'

Having negotiated the Kintbridge one-way system they had finally reached the main road heading west and were picking up a bit of speed.

'There was something else I wanted to talk to you about, Jas.'

'What's that?'

'This operation you said you're having. What is it exactly?'

Jasmine turned to look at Tom as he concentrated on the road ahead. He glanced at her and she saw his face redden.

'There's no need to be embarrassed, Tom. It's pretty straightforward. I am having my testicles removed as a preliminary to having the full sex-change. A, because it means I can reduce the amount of hormones I'm taking which are mucking me about and, B, because I'm nowhere near the top of the queue for the full works, and it could be years before I get there.'

She saw Tom's thighs tense as she spoke.

'Back at the path lab you seemed to imply it was a minor op. Sounds pretty major to me. Are you going to be able to carry on working?'

'I'll just have to take it easy for a few days. It is minor, a day in hospital, that's all, but it's a massive step for me. After I've had it there's no turning back. I'll be that one very important stage closer to being a woman.'

'And that's why you have it in for these she-males? Because they keep their balls?'

'I don't understand them, Tom. I want to look like and be a woman. I don't want a cock jerking to attention every five minutes.'

'Chance would be a fine thing. No, I'm joking. I think I sort of get it.'

'Thanks. Look I know it's hard for blokes. You get squeamish at the thought of losing your nuts. But for transsexuals it's one of the most important parts of transitioning. For the lucky ones, who can go private, it all happens at once and you come out of the operating theatre with a serviceable vagina instead of a penis and scrotum, but for others, like me, it has to be done step by step.'

'So where, when?'

'9 a.m. Monday morning. Charing Cross hospital.'

'And you come out the same day?'

'By lunchtime, I expect. Although I may not feel like it - lunch that is.'

'No. I can't imagine you will. How are you getting there?'

'Train, I suppose.'

'And coming back?'

'I need a lift. You couldn't...'

'Oh, Jas, I'd really like to help, but unless we get this case solved by the weekend I think I'm going to be pretty busy.'

'I thought you'd say that.'

'We're here.' Tom slowed the car and turned off the road, through a pair of new wrought iron gates and drove up a recently tarmacked driveway. Ahead was a low modern bungalow which seemed to have had a number of recent extensions.

'Looks as though they're doing pretty well for themselves. Profits from property or prostitution?' Tom commented as they drew to a halt behind a shiny new Jaguar outside a porticoed entrance.

They both got out of the car and mounted the two steps to the front door, Jasmine a little behind Tom. He pressed the doorbell. A complex electronic chime sounded in the distance. Over a minute passed before the door opened. Jasmine was struck by the woman who looked at Tom briefly, then transferred her gaze to her. She was taller than Jasmine, slim, with a severe black bob and looked to be in her late forties. Her tan looked dark above a white silk shirt. The puffed sleeves gave her a broad-shouldered appearance. Despite it being a warm day she was wearing tight-fitting, tan leather trousers. Her immaculate red fingernails were as pointed as talons.

'Yes?' she said in a bored voice.

'Police,' Tom waved his ID. 'I'm Detective Sergeant Tom Shepherd. Are you Mrs Taylor?'

'Yes, I am.' She made no move to invite Tom and Jasmine in. 'And this is?' She nodded to Jasmine.

'Jasmine Frame. She is assisting us. I've come to speak to Mr Taylor about a property he owns.'

'*We* own. I suppose you mean the Bredon Road flat which had the fire yesterday?'

'Yes. Can we ask you and your husband some questions?'

'If you must. I suppose you had better come in. Follow me.' She released the door and turned away. Jasmine followed Tom into a spacious hall opulently decorated with antiques and hurried to keep up with Tom and Mrs Taylor as they entered another room.

'It's the police, Kelvin. They say they've got some more questions about Bredon Road.'

A middle-aged man rose from a plush, floral sofa. He was bordering on obese.

'Oh, I thought I told you everything yesterday evening,' he said with a look of mild irritation. 'When can we get back into the flat? I imagine it needs some re-decoration after the fire.'

'It is still a crime scene, Mr Taylor,' Tom said. 'We have some questions about the occupants of the three flats.'

'I gave you their names yesterday. Miss Jones on the ground floor and Miss Newman on the top. The middle flat is empty. I hope we can have access pretty soon. We need to get new tenants in.'

'I understand that, Mr Taylor, but this is a murder investigation.'

'Murder? I thought the silly girl set fire to herself. Last night your colleague said she was found dead on the bed when the fire was put out.'

The four of them were standing in a loose circle in the centre of the room. Kelvin Taylor looked up at Tom, red-faced.

'I think, Mr Taylor, it would be a good idea if we sat down and discussed this calmly.'

'What? Oh, alright.' Taylor flapped his hands and sat back down on the sofa. His wife stood quietly behind him. Tom looked around and decided to sit on an armchair alongside the sofa. Jasmine chose a chair on the opposite side where she could watch all three from a slight distance. It would be better to let Tom do the talking while she listened and observed. Tom took his pocket book out of his jacket and flicked it open.

'Last night all we knew was that a body had been found in the top floor flat of your property and that there had been a small fire.'

'Yes. That's what your man said,' Taylor nodded his head.

'The victim was identified as your tenant, Xristal Newman. Today, it has been confirmed that Miss Newman was dead before the fire started and that she was probably smothered. We are therefore looking for the person who killed Xristal and started the fire.'

Sweat appeared on Taylor's forehead. He shook his head vigorously.

'Well, I don't know anything about it.'

'Of course not, Kelvin,' Mrs Taylor said, 'the police only want to know a bit more about Xristal.'

'Thank you, Mrs Taylor,' Tom said. 'Did you know Miss Newman by any other name?'

'Other name? No, she told me her name was Xristal. Funny name, but some kids have strange names these days don't they. That was the name on her tenancy agreement.'

'How did she pay her rent – cheque? Cash?'

'We don't accept cheques,' Mrs Taylor said, 'They bounce too often. Miss Newman paid by electronic transfer from a bank account.'

'Her payments were on time?' Tom asked.

'Yes. She was one of the better tenants,' Mrs Taylor

answered.

'Do you know how she got the money to pay the rent?

'Look, we don't go digging into our tenants' affairs, sergeant,' Mr Taylor said, 'Xristal Newman paid on time and that was all we cared about.'

'So you had no contact with her?'

'Not once she'd moved in.'

Jasmine had been listening patiently, but felt she had to interject.

'What about the bed?'

Mr and Mrs Taylor both looked at her.

'What about it?' Mr Taylor asked.

'The king sized bed in Xristal's flat doesn't look like the usual thing for a furnished flat.'

A flicker of a memory passed over Mr Taylor's face, while his wife glared at Jasmine.

'Oh yes, the bed. Miss Newman asked if she could replace the bed we provided. She said she needed a different bed to help her sleep. We agreed and she arranged the removal herself. Actually, I think it went into the ground floor flat to replace one that had seen better days.'

'So you think the bed was just to help her sleep, Mr Taylor?' Jasmine said.

'Well, yes,' Kelvin Taylor looked confused.

'You didn't agree to it because it helped her in her bondage games with her clients?'

'Bondage? Clients?'

'You weren't aware that Xristal Newman was a prostitute specialising in BDSM?'

'No!'

'Or that she was a transsexual?'

'Trans...No!' Taylor's face was red and glistening with sweat. His wife gave Jasmine a dark look.

'As my husband told you, Miss Frame, we have had little contact with Miss Newman since she moved in, did not see this bed you mention and certainly had no knowledge that she engaged in sexual activities for money. Nor did we know she was transsexual. My husband dealt with her tenancy agreement and made no mention of anything other than that she was a young woman.' Mrs Taylor stared fixedly Jasmine, as if daring her to contradict.

'Thank you, Mrs Taylor,' Tom intervened. 'I am sure you are aware of the consequences if it is found that you were benefiting from prostitution at any of your properties.'

'Of course, Sergeant.' Mrs Taylor gave Tom a broad but humourless smile.

'We just provide accommodation for those that need it,' Kelvin Taylor said, slumped on the sofa.

'What can you tell us about Honey Potts?' Tom asked.

'Ah, now she's a different case. She owes us money.' Mr Taylor had become animated again.

'What for?'

'She left with no warning. Just disappeared a fortnight ago owing us a couple of months' rent.'

'Did she leave a forwarding address?'

'Of course not, Sergeant,' Mrs Taylor said. 'She doesn't want us pursuing her for what she owes. And before you ask, she's changed her phone. The number she gave us is no longer operative.'

'Doesn't her deposit cover her rent?' Jasmine asked.

Kelvin Taylor snorted, 'Barely covers the cost of cleaning the flat and preparing it for the next tenant. She should have given a months' notice. We've lost all that.'

'Couldn't Xristal tell you where she'd gone?' Jasmine asked.

'I did ring Miss Newman,' Taylor said, 'but she either couldn't or wouldn't tell me where Honey Potts was.'

'Perhaps you could trace her through her bank?' Tom asked.

Taylor snorted again. 'Oh, she was a clever one. Had us there. Paid by cash, monthly. Perhaps I'm too trusting but some tenants prefer to pay that way. It doesn't usually cause us any bother.'

'How did she pay the rent?' Tom asked.

'Sometimes she dropped it off here. Sometimes my wife went to collect it.'

'Oh, so you did go round to Bredon Road, Mrs Taylor, and met Honey?' Jasmine said. This was interesting - surely Mrs Taylor must have noticed something different about Honey Potts' statuesque, well-endowed figure.

'A few times, that's all.' Mrs Taylor waved the question away.

'And you didn't find her appearance unusual?'

'What do you mean? I suppose she was a big woman.'

'You didn't think that she might be transsexual too?'

'Do you see transsexuals everywhere, Miss Frame?' Mrs Taylor spat out Jasmine's name. 'No, I never gave it a thought.'

Kelvin Taylor looked at his watch and heaved himself off the sofa. 'Are there any further questions, Officer? I have another appointment.'

Tom glanced at his notepad. 'We may have more questions, Mr Taylor, but I think that's all for now.'

'Good. My wife will see you out.'

Tom and Jasmine stood up and were ushered towards the front door. As they were leaving, Jasmine turned to Mrs Taylor.

'Xristal and Honey were she-males. Were you aware of that, Mrs Taylor?'

'What a strange term. What does it mean?'

'They had the appearance of women, but the working genitals of a man.'

'What a disgusting thought. Of course I had no idea. Goodbye.' She closed the door on them.

'Why did you ask that?' Tom got into his car.

'I wanted to see how she would react?'

'And?'

'Well, she's a stuck up cow, but she's either a consummate liar or a complete innocent if she wasn't intrigued by Honey Potts' augmentations.' Jasmine plugged in the seat belt.

'Perhaps they do know more about the prostitution angle. We'll have to check their other properties.'

'And definitely put them on your suspect list.'

'What motive would they have? Xristal was apparently paying her rent regularly so why should they want to lose that? There's no evidence linking either of them to the scene. There's not even proof that Xristal and Honey were prostitutes. We need to track down some of their clients.' Tom turned the car back towards Kintbridge. 'Do you think they shared any of Tilly's punters?'

'Tilly caters for a totally different clientele,' Jasmine said. 'Her punters like young-looking girls, not big women with pricks!'

Tom dropped Jasmine off in St Benedict's Street and she sauntered back to Bredon Road. She passed her car and walked the full length of the street. Parfitt's SUV was back in its regular position, but there was no sign of him. Another chance of snapping him missed. Feeling fed up with the chore of surveillance, Jasmine returned to her Fiesta. Sighing frequently, she tried to focus on watching Parfitt's house, but her attention kept wandering. Thoughts of her impending operation and who could pick her up from the hospital, jostled with images of Xristal's remains on the hospital slab and wondering about Xristal's life as a she-male bondage specialist whore. Her mind flicked from one problem to another with no solutions to her questions.

To break the pattern and stop herself nodding off she got out of the car and went for the familiar short walk up and down the street. It was late afternoon by now and there was no movement in Parfitt's house. Her phone rang from inside her bag. She scrabbled for it, hoping it was Tom with some news and perhaps another, more interesting task. Once she had it in her hand she swiped the screen not noticing who the caller was.

'Hi. Tom?'

'No, it's Angela, Jas.'

'Oh. Hi. Sorry I wasn't expecting you...'

'No, well it has been a while hasn't it?' A while! It had been

61

over a month since Jasmine had heard from Angela, and they'd only seen each other once in the nearly three months since the divorce had come through.

'I suppose you've been busy, Ange.'

'Yes. You too?'

'Yeah. I've got quite a bit on.'

'That's good.' Angela's sympathetic tone rankled a bit because it always seemed she doubted that Jasmine could make a go of living and working alone. But, she reflected, they'd had good times together and Angela understood her better than anyone else.

'Look,' Angela went on, 'I haven't got long, but I thought it was about time we met up again, don't you think?'

'Yes. That would be nice.' They always had plenty to talk about whenever they met and, now the divorce was out of the way, there was no more of that irritating legal business to sort out. Perhaps Angela would be free to pick her up from the hospital on Monday?

'How about tomorrow evening, Jas? We could meet in a pub. It's short notice, I know, but…'

'That will be fine.'

Angela would now guess that she still didn't have much of a social life and could come out whenever she called. Well, that was true enough. She was free unless something came up with the investigation, in which case she'd just have to put Angela off.

'Where do you suggest?'

'How about the Earl of Pembroke in Whitclere? Do you know it?'

'Yes, of course.' Jasmine couldn't remember ever visiting the pub, but she knew the area.

'It does good food and it's the type of place where you can have a decent chat.'

'That's good.'

'Shall we say eight o'clock?'

'Fine.'

'Oh, by the way, I'll have a friend with me. His name's Luke.

He's looking forward to meeting you.'

A friend? A boyfriend? Jasmine was surprised at how the news affected her. She knew that now she and Angela were divorced there was nothing stopping Angela finding another man. There hadn't been anything in her way before, to be fair. They were no longer partners and hadn't been lovers for considerably longer but, nevertheless, the thought of Angela being with another man depressed her. Angela would no longer be her soul mate.

'Jasmine? Is that OK? I've got to go.'

'Uh. Yes. I'll see you both tomorrow.'

'Good. Take care.'

Angela hung up. Jasmine found herself standing on the pavement staring at the phone. Why was Angela so keen to meet? Was it to show off her new boyfriend, to prove that she had moved on, that they were no longer an item? The divorce had been a legal necessity rather than a sign that they had stopped loving one another - although in reality their relationship was over. She still loved Angela, although the need to be a woman was a stronger emotion and had put an end to their married life together. She returned to the car, wondering what this Luke would be like and feeling that another thread connecting her with her past life had snapped. Sitting watching nothing happen seemed a pointless exercise and she felt restless. Enough of waiting for Parfitt to appear, she needed to do something. Her mind turned to Xristal and Honey and how they earned the money to support their lifestyle. Were they working on their own or were their clients provided for them by a pimp? She didn't know the answer, but she thought she knew how to find out - and it didn't mean travelling far.

She started the engine and drove slowly along Bredon Road. It was a long road running west from the centre of Kintbridge. At the town end, the houses were elegant Edwardian terraces now somewhat dishevelled and mostly divided into flats. Further along, there was a mishmash of twentieth century architecture, from thirties suburbia through sixties concrete modernism to nineties brick and tile uniformity. Jasmine pulled up outside a detached 1930s house with a drive and a scruffy lawn. Curtains obscured the bay windows on both sides of the front door on the ground floor and above, giving no hint as to whether the house was occupied or what went on inside. But Jasmine knew. She had been here once before.

It had been a drugs raid early one morning, not long after she had transitioned. Unusually, Sloane had her included her in the team on the ground, probably because he needed every body he could get. They hadn't found the drugs they expected, so in most respects it had been a failure. Sloane's mood had been evidence of that. What they had discovered was a brothel occupied by half a dozen working girls, most of whom could barely speak a word of English. The girls were carted off and dispersed, but with no sign of the pimp not a lot happened. The business had been allowed to re-commence, with the police keeping a watchful eye. It was better to know where things were going on rather than them taking place out of sight.

Jasmine recalled the stampede into the house after the door was battered down; the search through the rooms for stashes of drugs; beds overturned, drawers and wardrobes opened and their contents ransacked; the frightened girls, naked or wearing skimpy nightclothes. She remembered the adrenalin rush, the excitement of doing a job she loved. She also remembered the depression and disillusionment when she found herself left out of similar operations, sidelined to look after the desk back at base, the feeling that she wasn't wanted as part of the team anymore.

She dragged the wig off her head. No disguises necessary for this task. Tossing her bag over her shoulder, she got out of the car and walked up the drive to the front door. The one smashed in by the police had been replaced by a more secure-looking, solid wood door. She rang the doorbell and waited. It was difficult to hear anything through the thick door, but at last it opened a few centimetres. Jasmine shoved, hard. The door swung open and she stepped through into the hall. A woman stood backed against the wall, her hand still on the door handle. She was short and could have been anywhere between forty and sixty - her long greying black hair made it difficult to judge. She was wearing a black wraparound dress, but there was little of her to wrap around. Her thin bare arms and legs and hollow cheeks made her look almost emaciated. There was a look of surprise and fear on her face, which slowly turned into disdain as she looked at Jasmine.

'Who are you?' the woman asked, in a husky, eastern European accent.

'I'm a detective.'

The look of fear returned. 'Police?

Jasmine took her private detective's I.D. from her bag and waved it briefly at the woman, not giving her an opportunity to read it.

'Don't worry. I'm not going to arrest you. I just want information.'

The woman pulled herself upright, sniffed and pushed the door closed.

'What information?'

'Are there more of you here?'

The woman opened a door and entered one of the front rooms. Jasmine followed. Despite it still being daylight outside, the thick drawn curtains made the room appear as if it was night-time. A couple of standard lamps provided illumination. Jasmine saw three girls sitting on the sofa and armchairs that lined the walls of the room and were the only furniture, but for a small writing desk in an alcove and a large coffee table in the centre of the room. They were wearing flimsy negligées and stockings and suspenders. One was dark but the other two were pale and, though one was blonde and the other brunette, they looked like twins. They stared at Jasmine with indifference.

'Hi girls,' Jasmine said with a smile – no response. 'Look, I need your help. I wonder if you have seen either of these girls before.' She took her phone out of her bag and quickly thumbed the screen to bring up the image of Xristal and Honey. She walked around the room showing it to each of the three girls. They looked, but showed no flicker of recognition. Finally, she showed it to the older woman who screwed up her nose and shook her head.

There was the thud of the front door opening and steps in the hall. Jasmine dropped her phone into her bag and spun around in time to see a man enter the room. He was shorter than Jasmine by a couple of inches, wore a white T-shirt under a shiny grey suit and had short black hair and a moustache.

'Hey, who are you?' His voice was rough with an estuary twang.

'I'm a detective.'

He scanned Jasmine up and down from her blonde bob to her bare tanned legs.

'I know you,' he said. It was as if a light went on in his head. He smiled. 'Yes, that's it. Your mug was in the papers. You're that trannie who used to be a cop.'

Damn, thought Jasmine. Well, she had taken the decision to remove the wig.

'What are you doing here? Snooping?'

'I just want…'

'We don't have snoopers here. Especially freaks and cock sucking arsefuckers like you.'

He lunged at Jasmine with a hand stretched out, fingers spread to encircle her throat. She didn't think, just stepped aside, grabbed his arm, kicked his legs out from under him and pushed him to the floor, pressing his face against the thin carpet with her knee in the small of his back. The girls and the woman looked on impassively.

'I don't like being insulted by morons like you,' Jasmine said, 'especially when I was simply being polite and asking for information. I don't care what sordid little business you have going on here.'

The man struggled ineffectively, then lay still.

'What information?'

'Are you going to be sensible?' Jasmine asked with another

prod of her knee in his back and a twist of his arm.

'Ow. You're killing me.'

'You won't attack me again?'

'No. Let me up. I can't breathe.'

Jasmine released the arm and stood up. She stepped away from the man towards the exit and retrieved her bag which she had dropped. The man rolled over and sat up rubbing his arm.

'What do you want then if it's got nothing to do with this place?'

'I want to know if you know anything about the competition.'

'Competition?' His face was blank. He pushed himself to his feet.

'Yes. A couple of working girls in a house down the road.'

The man shrugged. Jasmine got her phone out again and held it up for him to look at.

'These two. Seen them around?'

The man bent close to examine the photo. He let out a bark of a laugh.

'They're geezers. Faggots with tits. Like you.'

Jasmine pursed her lips.

'No, not like me, but they are she-males.'

'I don't deal in perversions. My girls,' he waved his hand at the three sullen young women, 'offer a good honest service to straight blokes who want a bit of relaxation.'

Jasmine shook the phone to get his attention. 'But do you know them or anything about them?'

He screwed up his face in an expression of distaste. 'Nope. I've never seen either of them and I hope I never do, fucking perverts.'

'What about your clients?'

'I told you, my girls' clients are straight guys. They wouldn't touch those freaks with a bargepole. But I hope your old friends in the Bill run them out of town. I don't want this area getting a reputation for the kind of filth they get up to.'

'You want this area for yourself do you?'

'Why not? Can't a bloke make a few quid providing personal massage for hardworking guys?'

Jasmine accepted she wasn't going to get any more useful information. At least she'd found out that Xristal and Honey were probably working on their own without this or any other pimp keeping an eye on them.

'I hope it is just massage your girls offer. My old friends, as you call them, will be taking an interest otherwise.'

The man laughed again. He had regained most of his early swagger.

'I don't think old man Sloane will be in a hurry to come here again after the egg on his face he got last time. Get out of here you cock-teaser. Margot – show the man out.'

Jasmine bit her lip and dropped her phone back in her bag. Backing into the hall, she kept the grinning pimp in her sight. The older woman, Margot, squeezed past her and opened the front door. As she left, Jasmine whispered, 'Don't let him bully you or the girls, Margot. Get in touch with the police or me.' She held out one of her cards but Margot shook her head and made no move to take it. Jasmine shrugged and stepped outside. The door closed with a heavy clunk.

She returned to her car feeling dejected and dirty. Seeing women being abused as the three girls obviously were demoralised her. She'd let Tom know what she'd seen and he could decide whether another raid, this time for evidence of prostitution, was in order. But the point was she had found out little about Xristal. She sighed, started the engine and headed home.

Jasmine fidgeted and paced around her small, dreary flat. She hoped a hot bath would help her relax. Concentrating on shaving her legs and arms until they were smooth and hair-free occupied her for a while. Having dried herself, she dressed simply in a short cotton skirt and T-shirt, picked up cheaply from Primark, re-did her always necessary make-up and decided to look for something to eat. The fridge was, as usual, almost bare but she found leftovers of a spaghetti bolognaise in the freezer. She heated it up and ate it with a slice of bread. She told herself she must do some shopping. When? Tomorrow? It was Friday. She tried to sit down and watch TV, but she couldn't settle. Everything she had learned about Xristal that day kept going through her head.

How did she find her clients? Were they all off the internet or did she use traditional methods? Jasmine was impatient to find out. Sitting around doing nothing irritated her. Finally, she'd had enough. Slipping on her pumps, she grabbed her bag and left the flat. She got into her car and started to drive. Where was she going? No ideas occurred to her as she turned onto the main road heading into the town centre. It was while entering the one-way system she remembered. Some of the street girls used to assemble and tout for business near where Xristal had lived. She'd go and talk to them, see if they knew Xristal.

Back on St Benedicts Street again, she passed the turning to Bredon Road and drove on over the railway line. She pulled into a road on the right and found somewhere to park. She wandered casually back to the main street, crossed and turned into Railway Terrace. The road dropped down to the station, the lights of which were visible a couple of hundred metres further on. The original row of terraced houses was long gone, replaced by the long, windowless concrete wall of a disused retail warehouse, daubed with flaking graffiti. The pavement opposite ran along a fence bordering the railway cutting. The sun had already sunk behind the buildings to the west and the evening gloom was settling. Three women were loitering under a solitary streetlight. Jasmine crossed the road to join them.

As she approached, Jasmine noticed that two of them were very young, probably still in their teens. Both had long blonde hair. The other was visibly older, late thirties at least, with bleached hair. All three wore short, tight skirts, breast-hugging tops and high heeled sandals.

'What do you want?' The oldest woman said threateningly.

'I wonder if you can help me,' Jasmine replied, trying to

sound as mild and unthreatening as possible.

'Not a cop are you?' the woman asked. The younger women backed away, getting ready to make a run for it if necessary.

'No,' Jasmine said.

'Well, don't think you can muscle in. This is our pitch.'

The two girls glared as if daring Jasmine to contradict their companion. Was she offended by being taken as a possible rival? She found she wasn't.

'It's OK, I'm not looking for business. I'm trying to find out about someone. She may have come here looking for pick-ups.'

'Soliciting, you mean?' the woman sneered.

'Yes. Do you recognise her?' Jasmine held up her phone displaying the picture of Xristal and Honey.

'Which one?'

'The smaller one with dark hair.'

The woman leaned in to look closely. The two girls also peered at the photo.

'No. Don't know her. The other one though. I've seen him around here a few times.'

The girls nodded but said nothing

'Him?'

'Yeah. Did himself up like a woman, but I knew he had a cock between his legs.'

'What was she, he, doing here?'

'Looking for punters. What else do you think he was doing?'

'Did she have any success?'

'He got in a couple of cars. Most of the time though, the drivers just pulled away as soon as he took a step towards them.'

'She wasn't popular with you girls?'

'Complete shit, wasn't he? Told him to get lost, but he kept coming back until we said we'd put a pimp onto him.'

'You threatened him?'

'You bet. The stupid bugger was bad for business.'

'Did you get the pimp?'

'Nah. Try to avoid them if I can help it. They nose around here, but I wouldn't trust them an inch myself.'

'When was that?'

'A month or so back.'

'So, did Honey stop coming after that?' Jasmine continued.

'Called himself Honey did he? Can't say he looked that sweet. Well, he didn't appear again.'

That wasn't long before Honey left her flat, Jasmine calculated.

'Did you know any of the men she, uh he, went with?'

'Nah. If they were prepared to go off with a bloke in a skirt then they weren't looking for a real girl. So no, this Honey tosser didn't pick up any of our regulars.'

'You can't tell me anything about them?'

'No. I couldn't care less about them - wankers. Why are you so interested then? You after the same guys?'

Jasmine's heart thudded in her chest. Had she been read? Did this prostitute think she was like Honey? She was aware of the three women encircling her, but she needed to press on.

'So you do get kerb crawlers looking for she-males?'

'She-males!' The woman spat a gobbet of phlegm onto the pavement. 'Of course we do. Fucking pricks looking for every sort of excitement – girls, boys, boys who look like girls.' She leaned forward to peer at Jasmine. 'You are one aren't you? You got balls in your knickers?'

She reached forward between Jasmine's knees. Jasmine recoiled backwards but found the two girls behind her. They grabbed Jasmine's shoulders and held her tight. The older woman's hand groped between her thighs.

'No, I'm not! I'm not like them,' Jasmine shouted, unwilling to use her police training to free herself.

'Yeah. You fucking trannies. Think you look like women but you want to fuck like any bloke don't you?'

'No!'

The hooker's fingers reached up her thighs, touched the taut Lycra, failed to find her testicles dangling. They were tucked away, constrained in Jasmine's tight knickers. Jasmine twisted out of the arms of the younger girls, turned and ran back up

Railway Terrace. Tears blurred her eyes as she repeated to herself: I'm not like them, I am a woman.

4

FRIDAY

Jasmine hurried out of the flat, throwing her bag and camera over her shoulder. It was eight a.m. and she felt as if she'd been awake all night. Actually, she probably had. She tried to put the agonies of tossing and turning in bed out of her mind as she got into the Fiesta. Xristal Newman and Honey Potts were to be banished from her thoughts. She was just going to get on with the surveillance of Parfitt and with any luck get the evidence the Fraud Investigation Service wanted.

She turned the key in the ignition. The starter motor churned but the engine didn't start. The phone in her bag began to ring. Jasmine released the ignition key and groped for the phone.

'Good morning, is that Jasmine Frame?' Jasmine recognised the voice of her FIS contact.

'Yes. Hi.' She tried to sound bright and cheerful.

'We are still waiting for your report on the Parfitt case.'

'I'm sorry. I haven't completed my observation yet.'

'Why is it taking so long?'

'He's been very careful. He hasn't shown he can walk unaided.'

'Well, we can't hang around any longer. I need that report on my desk tomorrow or we will have to terminate the contract.'

'I'm on it. One more day.'

'Please email your report to me by four pm tomorrow afternoon. Goodbye.'

The phone went silent.

Damn. Jasmine glared at the display. It was just as well she was giving up on Xristal. She would have all day to get the evidence on Parfitt. One day to save her reputation, such as it was. She turned the key in the ignition again. Thankfully, the engine coughed into something resembling life and she joined the traffic crawling along the Bristol Road.

Her thoughts turned to the previous evening. How could she have been such a fool as to talk to those women last night? She shuddered in disgust and embarrassment at not only being so easily read as being transgender, but at being thought to be a she-male like Honey. It was that accusation that disgusted her most. How could the women have thought that she still wanted her male bits? She should have been easily able to handle the situation with the three women without having to resort to her self-defence training, especially as they were probably drugged up and teetering on high heels. Thankfully, she had got away easily enough, but hardly with her dignity intact. Still, at least she had found out that although Xristal hadn't been seen on the street, Honey actively solicited. Not surprising if Xristal specialised in the more sophisticated art of bondage - she would have made contact with selected clients much more carefully. Well, it was down to Tom Shepherd and the rest of DCI Sloane's team to trawl the internet for any leads on Xristal's clients.

Pulling into Bredon Road, Jasmine was pleased to find a parking space close to Parfitt's house. She was just about to get out of the car, when the front door of his house opened and Parfitt appeared on his crutches. He limped out to the road and got into his four-by-four. Jasmine hurriedly turned the key in her ignition, praying the hot engine would re-start. It did, reluctantly, and she performed a quick three pointer to follow Parfitt. Turning on to St Benedicts, two cars got between her and Parfitt and she was terrified that she might be caught by a traffic light and lose sight of him. She trailed him through the town centre and then he joined the dual carriageway heading north. Jasmine took a deep breath and relaxed a little.

Parfitt accelerated beyond the speed limit. Jasmine floored her accelerator. With the Fiesta's ancient engine screaming, she just managed to keep pace. The temperature gauge rose slowly but inexorably as the miles passed by. She prayed that Parfitt wasn't heading for Birmingham or even further north. Her poor old car couldn't keep up this pace for long and she didn't have enough petrol for a long journey.

They reached the outskirts of Oxford. Parfitt signalled and turned onto a slip road. Jasmine sighed with relief; perhaps they weren't going much further. They followed the ring road for a few miles then turned into a housing estate. Jasmine held back, hoping that Parfitt had not noticed her in his mirrors. He pulled up outside a three-bed semi. Jasmine shoved her foot hard on the brake and stopped fifty metres away. She grabbed her camera from the passenger seat. This could be her only chance to get a good shot of her target. Luckily there were no vehicles in the way. She had a clear sight through the viewfinder. She watched the car door open. Parfitt stepped out on to the road - without crutches.

Jasmine held the shutter down taking shot after shot as Parfitt walked easily and without any trace of a limp around the car and up the path to the front door. Moments later, he disappeared inside. At last she had her evidence, but it wouldn't hurt to get more. She'd wait to catch Parfitt again as he came out. First she would move the car and get into a better position.

Jasmine yawned. It had been three hours without any sign of Parfitt. She had left the Fiesta a short way down a side road just out of sight of where he had parked. The estate was pretty deserted. Most people must be at work or out shopping or watching daytime TV. Just a few cars had driven past and there had been even fewer pedestrians. At last the door of the house opened. Jasmine crouched behind the wall of the neighbouring house. She peered through the viewfinder and clicked off a series of shots as Parfitt sauntered back to his car turning to wave to whoever he had visited.

Jasmine hurried back to the Fiesta, sliding the memory card out of the camera as she did so. It was almost full and she was convinced that the FIS would be very happy with the evidence she had. She dropped the card into her bag and dug out her keys. As she put her car into gear, she caught a glimpse of Parfitt's car turning at the end of the road so she accelerated after him. As she followed at a discreet distance she was relieved to see him apparently heading back to Kintbridge. He wasn't taking his time though and she had to strain her poor little car to keep up. The return journey was uneventful and Jasmine was able to keep Parfitt in sight while staying far enough back so as not to arouse his suspicions. When she pulled into Bredon Road she was annoyed to find Parfitt occupying the final convenient parking space when she pulled into Bredon Road. She drove past him as he was getting out of his car with his crutches and watched in her rearview mirror as he limped across the road towards his house. Turning into a side road she saw a space just big enough for the Fiesta which she was able to manoeuvre into It was still only lunchtime, so a bit more waiting around wouldn't hurt if she could get even more evidence of Parfitt's fraud. She clicked a new memory card into the camera, cradled it in her arm and opened the car door.

The door was abruptly wrenched from her hand and an arm reached in and grabbed the front of her T-shirt. It was Parfitt, his crutches discarded. Jasmine allowed him to pull her out of the car to avoid her T-shirt being torn from her breasts. Off balance, she leaned against the roof of the Fiesta, her feet in the gutter with her toes squashed against the kerb.

'You've been following me, haven't you?' he growled. Jasmine pulled his hand off her chest, pushed his arm away from her, straightened her skirt and smoothed the creases out of her T-shirt. 'I know who you are - you're that detective that was in all the papers!'

Jasmine raised a hand to her head and felt her own hair. Shit, she had forgotten to put a wig on. There wasn't any point in denying anything. She had to find a way out of this. Parfitt's anger was mounting.

'You've been following me you perv. I've seen your wreck

around here for days. You followed me all the way to Oxford, didn't you?' His eyes dropped from her face to the camera still held in the crook of her arm. 'And taking photographs, you fucking scumbag. Give me that camera.'

He made a grab for it and pulled it from her.

'Give that back,' Jasmine shouted, 'or I'll have you done for theft as well as benefit fraud!' She reached for the camera. The back of Parfitt's hand slammed into her face. She fell sideways, grabbing the roof of the car to stop herself falling to the ground.

'Think you've got evidence do you?'

She looked over her shoulder and, through tears, saw him pull the memory card from its slot. He thrust the camera back at her. Jasmine twisted around and grabbed it from him.

'Here, cunt, you can have it.' He stepped back and looked at her again.

'You were at that fire in Xristal's place on Wednesday, weren't you? You had a stupid wig on then, but it was definitely you.'

'Xristal's place?' Jasmine felt her sore chin..

'The girl who died. It was you that broke in to her flat, wasn't it?'

'Yes. I found the body.'

'How was she?' Parfitt became almost conversational.

'What do you mean?'

'Was she, uh, tied up?'

A light went on in Jasmine's brain.

'Why? Did you tie her up? Did you kill her?' She straightened up and stepped towards Parfitt. She was taller than him. He backed away, realising that he'd said too much. His bravado ebbed away.

'No, no. It was nothing to do with me. I've not been near her.'

He turned and hurried away, picking up his crutches as he went.

'You'll be hearing from the police!' Jasmine shouted at his receding back.

She got back into the car and checked the camera for damage. The thought of Parfitt thinking he'd got her memory card with the incriminating photos brought a smile to her face. Pain shot through her jaw. Damn, she'd have a bruise. She got her phone out of her bag and thumbed Tom's number. He answered quickly.

'Hi, Jas. I was wondering when you'd get round to calling. You just got up? We've got work to do.'

'Actually, I have been working, and guess what?'

'What?'

'It looks like Parfitt knew about Xristal.'

'Parfitt?'

'My benefit cheat. The reason why I was outside Xristal's house.'

'Oh, him. Nothing came up in the house to house.'

'Of course not. He'd deny even knowing she existed; but it slipped out when we were having a slight contretemps just now.'

'A contra- what?'

'A fight, or a chat. Both really.'

'I thought you were just supposed to be watching him?'

'Yes, well he noticed.'

'Not so good.'

'Ah, but not before I got my evidence.'

'Oh, that's OK then. We can haul him in to answer a few questions.'

'Yes. Now what other work have we got?'

'Come round to the station. I'll meet you in the car park and tell you all about it. We're getting somewhere with Miss or Mr Newman.'

'OK, I'll see you in a few minutes.'

Jasmine dropped the phone into her bag. Tom might be expecting her soon, but before setting off she needed to make herself a little more presentable. She got out a mirror and examined her face. There was an ugly red mark on her chin. She did her best to cover it with some concealer and foundation, put on some lipstick and brushed her hair smooth and straight. The face reflected back at her looked just about acceptable even though she could feel the swelling. She dropped her make up stuff back into her bag and put it on the passenger seat. Now she was ready to meet Tom.

DS Shepherd was waiting on the steps of the Police HQ. Jasmine gave him a wave and he walked towards her as she pulled into a parking place. He was alongside by the time she had stopped, turned the engine off and grabbed her bag and camera from the passenger seat.

'That was more than a few minutes. The traffic isn't bad, is it?' he said as she got out of the car.

'No. I had to repair my make-up.'

Tom looked at her face in concern.

'Is that a bruise on your chin?'

'Damn! Is it showing already?' Jasmine reached into her bag for her mirror and once again examined the damage.

'Parfitt did that? What did he do, punch you?'

'A backhand. He might have had a ring on his finger which has made it worse.'

'Are you going to report the shit?'

'It's his word against mine, so probably not. But I've got my evidence on him, even though he thinks he's taken it off me.'

'Oh?'

'And he obviously knows something about Xristal. He certainly knows she got herself tied up from time to time.'

'I told Sloane. He was pretty pleased as we haven't got anywhere with identifying her clients yet. He'll get Parfitt dragged in for questioning while we're gone.'

'Gone? Where are we going?'

'Come and get in my car. I'll explain while we're driving.'

Tom led the way to his Mondeo and Jasmine settled into the passenger seat. After a morning in her old rust-heap Jasmine was envious of the comforts of the larger, modern car. They negotiated the town centre traffic and soon were on the A road heading east. Tom relaxed and spoke.

'The bank has been very helpful.'

'Great, what have they told us about Xristal?'

'Well, they only know him, her - I don't know which it should be, him I suppose - as Christopher Newman. He's had the account for years and they have a number of changes of address.'

'That may help us find people who know her.'

'Exactly. But it's the oldest address that's most interesting. We think it's his parents' home in Reading. The electoral role gives the names of the occupants as Mr William and Mrs Julia Newman. That's who you and I are going to see now.'

'Why me?' Jasmine felt excited and nervous. What would facing Xristal's mother and father be like? As a police officer she'd been the bearer of news of deaths before, but this was a bit different.

'Yes. Sloane thought you would know how to deal with the parents of a she-male.'

'Hmph. Making assumptions again is he? It all depends if they know about Xristal.'

'You think they might not?'

'It's a strong possibility. Christopher may have cut himself off from his past life when he became Xristal. Whatever he was, he'd probably come a long way from being the son his parents thought they knew.'

'Hmm, that's an interesting insight. You certainly understand a lot more about this sort of thing than we do.'

Jasmine was silent, thinking about how to play the meeting with Mr and Mrs Newman. Tom concentrated on driving.

After a few minutes Jasmine spoke again.

'Did anything else interesting come out of talking to the bank?'

'Yes. The account has been used a lot in the last couple of years. Xristal had been making fairly regular, sizeable deposits and also some large withdrawals. There was one to a private clinic in Hertford about two years ago.'

'About when she and Honey moved into Bredon Road?'

'That's right.'

'Could be when she had the boob job.'

'Maybe. And there were several payments to a beauty consultant recently.'

'Dr Winslade said she'd had electrolysis to remove her facial hair.'

'That's right. Actually the two biggest withdrawals were very recent. She'd almost cleaned out the account. One was to Etihad, the airline. We've checked it out. She had tickets in her female name to Suvarnabhumi.Bangkok airport for a couple of weeks' time. She was going out for a month.'

'Really? What was the other?

'It was to a clinic in Chonburi. We haven't been able to make contact with them to find out more yet.'

'Wow, that really is interesting.' Jasmine stroked her sore jaw.

'What was she up to? We've checked her current passport and it's in the name of Christopher Newman. She wouldn't have been able to use the flight tickets with that passport.'

'I think if you dig a little deeper you'll find she applied for a passport under her female name. It's probably in the system somewhere.'

'But he's still male.'

'You don't need a full gender reassignment to get a new passport. '

'What was he travelling to Thailand for then?'

'Xristal could have been going for some more cosmetic surgery. Hip and bum implants, for example.'

'What? To make his bum larger?' Tom snorted.

'Don't laugh. Real women have it done as well as trans-women.'

'What on earth for? Don't most women worry their arses are too big?'

'Actually, quite a lot of women want a more curvaceous look. One thing you can't change is bone structure, and men and trans-women have a narrow pelvis. Implants can give the appearance of wider, more feminine hips.'

Tom shook his head.

'How much was Xristal's payment to the Thai medics?' Jasmine asked.

'Um, about fifteen grand.'

'Well, it wasn't cosmetic surgery then.'

'Why not?'

'I don't think even a full bum and hip job would be that expensive.'

'What was she having done then?'

'I reckon she was going to have the full gender reassignment.'

'That's what you're having, isn't it?'

'Yes, but not yet. I can't afford that sort of money. The fifteen grand is probably only half of what the whole trip would have cost her.'

'I didn't realise it cost that much.'

'That's why I'm having to do it in stages on the NHS, Tom. It looks as though Xristal was going for the complete replacement of her male genitals with a vagina, the full works.'

'Right.'

'It's interesting. We, or at least I, have been thinking of Xristal and Honey as being the same: two aggressively promiscuous she-males, both perfectly content with their male organs, while flaunting the secondary female characteristics they'd given themselves. This suggests that Xristal wasn't like that. Perhaps in a few weeks she would have been physically and legally female.'

'Yeah, but so what?'

'Well, it would make a few changes to her business arrangements with her clients, wouldn't it?'

'What? Oh, I see, she wouldn't have a cock anymore.'

'That's right. Her clients probably wanted her to have a cock. What would they think about her changing sex?'

Tom let out a long low whistle. 'I wonder.'

'And then there's Honey. She and Xristal were obviously pretty close, at least until Honey left. Honey is a different character. Obviously male despite her enhancements, and happy to pick up guys at the kerbside.

'How do you know?' Tom glanced at Jasmine with a frown.

'I spoke to some of Kintbridge's working girls last night.'

'You did? Where?'

'Railway Terrace.'

'They still there? I thought we'd moved them on. It used to be as busy as the station itself.'

'There were just three of them last night. They recognised Honey but not Xristal. A bit pissed off actually, because Honey buggered up their own soliciting.'

'I can imagine. Hold on, I'm going to have to turn the volume up on the sat nav. It's a while since I've been to Reading.'

'But I'm pretty sure both of them were freelancing.'

'How do you know they didn't have a pimp?'

'I made enquiries at that brothel further up Bredon Road.'

'The one we raided for drugs?'

'That's right.'

'You went there? Sloane won't like that. We're keeping it under hands-off observation.'

'I know, but I don't care what Sloane thinks. I'm not a cop anymore.'

'Hmm, not sure he'll accept that argument. What did you find out?'

'There were a few girls and a maid looking after them. They all seemed to be from Eastern Europe and didn't look particularly happy. If I was Sloane I'd be exploring the trafficking angle.'

'I'm sure he is.'

'Well, then this guy with a London accent arrived. He wasn't very happy to find me there.'

'I'm not surprised. Was he a little guy with a moustache?'

'Yes.'

'Ah, that'll be the Colonel.'

'Colonel?'

'Rhyming slang. Colonel Blimp – pimp.'

'I see… but he's not…'

'No, of course not. He appeared a few months ago and took over the brothel. Sent by the big guys in London. We're keeping an eye on what he's up to. So what happened?'

'He went for me and I had to teach him a lesson.' Jasmine was quietly proud that she was still able to bring her police training into play.

'I bet that cheered him up.'

'Made his day, the nasty little shit.'

'Did you get anything out of him?'

'Only that he didn't recognise Xristal or Honey but saw immediately what they, or rather what Honey, was. He didn't like the thought of them operating on his patch even though they weren't taking any of his customers. I'm sure Xristal and Honey must have been getting their clients from a completely different source.'

'So, we're back to trawling the internet,' Tom sighed. They'd been driving through the suburbs of Reading for some time, but Tom at last drew to a halt outside a smart, 1930s detached house.

Tom rang the doorbell then stepped back to stand alongside Jasmine. She felt small and insignificant beside him and self-conscious that while he was in his dark, formal suit she was just in a short skirt and T-shirt.

The door was opened by a woman. Jasmine estimated that she was in her late forties. She had dark hair with a few flecks of grey and was smartly dressed in a pale blue dress that showed off a slim, well-cared for figure.

'Mrs Julia Newman?' Tom asked, 'I'm a police officer, DS Shepherd,' he held out his ID card. 'Miss Frame here is a special police advisor. May we come in please?'

Mrs Newman looked nervously at them.

'Oh, yes, of course.' She opened the door wide and stepped back into the hallway. Tom and Jasmine followed her into a light and airy sitting room where a pair of sofas were set at right angles around a fireplace.

'Please take a seat. Can I get you a drink, tea, coffee?' she said.

'No, thank you,' Tom said, sitting on one sofa. Jasmine sat beside him, tugging her skirt down her thighs and pressing her bare knees together. 'Please sit down, Mrs Newman. Is Mr Newman at home?'

'No, he's at work, in London,' Mrs Newman replied, as she sat down on the other sofa.

'I see. Is there someone, a relative or a friend, that you can get hold of?'

Mrs Newman turned pale and covered her mouth. 'Nothing's happened to William has it?'

'Your husband? No, not that we are aware of. We're here to ask some questions about your son.'

'Christopher?' She was shaking now. 'Is he all right?'

Jasmine looked at Tom. He was hesitating, wondering what to say. 'Well, we think we may have some news, but...'

'Have you seen Christopher recently?' Jasmine interrupted.

'No,' a sob began to shake Julia Newman's chest. 'We haven't seen him for six years, but we hear from him now and again. He sends postcards from all over the country.' She stood up and picked up a pile of cards from the mantelpiece. She handed them to Jasmine.

They were indeed pictures of places all over the British Isles but most had postmarks from the Thames Valley and Berkshire. The messages were brief and cheery and signed "Chris". She passed them to Tom.

'You don't know where he's been living?'

'No, although I don't think he's been far away as you can tell from the postmarks.'

'And you haven't been in contact with him?'

'No, he's never given us an address. All we've had are these cards to tell us he's still alive.'

'I can see that this upsets you, Mrs Newman, but do you

know why he's cut himself off from you?'

'No. We really can't understand it. He was such a bright, loving boy, but as he went through his teens he became more and more angry and unsettled. He should have been one of the top students in his year, but he only just scraped enough GCSEs to stay on for the sixth form. He left just before his A2s, not that he would have passed any. By then he was uncontrollable, spending nights out, hardly at home at all.'

'Did you try to get him some kind of help or support?'

'What kind of help? He wasn't ill. He wasn't on drugs or drinking; there was no sign of that. He wasn't getting into trouble with the police. It just seemed that he couldn't stand being here, at home - with us.'

'Did anything particular happen when he left for the last time?'

'No. His exams were coming up and it was obvious he hadn't worked for them. He just went out one day and didn't come back.'

'Did you report his disappearance?' Tom asked

'After a week. Every other time he'd come back after a few days. We went to the police, but because he was eighteen they weren't too concerned. Then we had the first postcard. The police lost interest once we confirmed that it was in Christopher's writing.'

'So legally he wasn't missing?' Tom said.

'Yes, but we still didn't know what to do. For a couple of months we waited, hoping he'd come home. There were a couple more cards, but they didn't tell us anything. I was in a terrible state, wondering where he was, how he was living. William tried to take it calmly, but I knew he was as worried sick as I was.'

'Did you do anything to try and find Christopher?' Tom asked.

'We hired a private detective to try and find him, no expense spared. But after three months he still hadn't found Christopher.'

'What information did you give the detective?' Tom questioned again.

Mrs Newman frowned. 'You are asking me a lot of questions. You must know something about Christopher or you wouldn't be here. What's happened to him? Where is he?'

Jasmine saw Tom redden beneath his tan. She knew he didn't want to tell Mrs Newman that Christopher/Xristal was dead, not while she was on her own. He pulled his mobile from his pocket. 'I need to make a call. Excuse me, please,' he said, getting up and leaving the room.

'Where's he going? Why didn't he answer my question?' Jasmine watched a flash of anger pass over Mrs Newman's face, quickly replaced by fear. 'Christopher's dead, isn't he?'

Jasmine felt trapped and at a loss. What should she say? Without official status, how could she inform this mother of the death of her son?

'I'm sure DS Shepherd will answer your questions when he returns, Julia. May I call you that?' Jasmine said as soothingly as possible.

Mrs Newman hardly seemed to register what Jasmine was saying. 'He's dead, isn't he? Christopher's dead?' she said in a barely audible whisper. 'Please tell me.'

Jasmine hesitated, then crossed the room to sit beside Mrs Newman.

'We have found a body,' Jasmine said, 'but we're not sure it's Christopher.' She struggled to maintain a poker face. She mustn't give the poor woman reason to be hopeful.

'I see. And you need identification so you can tell that it's not Christopher you've found.' Mrs Newman got up and crossed the room to a display cabinet. She slid the glass doors open and reached in for a framed photo. She returned to Jasmine and thrust the frame into her hands. 'That's him.'

It was a school photo showing a young man, a teenager, with long, thick black hair.

'When was this taken, Julia?' Jasmine asked.

'Eight years ago. Christopher was sixteen. It's the last

photograph I have. He hated having his picture taken.'

The boy looked younger than his years, his white school shirt revealing a slight build and flat chest. His face was pale with an expression that betrayed his discomfort at having his photo taken. Jasmine looked hard at his facial features, struggling to match them with those of Xristal. She thought that they were probably the same person, although eight years and cosmetic surgery had wrought significant changes. The photo alone was not enough to be one hundred per cent certain of the identification.

Tom entered and returned to his seat. 'The Family Liaison Officer is on her way,' he said. Jasmine sensed his discomfort and knew that he realised that he should have been prepared for the possibility of Julia Newman being alone.

'Julia guessed that we had some bad news,' Jasmine said, 'She's given me a photo of Christopher.' She leaned forward to hand the picture to Tom. He examined it carefully.

'The body you found, it's not Christopher? The photo is proof, isn't it?' Mrs Newman looked at him hopefully.

Jasmine saw the look of pain on Tom's face as he realised he had to tell her the truth.

'I'm very sorry to have to tell you this, Mrs Newman, but we have good evidence that the body we have is that of your son, and while this photo is insufficient for a positive identification it does show considerable resemblance...'

'What do you mean, considerable? It's only been eight years! He can't have changed that much. Surely you can tell if the body is Christopher or someone else?'

'I'm sorry,' Tom said, clearly having difficulty choosing his words, 'but Christopher's features have altered since this photo was taken.'

'Why? Has he been in an accident? Has his face been injured?' Mrs Newman sobbed and buried her face in her hands. Jasmine put her arm around her shoulders - the woman's distress was palpable. The most difficult part of any investigation was being the bearer of bad news.

'His face wasn't damaged when he died,' Jasmine said, being as honest as she could, 'but his appearance has changed since he left home.'

Mrs Newman looked at her through her tears.

'I know he's older now, a grown man, but how could he change as much as you say?'

Jasmine saw Tom looking at her with desperate eyes. Jasmine knew she had to delve into the Newmans' family life to discover how Mrs Newman would react to being told about Xristal – that she was a prostitute as well as being transgender.

'You said that Christopher was difficult as a teenager. Do you have any ideas why? What was the matter with him?'

'You say my son is dead, but you are asking why he was an awkward teenager!' Mrs Newman's sudden flash of anger took Jasmine by surprise.

'We do think Christopher is dead, Julia. I am very sorry, but we do need to find out why he died and who killed him.'

Mrs Newman's anger died instantly and she covered her mouth with her hands.

'Christopher was murdered? How?'

'He was smothered,' Tom continued. 'I'm sorry to have to tell you this, Mrs Newman, and we will try to answer all the questions you have, but there are things we need to know for the purposes of our investigation.'

'Smothered?' Jasmine was amazed at how quickly Mrs Newman recovered her composure. 'Then why had his appearance changed?'

'It may be related to his behaviour when he was growing up,' Jasmine said. 'You said he was difficult and didn't like being photographed. Did he dislike his appearance?'

'Yes. He hated seeing himself in a mirror or a photo.'

'He looks like an attractive boy. What didn't he like about himself?'

'He would never say, but how he looked was one of the problems, I suppose. My husband was always going on at him to get his hair cut.'

'Was there anything else that your husband found difficult to accept about Christopher?'

'Well, William always wanted a boy – someone who he could talk about things like sport and cars with. But Christopher didn't like any of those things.'

'So your husband didn't get on with Christopher?'

'William is…was a good father.'

'But…'

'No, William found Christopher difficult. They had rows. William said Christopher was gay.'

'Was he?'

'I don't know. I never thought so. Christopher never had any close friendships with boys but he was friends with lots of girls – not serious girlfriends, just girls he chatted with.'

'There was nothing else in Christopher's behaviour that you think caused him to move away as soon as he could?'

'No. We thought it was because he'd had enough of the rows with William. William was very upset when he realised he was probably the cause of Christopher going and tried everything he could to get him to come back.'

'Including employing a private eye?' Tom had been listening closely to the exchange. 'What information did you give him?'

'Well, there wasn't much. We showed him the postcards that Christopher sent and he had a look in Christopher's room, but as I said, he didn't get anywhere.'

'Is Christopher's room still as the private eye saw it?' Jasmine was hopeful that the answer was yes.

'Yes. It hasn't changed since Christopher left. I thought he would come back and would want his things. As time went on, I couldn't bear to go in there and change anything.'

'May I see it?' Jasmine asked.

'Yes, if you like. It's up the stairs and on the right, but I don't see how it can help you find out how why Christopher has been murdered.'

'You never know,' Jasmine said, getting to her feet. She left the room and climbed the stairs to the landing. There were four doors, but only one was on her right and it was closed. Jasmine turned the handle but had to give it a push to unstick the door in its jamb. It was as if the paint had sealed it after years of disuse. The room was dark because the curtains were closed. Jasmine pulled them open dislodging a thin veil of dust. She looked around. It was clearly a teenager's bedroom – single bed, desk, wardrobe, chest of drawers, a couple of bookshelves with books and ornaments - but surprisingly lacking any individual touches of a boy, or a girl. There were no model cars or aeroplanes on display and the walls were bare of posters of rock bands or computer games. Neither were there photos or mirrors. Jasmine was surprised at how sterile the room was. It told her nothing of the personality of its occupant. Perhaps Christopher hadn't wanted to reveal much about himself. She looked at the book titles. Most were classics - Austen, the Brontes, Alcott - but some were modern. Jasmine recognised some chicklit authors: Sophie Kinsella, Cecelia Ahern. She smiled to herself. Would a male private eye have seen the significance of those titles and authors? She thought not.

Jasmine slid the doors of the wardrobe open. There were jackets, trousers and shirts that looked like school wear, a few pairs of skinny jeans, but nothing else. She pulled open the drawers of the chest. One was filled with boxer shorts and socks, another had a pile of T-shirts and jumpers. There wasn't much space for anything else.

She got down onto her knees and peered under the bed. The space was empty except for a magazine. Jasmine pulled it out and read the title – "Seventeen" - dated over six years ago. She smiled again and tucked it under her arm.

Closing the door behind her, Jasmine retraced her steps down the stairs to the lounge.

'You weren't long,' Mrs Newman commented, 'Did you find anything?'

'Did Christopher take any of his clothes with him?'

'No. That's why we thought he wouldn't be gone long. The only thing missing was his laptop as far as I could tell.'

'Judging by the clothes in his wardrobe, Christopher seemed to wear jeans and T-shirts when he wasn't at school.' Jasmine said.

'Yes, he had no interest in clothes at all. I had a real struggle getting him to choose trousers and shoes. He never wanted to go shopping with me.'

Jasmine held out the magazine.

'I found this under the bed. It's a magazine for teenage girls.'

'I know. I thought one of his female friends must have left it behind. They did come over and see him now and again.'

'Did you speak to these girls when he disappeared?'

'Yes, we knew a couple of them that lived nearby. They couldn't tell us where he'd gone or why.' Mrs Newman stared at Jasmine. 'You know something, don't you? You and your partner,' she waved a hand vaguely in Tom's direction. 'You haven't just come to tell me that Christopher is dead.'

'That's right,' Jasmine said, while Tom started to open his mouth, 'but we wanted to know how much you knew before we said something that would shock you.'

'What could shock me more than telling me that my son has been murdered?'

'You're right, Mrs Newman,' Tom said, 'but the circumstances in which Christopher was living when he was killed may come as a shock to you. That is what I think Jasmine is trying to say.'

'Tell me! I want to know everything about Christopher! I need to know why he was murdered!'

'I'm afraid we can't answer that last question yet, Mrs Newman, but we can tell you some facts about Christopher.' Tom looked at Jasmine with an appeal in his eyes.

'You said you didn't think Christopher was gay,' Jasmine began, 'but do you understand the term "transgender"?'

'Transgender? I'm not sure. Do you mean men dressing up in women's clothes?'

'Sort of. I believe Christopher was transgender and at the time of his death he was living as a woman.'

Mrs Newman's eyes widened. 'You mean - he'd had a sex change?'

'Well, no, not exactly,' Jasmine was searching for the correct words to use, 'but she'd had some cosmetic surgery to make her look more feminine.'

'That's why Christopher didn't look like he did at sixteen,' Tom added.

'Cosmetic surgery? Do you get that on the NHS?'

'Sometimes,' Jasmine replied.

'But not in Christopher's case is what you're saying. Tell me everything you know. How did he pay for this surgery?'

'We think Christopher performed sexual services for money,' Tom said in his most official voice.

Now Mrs Newman was visibly shocked. She sobbed and covered her face. Jasmine wondered whether it was shame she felt more than the loss of her son.

'When? How?' she asked almost incoherently.

'I think Christopher was transgender from a young age,' Jasmine explained. 'For a long time he must have been confused about his feelings but didn't feel he could talk about them with you or your husband. That's not uncommon. Many trans people have difficulty in expressing their problems to their families and friends. But his friendships with girls, lack of interest in male clothes, the books he read, suggest that Christopher discovered his differences a long time ago but he kept them secret.'

Mrs Newman parted her hands and peered at Jasmine, examining her closely for the first time.

'You seem to know a lot about it, Miss Frame. Are you really a woman?'

'Oh yes, I'm a woman,' Jasmine declared, 'although physically I'm not there yet.'

'You're one of those trans people you were talking about! How can I know that you're telling the truth about Christopher?'

'I can show you,' Jasmine said pulling her phone from her

bag and swiping to the photo of Xristal and Honey. She passed the phone to Mrs Newman. 'Do you recognise Christopher?'

She stared at the picture silently and then tears started to trickle down her cheeks.

'Oh Chris, what have you done to yourself?' She looked up at Jasmine. 'Who is the other person in the picture? Is he a man too?'

'Her name is Honey Potts. She and Xristal…'

'Xristal?'

'That's the name Christopher used. She and Honey were friends, but we don't know anything about her or where she is?'

'Do you recognise her?' Tom asked.

Mrs Newman shook her head. 'She doesn't look familiar, but if she has changed her appearance too… But Christopher had no male friends or friends who were trans-whatever. Did this Potts person kill Christopher?'

'We don't know,' Tom answered, 'but we need to find her to discover what she knows about Christopher.'

Mrs Newman continued examining the photo closely. 'What changes did Christopher have done? I can see his hair is still black although he's had it styled.'

'She had her nose altered, her lips puffed up, ears pierced, and she had had some of her beard removed.'

'And these. These breasts he's showing in this bikini - are they real?'

Jasmine nodded. 'Xristal had breast enhancement.'

'This is what he wanted? To look like a whore?' Her voice suggested anger more than sadness or disbelief.

'I'm not sure what she wanted, Julia,' Jasmine said as softly as she could, 'We believe she was planning to have the full gender reassignment surgery soon to make her physically a woman.'

Mrs Newman shook her head. 'He paid for all this by selling himself?'

'We think so,' Tom said, 'but we are still collecting evidence.'

The doorbell rang.

'I hope that's the FLO,' Tom added as he hurried from the

room.

Julia Newman looked at Jasmine with a mixture of emotions flitting across her face. 'I can't begin to understand what Christopher was feeling but I see now that it could explain his behaviour and why he left. How was he able to go so suddenly and become this "woman"?'

'I don't think it was sudden,' Jasmine said. 'You said that for some time before he went missing he would go off for evenings, days even.'

'That's right.'

'I think Chris was meeting up with friends who understood her.'

'Other trans people?'

'Probably. Perhaps Honey Potts befriended her and helped her. She must have kept female clothes and cosmetics somewhere else. I think she had prepared to leave as soon as she was able to.'

'Do you think he was selling his body before he left?'

'I don't know, but we have to trace the people who knew her so we can discover what led to her death.'

'Will I be able to see him?'

'I'm sure DS Shepherd would like you to, so we can confirm the identification.'

The door opened and Tom returned followed by a female police officer in uniform. She looked from Jasmine to Mrs Newman.

'This is Constable Hargreaves,' Tom said.

'Call me Milly,' the officer said, holding out her hand to Mrs Newman. Jasmine thought she seemed a confident, competent, young woman eager to do her job.

'She'll stay with you until your husband returns. Longer if you like.' Tom said. 'I've told her what we know and what we've discussed. If you can tell her anything else that you think will be useful she'll pass it on to us. Otherwise she is here to look after you and answer your questions as far as it is possible to do so.'

'I won't get in your way,' Milly said, 'but I know you've had a big shock so I'll try to help you as much as I can.'

Mrs Newman looked at each of the three of them in turn, then began sobbing. Jasmine felt guilty that she had contributed to Julia's confusion and distress, but she didn't feel she could offer much more comfort. That was Milly's job.

'I'm sorry we had to bring bad news about Christopher,' she said. 'If I can tell you any more about what being trans might have meant to her, please give me a call.' She handed over a business card she had taken from her handbag.

'I've not only lost my son, I feel that our whole life as a family was a lie,' Mrs Newman said between sobs.

'I know it's extremely difficult for you,' Jasmine said, 'but I think Xristal still loved you or she would not have sent the postcards. They were to reassure you that she was well.'

'But he wasn't well! He was a mixed up trans thing, giving away his body and now he's dead!' Mrs Newman wailed in distress.

'I think we'd better leave now, Jas,' Tom said quietly. 'We've caused enough distress. Let Milly calm the poor woman down.' He faced Julia Newman. 'We'll leave you with Constable Hargreaves, Mrs Newman. Thank you for answering our questions. I expect we will need to speak to your husband and we will arrange for you to come over to Kintbridge to see Christopher's body.'

Mrs Newman wailed again and curled up in a ball on the sofa. Tom tugged Jasmine towards the door.

'Take good care of her, Constable. We'll keep in touch.'

Milly Hargreaves nodded and sat next to Mrs Newman with her arm around her. She nodded but said nothing.

Tom led Jasmine from the house and back to the police car. They got in and buckled up their seat belts. Tom started the engine and pulled away. They reached the end of the quiet suburban street before he spoke.

'Well, aside from causing a great deal of distress to that poor woman we didn't get much out of that, did we?'

'Oh, I think we did.' Jasmine said.

Tom glanced at her, 'Really?'

'Okay, we're no nearer to finding Honey Potts or whoever else Xristal was involved with, but I think we've learned a lot about Xristal herself.'

'Like what?'

'She was troubled about her gender for a long time and had made a life for herself away from home long before she moved out. She obviously felt that there was no hope of getting her parents to understand how she felt, so she found people who did.'

'Honey Potts?'

'Possibly, but I think people like Potts used her rather than understood her.'

'What do you mean?'

'From what I've seen and heard about Xristal's teenage years, she strikes me as a typical transsexual struggling to find an identity for herself. She doesn't seem like an in-your-face, extrovert, OTT, she-male to me.'

'No? Do you know many she-males?'

'No, I don't. I'm going by gut instinct. Xristal feels more like me, but somewhere along the line she got taken in by Honey Potts, or others like her, and persuaded to play a part like them and earn the money for a designer body in the way that they did.'

'Sounds feasible.'

'But she wasn't such an outgoing character. Perhaps that was why she got in to the BDSM. It required a different mind-set.'

'Can't say I know much about it. Anyway, where does it get us?'

'Not far, I know. We still have to find Honey and other people she knew on that scene, and her clients of course.'

'So we're still where we were before we met Mrs Newman?'

'In practice, yes, but I've now got a much better picture of Xristal and more sympathy for her.'

'You don't need sympathy in this job. It can get you into trouble. You know that, Jas.'

'If I was still a police officer, I'd agree with you. When I thought Xristal was a she-male, I didn't have much incentive for finding out who murdered her. Now I know more about her I really want to get her killer - and find those who persuaded her into becoming something she wasn't, as that ultimately led to her death.'

'That sounds more like a campaign than an investigation. What are you going to do?'

'It looks like a trawl through the internet-porn sites to find people who may have known Xristal. But first I've got to write a report that puts Parfitt firmly in the shit.'

5

FRIDAY EVENING

Jasmine hit "send" and leaned back in her chair. The report, together with the last shots from the memory card, began their journey through cyberspace. That would end Parfitt's money-spinning play-acting and complete her current contract with the FIS. It was a relief that one job was out of the way and that she could now devote herself fully to discovering why Xristal had been killed.

The washing machine rumbled to a stop, so she went to the kitchen to empty it. As she sorted the damp knickers, bras, tops and skirts, she wondered whether Xristal had relished this chore as much as she did. For Jasmine, each item of clothing hung on the dryer in the bathroom was a symbol of her femininity. How had Xristal seen herself – a man with tits or a woman with a penis? She presented herself as a woman, her wardrobe showed that, but did she think of herself as female? Perhaps her gender identity was still evolving, hence the ticket to Thailand and the appointment at the sex-change clinic. Was there any connection between her planned trip and the motive for her murder? Jasmine reasoned that the only way to find out was to search for Xristal's presence on the web, her main means of contacting her clients.

As she returned to the living room her phone rang. She grabbed it. Perhaps Tom had some more news.

'Hi, Jas.' It was Angela. 'Just checking you are still on for this evening?'

Making sure she hadn't forgotten more like – which she had.

'Oh, hi, Angela. Yes, of course. Eight o'clock was it?' She

glanced at her watch. It was already nearly seven.

'That's right. See you there. Bye.'

Just like Angela to check up on her before she actually was late, but just as well. The evening get-together with Angela and her new man had completely slipped Jasmine's mind. Now she hardly had any time to get ready - and a special effort was necessary to pass Angela's close scrutiny. She chucked the phone onto the sofa and ran into her bedroom, pulling off her T-shirt as she went. Having stripped, she hurried to the bathroom, showered quickly and gave her arms and legs a cursory swipe with her razor. A little more time and concentration was needed to give her face and neck a smooth appearance, and she sighed as she did every day with the forlorn desire to eliminate her facial hair. Shaving only made the hairs coarse and roughened her skin. She must have tried every moisturiser on the market, except for the ridiculously expensive ones, in the hope of finding one that really did the trick.

She gathered her towel around her and returned to the bedroom, trying to dry herself as quickly as possible. At last, satisfied with her dryness, she dropped the towel to the floor and examined herself in the long mirror. She averted her gaze from the dangling bits between her legs. The swelling of her breasts disappointed her, but she was relieved that her muscles weren't turning to fat. Her waist and hips showed a little more of a curve than prior to starting the hormone therapy, but she still had, and would always have, a boyish figure. She tucked herself into a clean pair of white knickers and slipped her breast enhancers into her bra.

Now the answer to the big question: what to wear to impress Angela and her man? What was his name? She'd forgotten. The weather had improved and it was now a warm and pleasant summer evening. She looked in her wardrobe. It was no contest really. Following the trannie-killer case she had been a little better off so had treated herself to something new and just a little more expensive than usual. It was a gorgeous Zara sleeveless dress, in a purple and white print. She pulled it over her head and the hem dropped to just above the knee. The dress flared out from the waist, which made her look more shapely than she really was, and had a high-ish neckline which hid her lack of cleavage. Spinning in front of the mirror she felt properly feminine. Next, make-up. This always took time and this evening she made sure that the tender pink bruise on her chin didn't show. Finishing with her favourite Maybelline red lipstick, she brushed her hair and put on some dangly silver earrings. She glanced at her watch, seven-forty. Okay, just time to get to Whitclere by around eight.

In the living room she searched for her bag, dropped her phone into it and drew out her car keys. A sudden shiver of apprehension passed through her. She was going out to a smart pub, mixing with other people who would look at her, perhaps eye her up, but that wasn't the cause of her nervousness. In the years since she had started going out as Jasmine, and since she had started her transition, she had grown used to being looked at and she had become fairly successful at portraying the young woman she felt that she really was. There was something else that was disturbing her. It wasn't meeting Angela. No, it was the fact that Angela was going to be with another guy. Her former partner and lover, her ex-wife, was bringing a man to meet her. For the first time since Angela had first rung to tell her, Jasmine wondered why. Angela didn't need her approval to go out with another man - after all, they had been divorced for about three months now. There was another reason for this evening's little gathering and, despite her uneasiness, she was going to find out what it was. Jasmine pulled the door closed behind her.

Her old Fiesta looked out of place between the Audis, Jags and BMWs in the car park of the country inn, but she didn't feel any jealousy. She was just glad to be herself. A glance in the mirror to check her lipstick reassured her and she stepped out of the car, smoothing the front of her dress. Jasmine recalled that she and Angela had visited the pub once before. It had been James accompanying Angela on that occasion, perhaps one of the last times that she and Angela had gone out as a male and female couple. A poignant smile flickered across her face at that memory.

She entered the pub and wondered where Angela would be. It was just past eight so there was no doubt that she would have already arrived. She was never late. The bar was spacious and not very busy and she soon spotted Angela waving at her from a leather chair by a window. She had obviously been looking out at the car park awaiting her arrival. As Jasmine approached, Angela got up and flung her arms around Jasmine. They kissed each other on the lips.

'It's lovely to see you, Jas. It's been a while,' Angela said, stepping back to examine her. 'You look great. I love that dress on you. I haven't seen it before. Is it new?'

'Yes, it is, from Zara. I thought I deserved a treat and it wasn't that expensive.' She didn't want to give the impression that she was spending more money than she had on clothes. Angela gave an understanding smile and turned to the man sitting beside her.

'This is Luke.'

He stood up and towered a good six inches above Jasmine and Angela. Luke looked to be a few years older – mid-thirties perhaps. He had short brown hair and brown eyes. A frequent visitor to the gym, Jasmine thought, examining and admiring his slim build. He raised a short-sleeved arm offering his hand. His arm was quite hairy. She couldn't remember when she'd last had hairs on her arms, or legs. Perhaps Luke was hairy all over? She had a sudden vision of Angela naked in Luke's bear-like embrace and shuddered. Why did the image appal her? Was it the hair or the thought of any man getting close to Angela?

Luke's hand closed around Jasmine's and squeezed – hard. Jasmine retaliated with her own firm grasp. Competitive handshaking is it, she thought. Is it a conscious thing or does he do it to every person he meets? She looked into his face. A smile hovered on his lips, but that was all. His eyes stared at her -

testing her.

'Pleased to meet you,' he said. Jasmine noted he did not use her name. 'Angela has told me all about you.'

'Oh, she has, has she?' Jasmine said trying to keep her tone light. Had she really told him everything that they had done and discussed over the last ten years?

'You know what he means,' Angela giggled. 'Why don't you get Jasmine a drink, Luke.'

'Of course. I'll be the gentleman,' Luke replied with another of his mouth-only smiles. 'What will it be?'

'A white wine spritzer, please,' Jasmine replied, 'with ice.'

'Ah, a girly drink,' Luke said, departing for the bar.

Jasmine settled into the third chair facing Angela.

'So, who is he?' Jasmine whispered. Angela leant forward.

'I've known him a few years. He's an accountant too and we're both in asset management. A few weeks ago we met up at a conference in London and got chatting.'

'Just chatting?'

'Well, no. I suppose after our divorce went through I felt something of a release and a need for a bit more. Do you understand, Jas?'

Jasmine knew that she should but it was so difficult to let go of her feelings for Angela – the only woman she had ever loved or made love to. Perhaps if they had not stayed together so long she would have transitioned sooner, but on the other hand, without Angela's support she may never have had the confidence to embark on her journey towards womanhood.

'Of course, Ange.' She hoped it sounded genuine.

'I knew you would. So, what's your news? Are you working?'

'Yes, I'm on an investigation.'

'Not looking for lost cats or snooping on wayward husbands?' Angela giggled.

Jasmine knew she meant it as a joke but it rankled a bit since that was exactly what she'd been doing until a few weeks ago.

'No, some benefits fraud cases and now I'm on a murder.'

'Another one! Not with Tom and Sloane?'

'Well, yes, actually.'

'Really? Well, take care of yourself. You nearly had it the last time.'

Jasmine could see there was genuine concern in Angela's face.

'Don't worry, I'll look after myself.' The memory of what the trannie killer had wanted to do to Jasmine was far too fresh in her mind. 'Oh, and I'm going to have...'

'Here you are. One white wine spritzer.' Luke leaned over Jasmine's shoulder and put the tall glass in her hand, 'and here are the menus. The waiter will be along in a minute.'

Luke took his seat while handing around the heavy leather-bound folders. Jasmine flicked the pages, glancing at the prices and groaning inwardly.

'This is on us,' Angela said quietly.

'Thanks,' Jasmine replied. 'The prices are a bit more than I can afford at the moment.'

'Detective work not paying well?' Luke said in, Jasmine noticed, a rather snide tone. 'I thought it was all brown envelopes shoved in your pocket, or handbag I suppose in your case.'

'It's all above board these days,' Jasmine said, as chattily as she could manage, 'but it takes a while to build up a client base.'

'Like in any business,' Angela added, smiling encouragingly.

The waiter approached and took their orders: a stereotypical steak for Luke; a complex fish dish for Angela; and Jasmine settled for a simple but filling chicken casserole. She was going to take advantage of the free meal.

'Let's go to the Ladies, Jas, while we're waiting,' Angela said rising to her feet, 'I need the loo.' She grabbed her handbag and headed off.

'That's right,' Luke whispered to Jasmine as she leant forward to reach for her own bag, 'Go and use the Ladies, you pervert.' Jasmine straightened, suddenly not sure she had heard what she thought she had heard, but the look on Luke's face confirmed his sneering disgust. Jasmine turned and hurried after Angela.

The Ladies was large with at least two free cubicles. Jasmine locked the door of hers, dropped her knickers and sat. She found herself shaking. Could it be that Angela's new man hated her? Every action he had made seemed to suggest, it although Angela appeared not to have noticed. She heard Angela's flush go and she hurried to restore her bits into their place and join her at the wash basins.

'Is Luke happy about meeting me here this evening?' Jasmine asked while holding her hands under the running tap.

'Yes, of course, he told me he wanted to meet you. Why? Are you uncomfortable with me being with another man? I do understand why it might be difficult for you.'

'No, it's not that.' Yes, it jolly well is, Jasmine thought, drying her hands. 'It's just that some men find trannies threatening, you know.'

'Luke? No. I don't think he'd find anything threatening. He's a modern guy.'

No, but he might be a threat, Jasmine thought and not as modern in his outlook as Angela might think. They stood beside each other looking into the mirror while swiping on lipstick.

'Look, Ange, there's something I'd like to say.'

'What's that, Jas?'

'I'm…'

The door opened and a middle-aged woman entered, glanced at the two of them and headed into a cubicle.

'What?' Angela asked.

'Um, I'm really pleased you're having some fun with Luke.' Damn, she couldn't go blabbing about her testicles with the other woman listening in behind the door of the loo.

'Well, thank you, Jasmine. We'd better get back to him or he'll be getting lonely.'

As they returned to the bar, Luke was rising from his seat.

'God, what do you get up to in there? The waiter has called us to our table.' He led the way into the crowded restaurant.

The waiter stood by an empty table. Luke dutifully ensured that Angela was sitting comfortably before moving to his own seat. Jasmine sat down beside Angela.

They ate and chatted about inconsequential matters. Jasmine was getting more and more concerned that she had had no opportunity to mention her operation next Monday but she felt reluctant with Luke sitting there. She hoped that he too would pay a visit to the loo but, despite sinking a second pint of beer, he stayed in his seat.

They were eating their desserts when there was a birdlike trill from Angela's bag. She muttered an expletive and dug in the bag for her phone. She glanced at the screen.

'Sorry, I've been waiting for this call; it's an important one. I was hoping to get it before we came out.' She got to her feet and walked out of the restaurant with the phone pressed to her ear.

Luke put his spoon down and leaned forward.

'I'm glad this has given us an opportunity for a little chat, just the two of us,' he said in a low voice that was almost a whisper.

'Really?' Jasmine wondered what on earth he could mean.

'Yeah. Look, Angela's a fantastic girl and I'm really getting on well with her, but she apparently still has some feelings for you. I don't understand why, the things that you've done, you trannie queer. But I'm telling you this. You keep away from her, stop bothering her and I'll let you be.'

A knot of anger grew in Jasmine's chest, but she wasn't sure how to respond to his threat.

She found her voice, 'Look I don't know what it is that Angela sees in you but she is free to do what she likes. I don't "bother" her, but I think she still wants us to be friends.'

'Well, you won't be when I've put her right about you, you cock-teasing apology for a man.'

'I'm a woman.'

'Don't give me that! You've got a cock between your legs! I expect you want the NHS to cut that off for you and give you tits and a girly voice and whatever else you want done. Design a new body for you - is that it?'

'I ...' Jasmine couldn't think of words to respond. Luke had distorted all her desires into a sordid-sounding perversion.

'Have it all done.   You'll still be a bloke with male chromosomes.'

'It's not all about chromosomes.'

'You'll still look like a faggot in drag.' Luke's face was contorted into a snarl and she thought that if the room hadn't been full he would have spat at her. She pulled her napkin from her lap, reached down for her bag and stood up.

'I'm not going to stay any longer to be insulted by you, even if Angela thinks we can all be friends.' She was half aware that diners at the adjacent tables were looking at her. 'I hope Angela realises what a bigoted bully you are before too long!' She strode off swinging her bag over her shoulder and marched out of the pub straight to her car. There was no sign of Angela.

She drove down the road away from Whitclere with her hands gripped tightly around the steering wheel, her jaw muscles taut and her eyes forced to stay open because one blink would set the tears flowing and then she wouldn't be able to see the road. What had happened? Luke was a fucking transphobe. That much was obvious; jealous of the affection between her and Angela that still existed despite their divorce and increasingly separate lives. Her grip on the steering wheel tightened. The wanker was obviously going to do his utmost to prevent the contact between them continuing, and she hadn't even told Angela about her impending operation. She still had no one to collect her from the London hospital.

Jasmine had to slow down as a tear escaped and obscured her vision. She couldn't lose Angela's friendship, she was the only person who really understood what she had gone through in the last ten years. She mustn't let Luke ruin that. But if Angela liked the man, loved him even, what right did she have to come between them?

Jasmine pulled up in her parking spot, turned off the engine, leaned on the steering wheel and sobbed. She had never, ever felt as alone as she did now.

6

SATURDAY

Jasmine lay in bed staring at the ceiling. Had she slept? It didn't feel like it. Another sleepless night. The things Luke had said kept going round in her head. Could it be that she was like Xristal and Honey? Seeking surgery to shape her body to the design she wanted? The thought of knives cutting into her flesh made her shiver, despite the cosy duvet, but she needed those operations to give her the body that she imagined was hers already. How was she different to Xristal and Honey? Well, neither Xristal, nor presumably Honey, were taking the hormones to turn them into women. They exulted in their continued masculinity, while delighting in their sculpted feminine shape. She was not like that, Jasmine told herself, and the thought of having an erection appalled her. No, whatever Luke had said, the work that she needed to have done on her body was to correct the defects she was born with - she was a woman while Xristal and Honey were she-males.

Her phone rang, interrupting her thoughts. The caller was Tom and the time was only 7 a.m. She tried to sound bright and cheerful, but she knew the night-long depression put an edge on her voice.

'Hey, Tom, this is an early call for a Saturday. What about the weekend?'

'Weekend? What's that? Surely you remember that we don't have days off when there's a case to solve.'

Jasmine did recall those adrenalin-stoked times when days passed without noticing. She missed them.

'So, has something happened?'

'No, nothing really. Are you OK? You sound a bit rough.'

Rough? If only the cause was something as simple as a heavy evening on the booze while having a good time with friends.

'Just a bit down. Tell you sometime. Why the call if there's nothing to report?'

'Well, that's it. Sloane's called a case conference as we don't appear to be getting anywhere.'

'I admit progress is slow, but it's only been a couple of days.'

'That's long enough for Sloane. He needs to decide what priority to give the Newman case.'

'Priority?'

'You know, Jasmine. If it's just a case of a prostitute coming to a sticky end then it's not worth much time and money.'

'Xristal wasn't a common whore, dosed up on heroin or cocaine, done over in some dark alley. She was in her own flat, on no drugs at all and contemplating gender reassignment.'

'Well, that's your conclusion. You have a point that you can put to Sloane.'

'At the case conference?'

'Yes.'

'When?'

'Eight.'

'Less than an hour?'

'That's right. Don't be late. You'll make Sloane cross.'

'He's always cross. Why does he want me there?'

'Have you forgotten? You're our special advisor on this case.'

'Oh, yes.'

'I'll let you get ready. See you soon, Jas.' The call clicked off leaving Jasmine staring at the screen. Sloane wanted her back in her old office, not just for a conversation with him or with Tom, but in a meeting. There would be the other officers to face, some of whom she may have known back when she was James and others she did not know at all but who, she was sure, would have been briefed about her. She felt a bit faint, the nausea for once not just caused by her drugs which, she remembered, she needed to take.

She leapt from the bed and took the tablets from their blisters, swallowing them quickly and gulping down the warm water from the glass she kept on the dressing table. Her tired eyes stared out of the mirror. Was there any point in dwelling on last night? Was this the way to build a career? Lying at home moping wouldn't do any good. She had to get out there, show that she was on top of the case, and that she didn't care what others thought. Emboldened, she ran to into the shower cubicle, washed quickly and dried herself, then pulled on her underwear. She dragged the curtains back and gazed outside. The cheerful summer evening and warm night had become a damp and dreary morning – a bit like her mood. Facing Sloane and his team this morning she would have to be business-like. She pulled on a white blouse and the little-used grey suit with the knee-skimming skirt purchased for these occasions. It was a little warm for high summer, but she could take the jacket off if the temperature rose in Sloane's company.

She had to spend time getting her face right so there was no time for breakfast before she hurried out of the flat, flinging her bag over her shoulder. As she got to her car she saw Viv also up and about. She gave him a wave, which he returned. It looked as though he was making his way towards her but she got in the Fiesta and turned the key. Miraculously, the engine started first time and she drove out of the car park leaving Viv standing looking a little bemused. She waved again and smiled, hoping that he would not think her rude to have run away from him.

The town was just getting busy and she glanced at her watch anxiously once or twice as she drove towards the Police HQ. Finding a spot in the car park, she galloped into the building through the mizzling rain, realising belatedly that arriving puffing, sweaty and rain spattered would not do her image as a confident and competent young woman much good. As it happened, she had to pause at the desk as the duty officer went through the usual rigmarole of checking that she had been invited by Chief Inspector Sloane and delegating a civilian to

111

guide her up to the meeting room. She glanced at the clock in the vestibule as they left: 7:58.

Her escort held the door open and Jasmine stepped into the familiar room. Four rows of desks faced the large whiteboard, most of them empty, and a small group of people were clustered in the far corner looking at pictures stuck up on the corner of the board. A couple of men, Tom and the other with his back to her, sat on the corners of desks, while a woman wearing a dark blue suit stood behind a black chair occupied by DCI Sloane facing the board. A small team. Obviously Sloane had already made cutbacks.

Sloane looked towards Jasmine, but no look of welcome registered in his features as he spoke. 'Ah, Frame. Join us.'

Tom rotated on his perch and smiled at her. Jasmine crossed the room and stood beside him.

'Good morning,' she said in as light and feminine tone as she could manage.

'You know DC Hopkins, of course,' Sloane said, waving a hand towards the other man, 'but DC Patel has just joined us. They both know why you're here.' Hopkins nodded his balding head imperceptibly. He had been friendly when she was the up and coming James Frame, silent and hostile when she became Jasmine. A thin smile flickered across the face of the woman and Jasmine knew that DC Patel had most definitely been informed about her.

'We're reviewing the lack of progress made on this case,' Sloane said in an irritated voice, 'despite evidence gleaned from a partially-burned corpse and a smoke-damaged room. Perhaps you'd like to tell us what you know, Frame.'

Why had he picked on her? Jasmine wondered where Sloane wanted her to start from. She looked from one face to another until Tom rescued her.

'We've already talked about the crime scene and how Mr Newman died.'

'Mr Newman? You mean Xristal?' Jasmine said.

'The victim was male. It says so on his bank account,

medical records, passport,' Hopkins growled.

'But Xristal lived as a woman,' Jasmine insisted.

'Just because he had tits…'

'Alright, Hopkins,' Sloane intervened, 'Use whichever name you like, Frame, but tell us about the victim.'

Jasmine took a deep breath and, glaring at Hopkins, began.

'Xristal Newman was twenty-four years old and had left home six years ago. We think that since that time she has lived as a woman. Probably for most of that time she has been working as a prostitute in the company of Honey Potts. As you know, she had had cosmetic surgery to make her look more feminine but had taken no steps to lose her ability to have sex as a male. People like her are known as she-males. Young, attractive ones like Xristal are popular with those who like sex a bit out of the ordinary.'

'Pervs.'

'Hopkins!' Sloane's cheeks flushed. 'Keep quiet if you haven't got anything to add. Go on, Frame.'

Jasmine felt uncomfortable thinking about the sexual practices Xristal must have indulged in and angered by Hopkins' rumbling prejudice.

'I think the evidence shows that Xristal was dissatisfied with her life as a call girl and her position on the gender spectrum and was planning on becoming a complete woman.'

'What do you mean?' Sloane asked.

'I mean she was planning to go to Thailand to get full gender reassignment surgery carried out.'

'So she wouldn't be a she-male anymore?' DC Patel said quietly.

'That's right,' Jasmine said, smiling warmly at her.

'That would have stopped her from, uh, servicing her clients in the way they had become accustomed,' Sloane said.

'Yes,' Jasmine almost added 'sir' but stopped herself.

'So did one of her clients do her in?' Hopkins asked.

'Perhaps,' Jasmine shrugged.

'This Potts person,' Sloane said waving his hand in the

direction of the photo stuck to the board, 'Was she the pimp? Did she have a motive for the killing?'

'Possibly,' Jasmine nodded. 'They appear to have been close for some time. Honey may have been controlling Xristal's business, but she disappeared two weeks before the murder.'

'And there have been no reports of her being seen in Kintbridge since then,' Tom added.

'Nevertheless, she could have gained access by stealth,' Sloane continued.

'Yes,' Jasmine agreed.

Sloane pointed at another photo stuck to the board. 'What about this Parfitt fellow we had in yesterday? Is he a suspect?'

'Patel and I interviewed him,' Hopkins said.

'And?' Sloane said, with a note of impatience in his voice.

'He was very open about it. Keen to tell us the story.'

'I bet.' Jasmine said. Hopkins frowned at her.

'He said he been looking at porn sites on his computer and came across this girl who he recognised as a neighbour.'

'What sort of porn sites?' Sloane asked.

'Ones offering sex with a she-male, with a little added bondage excitement.'

'So he went to try it out with her, did he?' Jasmine said, 'Or did he blackmail her, threaten to make public what she was doing?'

'No, none of that,' Hopkins said, 'Parfitt says he hasn't spoken to the, er, victim. He denied being a client or having anything to do with her.'

'Huh. A likely story,' Jasmine said.

'I think he was telling the truth. He's got a bad back.' Hopkins insisted.

'He's a liar and a fraudster,' Jasmine said, louder than she intended.

'Whatever he is or says, he is still a suspect,' Sloane said, 'If he has been in the flat then forensics may find evidence of it. Perhaps he has a motive as a frustrated client, or as Frame says, as a potential blackmailer. What about this website he found

Newman on?'

'He says he deleted it,' Hopkins said.

'But we've impounded the computer and we should be able to trace it,' Patel added.

'Good,' Sloane said, 'and that could lead us to other clients. So are there any others? Anybody else that knew Newman.'

'The only other people we know about are the ground floor neighbour, Tilly Jones, and the Taylors, the landlords,' Tom said.

'Are they suspects?'

'I can't see a motive,' Tom shook his head.

'The Taylors may be more involved in the prostitution than they admit,' Jasmine said, 'After all, they must have realised that the source of income of all three of their tenants in Bredon Road was sex.'

'I suppose that keeps them in the picture,' Sloane nodded. 'It seems we have three lines of enquiry. Following up the clients on the website, including Parfitt, is one. Finding this Potts person is the second, and tying up the loose ends with the landlords and any other acquaintances is the third. I can't give you any more personnel, so I suggest you get on with it.' Sloane pushed himself out of the chair and strode out of the room.

'Well, that's it, isn't it?' Hopkins said, standing and stretching, 'We can't do anything until the boffins have finished stripping Parfitt's computer.'

'Why do you say that?' Jasmine asked.

'Stands to reason. Potts did it. Fell out with her pupil or something, came back and killed him. But he'll probably be on the same website, so we'll have him. Let's have a coffee while we wait. You coming, Tom?'

'I think you've got it wrong,' Jasmine said.

'Where's you evidence?'

'I haven't got any, but I have a feeling…'

'Feminine intuition is it?' Hopkins sneered. 'Comes with the drugs you take, does it?'

Jasmine felt the heat rise up her neck and into her face.

'OK, Terry,' Tom said, reaching out his hands in a calming gesture. 'Go and get your coffee, while I work out who does what. You too Sasha, if you like.'

Hopkins nodded to Patel and they left silently.

'Hopkins still doesn't like me, does he?' Jasmine said.

'Diversity training didn't take too well with Terry, although he gets on OK with Sasha.'

'So, it's just me then is it? He feels I'm threatening his masculinity somehow.'

'Yeah, well, he's a bit stuck in a rut. Still a DC in his forties and moving from one team to another. But he's a good cop.'

'He let Parfitt off pretty lightly.'

'Do you think he did it?'

'Hmm,' Jasmine was thoughtful. It would be easy to hope that Parfitt, someone known to them, was the murderer. He was aggressive – her bruised chin was a testament to that. He was scheming – his benefits scam was evidence - but a killer? It didn't feel right. 'I think we need to keep him on the list, but I'm not sure.'

'I'll get Hopkins and Patel to go back and ask the neighbours if they ever saw Parfitt and Xristal together or saw him visit her flat.' Tom said.

'That will do his reputation a lot of good, when it comes out, along with him being had up on a charge of benefits fraud.'

'He's not going to be a happy bunny.'

'Serves him right.' Jasmine didn't usually gloat about the criminals she had nabbed but her tender chin made this one personal.

'So, what do we do about Potts? She or he looks as though they're top of the suspect pile.' Tom was thoughtful.

'I'm going to have to search the web, the trannie porn and sex sites, to see if she pops up.' Jasmine said, wrinkling her nose.

'Fun for some.'

'With all the drugs I'm taking fighting each other, my chances of having fun are about zero. I think I'm more likely to feel sick than sexy.'

'Well, you know what to look for.'

'Perhaps. What about the landlords, the Taylors?'

'Do you think they're suspects?'

'Well, they weren't entirely helpful the first time we spoke to them. I'm sure they must have known what their three tenants in Bredon Road were up to.'

'Let's go and ask them some more questions. Push them a bit more. Then you can get back in front of your computer and look at pictures of she-males. '

'Thanks.'

'I'll just leave instructions for Hopkins and Patel.'

Jasmine pulled up behind Tom's Mondeo outside the impressive entrance of the Taylors' house and joined him at the door. There was a wait of a couple of minutes before the door was opened. It was Marilyn Taylor again who greeted them. As before, she was dressed in a simple but elegant blouse and skinny leather trousers.

'Oh, it's you two. What do you want?'

'We have some more questions, Mrs Taylor,' Tom said in his polite, official voice.

'My husband is out,' Mrs Taylor pushed the door closed. Tom put a foot against it. She glared as the door stopped.

'I think you can answer the questions as easily as your husband, Mrs Taylor, as you are apparently joint owners of the property.'

There was silence for a moment as Mrs Taylor seemed to be considering what to do. Finally she let out a sigh and pulled the door open again.

'All right, but I haven't got much time. We still have tenants who are due to pay their rents today.' She stepped back and again led the way through the hallway to the lounge.

'Do you visit all your properties, Mrs Taylor?' Tom asked.

'Some. Occasionally.'

She stood in the centre of the lounge and indicated the chairs that Tom and Jasmine should sit on. Once they were seated she positioned herself in the centre of the sofa.

'So you are able to see what your tenants are doing in your properties?'

From the sneer that appeared on Mrs Taylor's face Jasmine could tell that Tom was not going to trip her up that easily.

'We don't inspect the properties on every visit, Sergeant, we merely call to collect the rent from the few tenants that pay cash. Some of our tenants appreciate what we do for them and invite us in, but for the most part the transaction is done on the doorstep. There is no need for my husband or me to enter.'

'You would need to know if any tenants were damaging your property?'

'We would inspect a property if a tenant gave notice. Any damage would be deducted from the deposit before it was returned to the tenant.'

'But not in the case of Honey Potts, I gather?'

Jasmine smiled as Tom elicited a pause and a frown from Mrs Taylor.

'She broke her contract by not giving notice. She will find it difficult to get another rental in this area, I can tell you, and there will be a debt recovery agency after her.'

'Do you insist you had no idea what your three flats in Bredon Road were being used for?' Tom continued.

'Used for?'

'Entertaining clients who paid for sex.'

'Certainly not. I told you that before.'

'Ah, but we have further evidence that the flats occupied by Tilly Jones, Honey Potts and Xristal Neman, were being used for that purpose. There is every chance of you and your husband being charged with living off immoral earnings at the very least. It would be better if you tell us all that you know now.'

Mrs Taylor took three deep breaths and then pulled herself up straight. She looked straight at Tom. 'I can assure you we had nothing to do with the careers of those three, uh, women and we took only what was agreed as the rent for the properties.'

'But you knew that Honey and Xristal were she-males?'

Jasmine asked.

'You asked me that before. Are you obsessed with them?'

'You didn't find their behaviour disgusting?'

'I knew nothing of their behaviour, disgusting or otherwise.'

'But you met both of them, particularly Honey. Didn't you find their appearance out of the ordinary?'

'Isn't that rather prejudiced? These days, landlords are not allowed to discriminate. It was no interest to us how our tenants want to present themselves.'

'Really. No interest at all? Two big-boobed, pouting tarts. They didn't make you wonder at all?'

'You really do have something against these she-males or whatever you call them.' Mrs Taylor's gaze ran up and down Jasmine's body. 'Your colleague said you were an advisor not a police officer. What exactly are you advising on?'

Jasmine wondered how she should answer such a direct question.

'The murder victim was transgender.'

Mrs Taylor spoke in a voice that was almost a hoarse whisper, 'And they picked you because you are too?'

Jasmine felt herself flushing, 'Yes.'

'So are you like them? Do you have false breasts and a penis? Are you taking your pills?' There was a nasty smile on Mrs Taylor's face now. Jasmine knew that she was enjoying seeing her squirm with embarrassment.

'I'm a woman,' Jasmine insisted.

'Huh. You may call yourself a woman,' spat Mrs Taylor, 'but you're not.'

'Right, that's all the questions we have for now,' Tom said rising quickly to his feet. 'We'll be going, but I remind you that given the nature of this inquiry there may well be further questions and possibly charges.'

As Mrs Taylor stood up, Jasmine was struck by how slim she was with a pert but not too large bust. It was figure she aspired to.

'My husband and I are not scared by your threats, Sergeant.

We have nothing to hide.' She shooed them out like a sheepdog snapping at ducks, and shut the door firmly behind them.

'Well, that went well – not.' Tom said, frowning at Jasmine, 'Why the hell did you let her wind you up like that?'

'I don't know,' Jasmine said. She felt stupid and miserable. 'I know at the moment I give myself away to people that look closely. That will change, I hope, when I've had the surgery and the hormones have taken their full effect.'

'But that wasn't what started it. You pushed her about the she-males.'

'I know. I'm convinced she must have been interested in Honey and Xristal. There's something about her. I'm sure she was more involved with Honey and Xristal than she's let on.'

'Well, we haven't got any more evidence yet. And that's what we need. Real evidence of who did know Xristal and where Potts is now.'

'I'll get right on it.' Jasmine hurried to her car, unwilling to spend any more time on the Taylors' property or speak to Tom when she felt she had behaved like an inexperienced trainee. She got into the Fiesta. On the third twist of the key the engine started and she pulled out around Tom's car while he was still belting up.

7

LATER SATURDAY

Jasmine paused and rubbed her eyes. Floating in front of her eyes were an array of stiff cocks and huge, spheroidal breasts that she'd been peering at in the hope of seeing Honey Potts' round face and collagen-filled lips. Hours spent flicking through endless galleries of she-male porn and contact websites had passed without success. She was getting more and more angry looking at these men pretending to be women. No, that was wrong. They couldn't be pretending to be women with those erect penises on show. What were they? How did they think of themselves? Her anger and the prejudice she felt against those she-males living like that annoyed and disappointed her. She wanted to be liberal and accepting, but there were enough misunderstandings about transsexuals without these she-males muddying the scene with their rampant sexualities. She stretched her back making the old dining chair creak ominously.

Suddenly, there was a loud noise outside - the sound of a heavy object meeting glass. Jasmine jumped up, reached for the door knob and pulled the door open. She stepped onto the small concrete landing at the top of the steps to her flat and looked down into the car park. There was no-one there amongst the half dozen or so cars. What had made the noise? A lump of rubble lay on the tarmac beside her car.

She hurried down the steps, sensing that the noise related to her. She was right. When she reached the old Fiesta she saw a spider's web of cracks radiating from a dent in the windscreen right in front of the driver's seat.

'What's happened?'

Jasmine recognised Viv's voice and turned to see him approaching her.

'Someone's decided to lob a large stone at my car,' she said, stating the obvious.

'Someone? Who'd want to do that? It's not kids is it?'

No, Jasmine thought, she hadn't had trouble from kids in all the time she had lived here although she had heard of trannies who were tormented by young people. But she could guess who had done it.

'I think it was probably a shit called Parfitt.'

'Who's he? A neighbour?' Viv looked around at the low-rise blocks of flats along the Bristol Road.

'No. He's someone I've been causing some problems for.'

'How did he know which car was yours or even where you live?'

'He's seen me in the car,' Jasmine looked at her sad, old Fiesta, 'and he probably found out where I live from looking at those old news items from when I was briefly famous.'

'Oh, yeah. That's how I recognised you.'

Jasmine recalled that Parfitt's computer had been taken away for checking. He must have borrowed one or gone to a library or somewhere. He was obviously seriously pissed off by the trouble she'd got him into. She noticed that Viv was looking at her with a concerned expression.

'Are you feeling all right, Jasmine? You look pale. Have you eaten?'

Had she missed lunch? There were those two almost sleepless nights, she was getting nowhere in the hunt for Honey Potts and in just over a day she was going to have to face a knife – well, a scalpel. Now her car was out of action. Wasn't that reason enough to forget to eat?

'You haven't, have you?'

'Uh, no.'

'Right, I'm taking you out this evening. I've just found that there's a restaurant in Kintbridge that does really good Mexican and Caribbean food – the closest I'm going to get to home cooking. How about it?'

'Um. I've got work to do and now I'll have to get the car sorted out.'

'Look, give me your insurance details and I'll get your windscreen replaced. You call your friends in the police and tell them what's happened. Then I'll take you out for the evening to take your mind off all this.'

'Well…'

'I won't take no for an answer.'

Jasmine saw the grin on Viv's face. Perhaps it would be good to have an evening in someone's company before she headed to London for her appointment.

'OK. That's very sweet of you, Viv, but I must do some more work first.'

'Fine. Now let's get your insurance details so we can get your car fixed.'

With Viv equipped with her documents and a call made to the police station to get a crime number, Jasmine settled back down in front of her laptop. She couldn't face looking at more naked flesh. Her mind wandered to Viv's invitation. Perhaps an evening out would be good for her, take her mind off the case and her impending surgery. It was very kind of him to sort out the car but, of course, she wouldn't need it for her trip to London. She gasped as she recalled she still had no arrangements for getting home. Angela had been her last and biggest hope, but she hadn't even managed to tell her that she was having the biorchidectomy. Neither had Angela called to find out why she had left the pub so suddenly last night.

Jasmine reached for her phone but paused. It was the weekend, Angela would probably be with Luke. What story had he told Angela about her hurried departure? What poison was he injecting into the relationship that she and Angela had shared, destroying the rapport that existed between them despite the divorce? Jasmine put the phone down, the sadness a weight on her chest. She would have to try and contact Angela when

123

she knew she was alone, at work perhaps.

Jasmine glanced at the time on her computer screen. 17:30. Two hours till Viv said he would be calling to take her out. She must try to trace Honey before she had to call it a day. But no more she-male sites. Perhaps general trannie sites. They had gallery after gallery of photos. She started to click and search.

Time passed and she found herself on the website of a London club that did special nights for trannies, especially the younger transvestites that liked a good night out. There were pictures of performers. Could that be Honey? She looked closely. The picture showed a large, full-breasted female figure in a long, white sequinned evening dress and white feather boa. The face was heavily made up but the build and the features matched Honey Potts. The performer was named as 'Miss Havana Goodthyme'. Jasmine felt her heart racing as she scrolled through the website. It appeared that Miss Goodthyme was a regular performer at the club particularly at weekends. Her act looked to be that of a traditional female impersonator with hints that it went beyond Danny La Rue or Lily Savage. If Honey was going to be at the club tomorrow then she could perhaps go and meet her and find out what she knew about Xristal's death. She tapped the address into her phone and found the location on the map app. She'd travel up by train, check in to a cheap hotel not too far from the hospital, then go out to meet Honey Potts. There, she had a plan.

Excitement made her palms sweaty and her heart thump. Perhaps it was a good thing that Viv was taking her out. It would calm her down and pass some time. Time? What was it? 19:00. She jumped up – only half an hour to get herself ready. It would never be enough.

It wasn't. She'd showered and dressed, the Zara dress again, (well, it was her best, new outfit and she loved it) but still had her face to do when the doorbell rang.

'Give me ten minutes!' she hollered in a most unladylike voice.

'OK,' came the muffled response.

Jasmine hurried to apply her foundation as smoothly as possible, then eye shadow, a No.7 shade that went with the dress, powder and lipstick. She looked at herself one last time. Why was Viv so keen to take her out? It couldn't just be concern for her health. Was there more?

She grabbed her bag, looked inside to confirm her keys were there and hurried out of the flat pulling the door closed behind her. It was a fine, sunny evening, the air heavy with smells of grass and blossom carried by the water vapour evaporating from the morning's drizzle. Viv was lounging against his big Audi.

'Sorry, I've kept you waiting,' Jasmine said almost tripping on her heels.

'No worries. I expect to be kept waiting by a pretty girl.'

Jasmine felt herself flush. Pretty girl? She wasn't sure she'd ever been called that.

She giggled in a flirtatious manner that didn't come naturally. 'Now you're just flattering me.'

'No, I mean it. You look great. Really pretty. Come on, get in.' He pulled the passenger door open and held it as she bent to get in. The hem of her dress rode up her bare thigh. Jasmine was embarrassed and tugged it down as she squirmed into the passenger seat. Viv carefully closed the door and moved around the car to get in.

'It's not far. Just the other side of the town centre,' he said, as he started the powerful engine. 'I hope we can park close by.'

Jasmine found herself being driven through the familiar streets into St. Benedicts and then Viv turned into Bredon Road.

'Perhaps we can park down here,' he said.

'No!' Jasmine said, feeling an unfamiliar fear, 'Not here. I've been here too often the last few days. Parfitt lives down here.'

'The bloke that smashed your window?'

'Yes.'

'Perhaps we should call on him and tell him we're onto him?'

'Oh, I'm onto him all right, but there's no proof that it was him that chucked the rock at my car. I don't want to see him again and I don't want him seeing you.'

'Well, OK.' Viv turned the car and headed back to the main road. Jasmine didn't point out where Xristal had died. Murder wasn't an appetiser.

Jasmine directed Viv to another side road where they found a parking space and together they walked back into St. Benedicts. They stopped outside The Cancún Restaurant.

'Been here before?' Viv asked.

Jasmine looked at the colourful Mayan designs on the frontage and shook her head.

'No. I didn't even know it existed. I haven't had many invitations to eat out since Angela and I split up.'

'Well, I don't know if it's up to much but we'll try it out.' He held the door open for Jasmine to enter. It seemed popular enough as half of the dozen or so tables were occupied. Jasmine was relieved. With the place busy she felt less likely to stand out. A few people glanced at them as they entered, but they returned to their conversations or their food. A waiter approached them and Viv spoke briefly to him, before he escorted them to a table at the back of the restaurant.

'Will this do for you?' Viv asked. 'I didn't think you would want to be by the window.'

Jasmine was surprised. Had Viv really taken the trouble to choose a table at which she would not feel too conspicuous?

'This is fine,' she said, sitting in the upholstered chair. Viv sat opposite and the waiter brought menus.

Jasmine barely noticed the food. It was hot and spicy and she enjoyed it, but her attention was taken by Viv's conversation. He told yet more stories of his mixed-race childhood in Birmingham. Even when they were about occasions when he had been bullied and threatened he managed to turn the story against his tormentors with a joke. Not one story was familiar from their previous evening eating the takeaway. It seemed Viv could talk about his life for ever, but he didn't just talk about himself. He also asked Jasmine plenty of questions and she found herself telling him about her life with Angela, coming to the realisation that she was transsexual, the trauma of transition. She struggled to match Viv's humour as she recounted the events leading up to her resignation from the police force – the promotion missed, being side-lined on cases and left to the tedious in-office jobs that everybody had to do but were usually shared out evenly. It sounded so trivial as she recounted it, but she remembered how over-wrought she had become, depressed and suspicious, comparing her experiences as a male and female detective. She had begun to doubt that the lawyers would ever be able to put together a case for constructive dismissal.

Viv didn't let her become maudlin. He was off again with another anecdote that soon had her smiling. She wondered, was this what normal life was like – a man and a woman enjoying each other's company over a tasty meal? It was the first time she had been out with someone other than Angela who treated her as a woman and not as a man in drag.

They completed the meal with coffee and Viv asked for the bill. Jasmine tried to pay her share even though she knew her bank balance was looking pretty sad, but Viv refused.

'I've left all my friends and family up in the Midlands. You're the first person I've got to know down here that isn't a business contact, so please let it be a thank you for being who you are and a hope that it's the first of many.'

Jasmine felt so happy and flattered that she couldn't argue any further. Viv reclaimed his credit card and escorted her to the door. It was still light as they stepped onto the street and began the short walk back to the car, arm in arm.

'Oy, you! You! The trannie!'

Jasmine spun on her high heels to see Parfitt leaning on his crutches.

'Call yourself a private dick? Private dickless more like!'

Jasmine found herself staring open-mouthed and speechless.

'Or are you like that dead tart? A bloke with boobs?'

Viv, released Jasmine's arm and took a step towards Parfitt. 'Shut it, you! You'll need more than crutches if you carry on like that!'

Jasmine regained her voice. 'No, Viv. It's Parfitt. He can't do anything.'

'The arsehole who smashed your window?'

'Who I suspect smashed the window…'

Parfitt swayed on his crutches just out of reach.

'Got the cops on me, you did. I'll make you pay for that!'

'No you won't, Parfitt! Not unless you want a stretch inside.' Jasmine felt her training as a police officer start to resurface. 'Unless it was you that killed Xristal, in which case you'll be put away for a very long time.'

Parfitt backed away, fear creasing his face. 'That wasn't me. I told them that. I never went inside her place.'

He turned and limped away. Jasmine took Viv's hand and dragged him away towards the street where his car was parked. She was conscious of passers-by looking at them - at her - with interest.

'Let's get away from here. I don't like the looks I'm getting,' she said.

'Nor me,' Viv replied, quickening his pace.

They reached the car and Viv drove off as soon as Jasmine was in her seat. 'Now what was that all about?' he asked.

Jasmine described her extended surveillance of Parfitt, resulting in getting the proof that he wasn't as disabled as he claimed. She explained how this led to the exchange where she had discovered that he knew about Xristal.

'Who's Xristal?'

'Hasn't it been on the local news?'

'I don't listen to the news.'

Jasmine hadn't had the opportunity to follow the media in the last three days either, so she had no idea how much information had been released to the press. Perhaps the circumstances of Xristal's death had even reached the national media. Jasmine described the main facts that she knew of.

'This is the case you're working on now?'

'That's right. Sloane has taken me on as an advisor.'

'Sloane's the Chief Inspector that you're accusing of discrimination?'

'That's right'

'Not the most comfortable of working relationships.'

'No. I suppose we suffer each other.'

'But Sloane must think quite a bit of you to take you on while you are preparing this case against him.'

'Sloane thinks I'm the only person who can explain what being transgender means.'

'Perhaps he's right.'

'I don't know. There are lots of transsexuals like me around.'

'Not many with experience of working in the police.'

'Well, no. I suppose not.'

Viv turned into their car park and stopped in his space.

'Fancy a drink? We only had one glass with the meal and I've got a bottle of rum and some wine.'

'Rum?'

'Yeah. It's a taste I learned from my pa who got it from his pa. The flavour of the Caribbean.'

Viv showed her into his flat. It was similar in size and layout to hers, but the furniture was newer and better and it was freshly decorated.

'This looks a lot nicer than my place,' Jasmine said.

'Well it's not my doing. It's a furnished flat. My stuff's in storage until I get my own place. Wine or rum?'

'Rum and what?'

'Oh, I drink it neat.'

'Really? Not sure I've ever drunk neat rum. I'll give it a go.'

'Good girl!' Viv took two small glasses and a bottle from a cupboard and placed them on a low table in front of the pale grey, leather sofa. He pulled the stopper from the bottle, poured the dark liquid into the glasses and offered one to Jasmine.

'Here. Take a seat.'

Jasmine sat at one end of the sofa and crossed her legs. Viv sat on the other side of the sofa.

'Cheers,' he said, downing the drink in one gulp. Jasmine

sipped hers. It was strong with a flavour she wasn't sure she liked, but she took another sip.

'So,' Viv said, as if returning to an unfinished conversation, 'you were telling me all about your, what was it, transition? It sounds like a drawn-out process. Can't you have the sex-change op and get it over with?'

'I wish!' Jasmine snorted. 'I'm with the NHS gender reassignment clinic. I'm taking the hormone tablets but it could be years before I reach the top of the list for surgery. Gender reassignment is expensive and the NHS doesn't fund many each year. In the meantime, I have to live as a woman to stay on the programme.'

'During which time, people like that shit Parfitt can lob insults at you.'

'Yes, but he had a point. There are people like Xristal who are happy to alter their bodies but keep their male bits. I don't want that and the mixture of hormones has side effects which are making me ill.' Jasmine put the glass of rum down. She wasn't sure the strong spirit was doing her any good.

'Isn't there anything your doctors can do?'

'Well, yes, there is.' Jasmine explained about her forthcoming biorchidectomy. Viv's face lost some of its colour.

'And that's just an out-patients job?'

'Yes. Except I need someone to pick me up and bring me home. I won't be able to drive for a day or two.'

'No, I see that. So who's collecting you?'

'No-one.'

'What do you mean, no-one? You said you have to be picked up from the hospital.'

'Yes, but I haven't got anyone.' Suddenly the reality of the situation hit Jasmine. Ever since she'd received the letter she'd been too busy to really think about the procedure and how she'd get home.

'My doctor, she's a good friend, can't. Tom's too busy on the case and I never got round to telling Angela. I haven't got anyone else.' A sob forced its way up her throat.

'I'll do it,' Viv said forcefully.

'But you're working. You hardly know me.'

'I can take a day off, no problem. And I think how well I know you is for me to put right.'

'Well, if you're sure.'

'I'm sure. Now, what are the arrangements?'

Jasmine dug the letter out of her bag and showed Viv. He noted the address and times.

'How are you getting there?'

'Oh, I thought I'd go up by train tomorrow and stay in a cheap hotel.'

'I could take you Monday morning. We could leave early enough.'

'No thanks. There are things I want to do in London tomorrow before I have the operation.' She didn't want to tell him about the possibility of meeting Havana Goodthyme. She didn't want anyone to know that she had traced Honey Potts – not yet anyway.

'That's a shame. I'm going up to Brum tomorrow to see my ma.'

'No, that's fine. I can get myself there, it's just the getting back that's the problem.'

'Right, it's settled. I'll be at the hospital by midday. Now would you prefer wine?' Viv got up and opened the cupboard.

'Um, yes. I'm not sure rum's my drink.'

'An acquired taste, I know. Will red be OK?'

'Yes, please.'

There was the click as a screw-top seal was broken, then the sound of a glug of wine being poured generously into a glass. Viv turned holding out the glass.

'Here. Take a mouthful of that, then tell me a bit more about yourself.'

Jasmine took the glass from his hand and sipped it. The fruity flavour washed away the harsh taste of the rum.

'You know about me.'

'I know you are a woman and I know a little of what you are

131

going through.' Viv sat beside her with a re-filled rum glass.

Jasmine felt a warm glow inside her when he used the word, 'woman'.

'I want to know about you,' he went on. 'What are your likes and dislikes? What hobbies do you have?'

'Hobbies?'

'Yes. What do you like to do in your spare time?'

'Spare time?' Jasmine was stumped. What did she do with the time when she wasn't working? 'I'm not sure. Waste it, probably, watching TV, old films mainly.' Jasmine took a larger mouthful of wine.

'Oh, you like films. Me too. Go on.'

'Well, I like to run.' Jasmine realised that she hadn't actually been out for a run for a week or two. She'd felt off colour, nauseous, listless – thanks to the hormones battling inside her.

'Just jogging or are you a marathon runner?'

'Oh, just jogging now. I used to be good when I was at school, and at university. Middle distance. Athletics seemed to be an asexual sport even though men and women compete separately. Even when you're in a team event it's still you as an individual competing against the rest, so there's none of the "team bonding" that goes on in games such as football and rugby.'

'I know what you mean. I played in a cricket team as a youngster - for my Pa, I suppose, living up to my name. I wasn't very good, but it was fun. The banter was always good.' He paused, 'So, do you still compete?'

'Oh, no. Once I joined the police force there was no time for competition training. Then getting married and starting to transition... well, running became just a way to keep fit. It's something I can do without going to a gym and being on show.'

'Yes, I see.'

'Apart from that, I suppose I spend a lot of my time just learning how to be a woman.'

'What do you mean?'

'I have to make up for the time I lost, particularly as a

teenager, when girls experiment with make-up and fashions and hair styles and all the other things that help turn them into the women they become.'

'Now you mention it, I remember my little sister, Debs, when she was in her teens. She was always with her friends, swapping clothes, sharing lipsticks. She got into huge trouble when she bleached her hair. Ma made her dye it dark again.'

Jasmine laughed. 'You see – I missed out on all that even though I've got a sister too, but she's older. Angela was a great help, but I'm still catching up.'

'How do you do that?'

'Oh, reading magazines, looking on websites, window-shopping, reading chicklit – when I've got time and not feeling too tired.'

'Well, I won't join you in that and I'm no runner, but if you like films we can go to a movie together.'

Jasmine had a vision of sitting in a darkened cinema next to Viv, hand in hand, perhaps his hand on her knee, wandering up her thigh. She stopped herself. What was she thinking? Could Viv really be attracted to her as a woman? The image was satisfying though. It made a tingle run up her back.

'I'd like that,' she said.

'Good. I'll have a look to see what's on later in the week when you're up and about again.'

Viv's words reminded Jasmine that she had the operation to face. The thought of the scalpel sent a shiver the opposite way down her spine. She took a gulp of wine then put the empty glass down on the coffee table.

'That'll be lovely, but I think I'd better go now. Things to do before I travel tomorrow. You know.' She stood up pulling her dress down and smoothing it over her hips. Viv stood too.

'I understand. Look, thanks for this evening. I've really enjoyed it.' He put his hands on her shoulders.

'Yes, me too.'

'We'll make a date for next week - a celebration.'

'Um, yes.'

He leaned forward. Jasmine expected a peck on her cheek, but their mouths met. He pressed his lips against hers and she felt his tongue exploring tentatively between them. She didn't flinch or pull back, but wondered how far he would venture. His tongue touched her lips and she felt something like an electric shock. Would he force his way into her mouth? No, his tongue withdrew and he moved away. Jasmine breathed again. She looked at him. He was smiling.

'That was nice,' he said.

'Yes,' she replied in a whisper. She bent down to pick up her bag.

'I'll see you on Monday, Jasmine. Whatever time they let you go.'

'Thank you. I really do appreciate it.' The gratitude that Jasmine felt was overlaid by something else. Was it desire or longing to see Viv again?

'It's my pleasure. I hope we can find time to spend together.'

Jasmine turned towards the door. Viv leapt in front of her and held it open for her.

'Look after yourself,' he said as she passed by him.

'Thanks, and you too.'

Jasmine went down the steps, out into the car park and across to her own block. She didn't hear the door close behind her so guessed Viv had watched her departure. She didn't want to look around to check if he was still looking. She just wanted to relish the feeling of having someone care for her.

8

SUNDAY

Jasmine heard her phone ring above the whirr of the air conditioning and the rattle of the wheels on the tracks. She reached down to the floor of the carriage to retrieve her bag. With her knees pressed against the seat in front it wasn't the easiest of manoeuvres. She drew the phone out. It was still ringing and she saw it was Tom calling. At least there weren't many people on the train to be disturbed by her conversation.

'Hi, Jas. Where are you? It sounds noisy.'

'I'm on the train.'

'Train? Why?'

'I'm heading to London. You know, my surgery tomorrow.'

There was a pause. Jasmine imagined Tom recalling what she was having done on Monday.

'Did you get your pick-up arranged for after the, uh, operation?'

'Yeah, all sorted, thanks.'

'You've set off early. It's only three o'clock.'

'Yeah. I wanted to get into the hotel, get settled, prepare myself.'

'Oh, yes, of course.'

'Look, why did you call?' Jasmine was sure Tom hadn't rung to see how she was.

'I wanted to give you the news.'

'News?'

'Yes. The tech guys have got into Parfitt's computer and found the website that Xristal advertised herself on. He'd deleted it, but you know they can dig out old stuff.'

'Yes, I know. Go on. What does it show?'

'There are pictures of her dressed in leather and some of her naked showing, well, you know what, and some of her in bondage positions.'

'Hard core?'

'Well, not your soft focus, glamour shots. They look as though they're taken in her flat, not very professional, but anyone with a decent digital camera can take porn photos, can't they?'

'I suppose so. Anything else? Contact details?'

'Yes, she lists the services she offers and an email address.'

'Did Parfitt contact her?'

'The guys haven't found any record of an email exchange between them. Not on this computer anyway. They're getting the email records from the ISP to see if we can make up a list of clients.'

'Who would all be possible suspects?'

'That's right.'

'Could be a long list.'

'Perhaps, perhaps not. What Xristal was offering was pretty specialised – a she-male into BDSM. I can't imagine there are too many blokes into that.'

'You may be right.' Although Jasmine secretly thought that even the oddest sexual deviation usually attracted a host of followers.

'There's nothing about Potts on this website. Perhaps she'll turn up in the emails.'

'Perhaps.' Jasmine stopped herself from telling Tom what she had found out about Honey Potts alias Havana Goodthyme. She wanted to find her first before revealing what she had done.

'Yeah, well, we should have the names later today or tomorrow and we can start interviewing them. I'll let you know how things are going. Perhaps we'll have the case sewn up before you are.'

Jasmine shivered and groaned audibly.

'Sorry.' Tom did sound contrite. 'I shouldn't have put it like that. I hope it goes well for you tomorrow.'

'Thanks.'

'I'll phone as soon as I have any more news.'

'That'll be great.' Perhaps Sloane wouldn't have any more need for her services as an advisor if one of the clients confessed. She hoped not. She wanted to be the one to catch Xristal's killer and to find out why she was murdered.

'Bye.' The call ended and Jasmine dropped the phone back into her bag. She held the bag on her lap and leaned her head against the window. It wasn't very comfortable as the carriage rocked but it was marginally better than the headrest. She thought about Xristal and imagined what the pictures of her showed. Her experience of searching through similar websites in the last few days gave her a pretty good idea. Intimate shots revealing her gender-confused, cosmetically-enhanced body. Photos and videos of her engaged in sexual acts. Why would a young person like Xristal sell her body in that way? Was it just to get the cash to pay for her cosmetic surgery or had she actually enjoyed it? How had she felt about herself if, as Jasmine suspected, she had been preparing for gender reassignment? Jasmine couldn't answer the questions. She-males and their apparent delight in their male genitalia baffled her. Perhaps if she made contact with Honey she would provide some answers.

Getting rid of the appendage between her legs was her own top priority and, while the thought of the scalpel slicing through her skin made her tremble with fear, she was steeling herself for the next morning's operation as a step along her path to full womanhood. The tender kiss with Viv the previous evening had enhanced her feeling of femininity. The memory of the touch of his lips and his warm, moist tongue between hers gave her a feeling that she had not felt for years – not since she and Angela had still been in love or, more accurately, in lust. What were Viv's feelings for her? Could it be that he actually desired her despite knowing her background and her in-between status? She still wasn't sure what he wanted. Perhaps he was just lonely, having left his home town, and her company was better than nothing. The negative thought somewhat dampened the sexual ardour she had felt. Nevertheless, she resolved to give Viv the opportunity to make his feelings clear. Whatever the outcome, she would be grateful for his willingness to meet her from the hospital.

She had woken up in the morning with the usual thoughts circulating through her mind, but feeling a lot better than she had done for days. The memory of her conversation with Viv and a renewed feeling of energy had given her the incentive to go for a run. She had taken her usual route through the houses and open ground to the canal and then out of town for a mile or two. It had been quiet as always, but being a Sunday there had been a few other runners, dog walkers, and even a couple of narrowboats cruising along the canal with engines rumbling. She had passed a couple of locks before turning and retracing her steps. No-one had taken any notice of her – a young woman in shorts and sports bra holding her (imitation) breasts firmly. Stretching her legs, sucking cool air into her lungs, her heart beating a little faster than normal – a feeling of being truly alive. She had returned hot and sweaty but exhilarated – the nausea had come a short while later.

The train pulled in to Paddington station just about on time, despite the usual Sunday engineering work. Jasmine lifted her small case down from the luggage rack. It was almost unnecessary as it only contained a few overnight essentials, but she felt it looked better than a carrier bag. She sauntered through the station and down to the Underground where she had what seemed to be an interminable wait for the Circle Line.

She got off the tube at Gloucester Road and walked through the quiet streets to a Victorian terrace which had seen better days. A phone call before she left had reserved a room for the night in the small hotel spread across two of the five storey premises. It wasn't the plushest, cheapest or even the cleanest of hotels but having stayed once before, admittedly a few years earlier, she knew she would feel safe. It was used frequently by transgender folk making a trip to London to sample the clubs that welcomed their presence – and their cash.

An elderly woman was seated behind the reception desk reading *The Sunday Mirror*. She looked up and gave a smile of welcome as she pushed a registration document towards Jasmine, together with a Yale key.

'There you are, love. That's for your room, number seven, and the front door. Make sure you close the front door after yourself if you leave after nine p.m. We don't want riff-raff coming in off the street.'

'No, of course not,' Jasmine said, signing the form. She picked up the key and her case.

'Take care, darlin',' the woman said, returning to her newspaper.

'Thanks.' Jasmine trudged up the first flight of low-rise stairs covered in a threadbare red carpet. She found her room easily enough on the first floor. The bed, a small double, looked as though it had seen some action, and the curtains at the tall window had been washed so many times that the colour had almost gone. The other furnishings were dated but functional. Jasmine dropped her bag on the bed and pulled open the door to the ensuite bathroom. At least all the facilities were there – a loo, wash basin and old enamelled bath. It would do for one night, but the room was too depressing to stay in for long.

She returned to the dull, drab corridor making sure that the door to her room was locked, dropped the key into her bag and strolled out of the hotel. It was well placed for all the central London attractions but she didn't imagine that many of the guests visited the familiar tourist haunts like the Tower, the museums or the Eye. They were most likely to have come up to town for a show or, more likely, a club – or, frequently, for the same reason as her, to visit the hospital just a short tube journey away.

It was too early for her to go to Honey Potts' club and the nausea that came on after her run meant that she hadn't eaten before she caught the train. She needed to find a cheap restaurant. Cheap? In London? She must be daft, she thought. She retraced her steps from the tube station and came across an Indian restaurant. It was open all day, appeared clean and bright and the prices didn't look too extortionate. Even though it was late afternoon there were a couple of diners. She was shown to a table and settled down for her lone meal.

The boiled rice and a curry that was mostly potato left her feeling bloated, but it would be her last meal until after her operation – longer if the anaesthetic made her feel ill. Jasmine felt conspicuous as a lone diner so she didn't linger in the restaurant. It was nearly half past six so she decided to make her way to the club where Honey performed.

She descended to the tube and after a slow journey on the District line got off at Whitechapel and emerged into a part of the city some distance from the popular tourist haunts. A few minutes' walk took her into an area which seemed to have suffered all the agonies of post-war re-development. There were a couple of speculative new office blocks, lots of sixties flats and shops and even some gentrified mews properties. There were even some early twentieth century, brick-built business premises on narrow streets with stone kerbstones. The buildings displayed signs in languages she did not understand, advertising products and services she could not recognise. That was until she came to a large corner block with a sign above the steel door in lurid purple and pink announcing *Transgression! The club that breaks the rules of gender.* Boards filled in the old window frames and were covered with photographs of clubbers and performers in stylised and stereotypical female dress. There was plenty of flesh on show but nothing actually indecent. Jasmine approached the grey door. It was locked, but there was a poster stuck to it with duct tape announcing that the Open Club Night would start at nine p.m. There was still over an hour to go and it didn't look like there were any eager punters queuing up yet. Jasmine imagined that the club probably didn't liven up until around midnight when more upmarket clubs were either closing or charging high entrance fees.

She wanted to try to see Honey Potts before the show started, as the thought of mingling with a boozed and drugged-up, she-male-fancying crowd did not appeal to her, particularly as in her plain skirt and top she would stand out like a goose amongst peacocks. She walked slowly to the corner and looked down the alleyway between the club building and the adjacent block. There appeared to be another entrance about thirty metres away. Jasmine stepped into the alley, shivering as she immediately moved into shadow. There was the usual litter of discarded cans and crisp packets. The club building itself was forbidding with all its windows filled in and painted black. The entrance, when she reached it, was another grey steel door. She turned the handle. The door didn't budge. She rapped on it, making a dull clanging sound.

The door was opened immediately by a person of indeterminate gender wearing jeans and a sweatshirt. He or she was about Jasmine's height, but there the resemblance ended. He - Jasmine decided 'he' was probably the correct pronoun - had lank, shoulder-length hair, a waist and chest about twice hers in girth and arms with bulging tattooed biceps. He looked at Jasmine with a sneer.

'Who are you? You're not a member.' Jasmine guessed that the members of Transgression were instantly recognisable by their dress and appearance.

'No, I'm not.'

'The Open Club Night doesn't start till nine and the entrance is round the front.' He tried to push the door closed. Jasmine wedged herself in the opening.

'I know. I'd like to speak to one of your performers.'

He stopped pushing the door as if a little confused. 'Who?'

'Havana Goodthyme, Honey Potts.'

'She expecting you?'

'No.'

He made his decision and started pushing the door closed again. 'Well, she's not going to see you then.'

'Please,' Jasmine put her weight against the door to prevent herself being squashed. 'Give her a message.'

The bouncer stopped pushing. 'What?'

'Just say, I've come about Xristal.'

'OK. Now get out!'

He renewed his effort to close the door. Jasmine stepped back and the door slammed shut with a reverberating thud.

Would he pass on the message? Jasmine didn't know but resolved to bang on the door again after five minutes if there was no other response. She looked up. The strip of sky above her was still bright and blue but down here in the narrow alley it was as dark as twilight. She glanced at her watch noting the minutes passing. The five minutes were almost up when the door was wrenched open again.

'Come in. She says she'll see you.'

Jasmine stepped into a small foyer with a counter on the right. The walls were covered in purple flock wallpaper and posters of performers in flamboyant female dress. She didn't have time to search for one of Honey. There were two stairwells in front of her, one leading down into a dark underworld illuminated by small yellow wall lights. The other, leading up, was wider and brighter.

The bouncer closed the door. 'Follow me.'

They climbed several flights of stairs until they reached the top floor of the building. The bouncer pointed down a corridor. 'Dressing room C,' he said, before turning and heading back down the stairs.

Jasmine walked slowly down the narrow, dimly-lit corridor examining the doors on the left. The first two said A then B, the next, logically, said C. She tapped.

'Come in,' a voice called, high-pitched for a man but low for a woman. Jasmine pushed the door open and stepped into a brightly-lit room. There was a figure sitting in a swivel chair facing a mirror with a strip light on either side of it. Jasmine instantly recognised Honey's face in the mirror despite the long blonde tresses of the photo now being replaced by short mousy hair. There were other subtle changes that Jasmine couldn't identify immediately.

The chair swung around giving Jasmine a full view of its occupant. She had broad, fleshy shoulders and huge boobs that were only just held in check by the cups of a white basque which was covered in glistening pearls. A similarly be-pearled pair of knickers covered her very obvious manhood, but the basque gave her a totally feminine figure and her bare arms and legs were hairless.

'Who are you? And what do you know about Xristal?' As Honey opened her mouth to speak Jasmine realised what was different about her now compared to the photograph. Her chin was smaller, cuter.

'I'm Jasmine Frame and I found Xristal's body.'

The colour drained from Honey's face and drops of sweat appeared, glistening, on her forehead.

'Are you the police?' Honey's voice trembled.

'No, but I work with them and they are looking for you.'

'Why are you here then?'

'I want to ask you some questions before I tell the police where to find you.'

'You'd better close the door and have a seat.' Honey indicated the couch against the wall behind the door. Jasmine pushed the door closed and sat, placing her bag on the floor between her feet. Honey stood up revealing her full height which Jasmine estimated as about 6 foot three or four. She was quite impressed by Honey's hourglass figure, her massive boobs balanced by her large but firm buttocks.

'Would you like a drink? I think I need a whisky?' Honey crossed the room to a chest of drawers beside a washbasin. She reached for a bottle that stood on top of the chest and poured the amber liquid into a tumbler.

'Just a water, please,' Jasmine replied. Honey filled another glass from the tap and handed it to Jasmine. She sat again in her swivel chair.

'You knew Xristal was dead?' Jasmine said.

'I heard it on the radio,' Honey replied.

'But you didn't come forward?'

'I didn't know anything about what had happened to her.'

'But you have lived close to, if not actually with, Xristal for years. You knew her well.'

'Yes, but we split up a while ago.'

'Only a fortnight. That's not long. The police are having trouble finding out much about her. You could help them. That is, if you didn't actually kill Xristal yourself.'

Honey did not reply but her face took on an expression of deep sadness and she said nothing for a few moments. Finally she spoke.

'Xristal and I were close, but when I left two weeks ago we weren't exactly on friendly terms. If you know anything about the life we lead then you'll realise that I don't particularly relish questioning by the police.'

'I know you and Xristal were she-males working as prostitutes.'

Honey pulled herself up straight. 'That's in the past. I'm a performer now.'

'And Xristal – was being a she-male in the past for her?'

Honey sucked her lip. 'Almost. She'd decided that she wanted to become a complete woman. That's one reason why we had a row. I loved her as she was, with her gorgeous cock.'

Jasmine felt a little sick and also surprised at how disconcerted she felt at Honey's attachment to Xristal's male attributes. 'So, you killed her?'

'No!' Honey jerked upright and her nostrils flared. 'I said I loved her. I meant it but...' she subsided and sighed, 'well, if she was going to get the chop then there was no point sticking together. And there was the other reason.'

'What other reason?'

'I was offered the gig here.'

'You're going to have to be a lot more convincing if you want to persuade the police you didn't kill Xristal.'

Honey looked at the small clock on her dressing table. 'Look,

I'm the first act of the opening show. I've got to get ready.'

'But I need to know more. I've got to know who murdered Xristal.'

'Why? What are you doing here if you're not with the police?'

'Because ...' Why was she so desperate to solve the case? 'Because I'm trans too and I want to know why she was killed.'

'I thought so. Are you pre- or post-op? You don't look as though you've had much surgery. Are you on the hormones?' Jasmine recoiled from the questions fired at her.

'Pre-. I'm taking the tablets and I haven't had any surgery – yet.'

'Hmm. Well, how about this. Let's meet after my first show and I'll tell you what you want to know, on condition that you tell the police I wasn't involved in Xristal's death.'

'OK.'

'Right. Off you go then.'

'Where?'

'To watch the show!'

'How do I get there?'

'Go down two floors, then along the corridor. The end door will bring you out at the back of the stage. From there you can get into the auditorium. It'll be filling up now.'

Jasmine picked up her bag and stood up.

'Right. See you after your performance then.'

'OK. Oh, make sure you don't blunder through any of the other doors. You may not like what you see. You don't seem the kinky type.'

Jasmine's recent internet research meant that she was inclined to agree. She pulled the door open and left Honey already dabbing make-up on her face.

She followed Honey's directions carefully. After descending two floors she walked along a corridor with loud muffled rock music emanating through the wall to her right. She wondered if there was already action going on behind the closed doors on the left. At the end of the corridor she found the unlocked door and stepped through into a dark, high-ceilinged area. There was a raised stage to her right and a curtain in front of her from beyond which came the sound of voices striving to be heard over the booming music. Moving slowly forward she carefully pulled the edge of the curtain to the side and looked through the gap. There was a large room with small circular tables and chairs and, on the far side, a bar. In the gloom cast by a few wall-lights she could see a number of people sitting, standing, moving around. More were coming through double doors to the side of the bar. Honey was right, the club was certainly filling up.

Jasmine slipped through the curtain trying to be as unobtrusive as possible. She regretted wearing her light-coloured skirt and top as even in the semi-darkness she felt conspicuous. No-one seemed to notice her, however, so she tried to walk confidently and naturally towards one of the few empty tables that were left and sat down. There were a few tables between her and the stage but she felt that she would have a good view when Honey Potts, or rather, Havana Goodthyme, made her appearance.

She looked around at the clientele of the club. The majority were in female dress, well, a type of female., some drag, most not. There were lots of bright colours, sequins and shiny fabrics. Hems were high or slit to the hip. Bare arms and shoulders and impressive cleavages were on display, but further inspection made Jasmine wonder how many were real and how many were silicone. The voices were lively and predominately sounded alto or lower. As Jasmine had expected, most of the clientele of *Transgression* were transgender but she was not sure whether they were transvestites, she-males or transsexuals. None, however, were as modestly dressed and blandly made-up as her.

There were a number of men present. Real men or trans-men, Jasmine wasn't sure. Some were with the feminine characters as a couple, others in groups, but a few seemed to be standing alone with a glass in their hand checking out the growing audience. To Jasmine's horror a single man's eyes caught hers and he immediately started making his way across the room towards her, weaving his way through the tables and clubbers. He was bald-headed but looked to be late 30s, early 40s and was wearing groin-hugging jeans and a tight white T-shirt. His lack of a belly suggested a degree of fitness.

'Hi,' he drawled over the ear-numbing beat when he reached her table. 'You seem to be on your own. Mind if I take a seat? The show will be starting soon.'

Jasmine couldn't think of a reason to refuse since she was obviously alone. She signalled to an empty chair and shrugged. The man sat down next to her, put his beer glass on the table and leaned over to speak into her ear.

'I'm Greg. Who are you?'

'Jasmine.'

'Hi, Jasmine. Can I get you a drink?'

Jasmine wanted to get away but did not have time to answer. The painfully loud rock music suddenly stopped and was replaced by a fanfare, obviously announcing the start of the show. The lights dimmed and spotlights lit up the red satin and velour of the curtain. A man in a sparkly blue suit stepped out from behind it, and walked to the centre of the stage as the music faded.

'Hi there guys and gals, and guys that want to be gals and gals that want to be guys!' The audience cheered excitedly. 'What a show we have for you tonight!'

Jasmine's attention drifted as the MC launched into his innuendo-heavy introduction. She looked around the packed auditorium. Every chair at every table was filled and at the back the crowd was so thick that the bar could no longer be seen. Everyone was focused on the stage and cheering every rude joke. She half-heard a line about she-males and cocks and felt a weight on her knee. Looking down, she saw Greg's hand resting there. He leaned close to her again and his hand dragged up her thigh, ruffling the hem of her skirt.

'What about you, Jasmine? Have you got a dick under there?'

She shoved his hand off. What could she do? Getting up would draw attention to herself. The MC had already made lewd comments to members of the audience nearest the stage. It would be difficult to get out unseen and she needed to stay, to see Honey's act and get back to question her.

'Wait!' she said, hoping that would be enough to delay Greg's exploration.

'And now,' continued the MC, 'the one you've come for or would come over given the chance, Miss Havana Goodthyme!' The music changed to the opening bars of *Diamonds are Forever*, the MC skipped off the side of the stage and the curtains opened to reveal the impressive figure of Honey Potts just as she launched into the first line of the song.

Jasmine had to admit that she looked and sounded the part. Her height was now increased by a foot or more by silver platform-soled, stiletto-heeled shoes, together with a towering blonde wig. A sparkling silver satin dress clung to her vast bosom, wasp waist and immense hips. She looked like a giant Amazon of a woman. She stepped forward to the front of the stage, moving amazingly steadily on the outrageous shoes as she belted out the song, the slit in her dress parting to reveal white stockings flecked with silver held up with silver suspenders. Jasmine had never been particularly fond of drag artistes, but had seen quite a few on her visits to gay and trans clubs. There was no doubt about it - Havana Goodthyme was breathtakingly good. Honey Potts obviously had considerable talent.

The crowd hooted and whistled as Havana continued into her second and third numbers – classic Tina Turner and Alison Moyet songs. She moved, seductively at first, then with raunchier movements of her hips and bust, showing off her amazing figure. She kicked up her legs giving a glimpse of bare upper thigh and a hint of the bulge at her crotch.

The numbers got faster and louder and Havana's dancing raunchier. Jasmine failed to see how it happened, but the silver dress became undone and slowly, sexily, Havana slid the sleeves from her arms and threw it back off her shoulders. She stood, centre stage in the combined light of four spotlights, feet a metre apart, thrusting her manhood forward encased in the pearl-covered pouch of her knickers, hands on her broad hips and light glinting off the pearls scattered across her torso. Jasmine imagined that this was the climax of Honey's act, but she moved smoothly into another number with another heavy bass rhythm. Her voice soared to hit the high notes, reverberating through the auditorium as she moved, gyrated and bent over showing off her magnificent physique. Then she began to wiggle herself free from the confines of the basque. With a flourish she discarded it, revealing the tasselled nipples of her high, melon-sized breasts. She came to the front of the stage, still singing, and leaned out to the audience. Jasmine wondered how she managed to maintain her balance; how the weight of her tits didn't make her topple to the floor. Perhaps it was the counterbalance provided by her buttocks that did it. Still singing, she did a one-eighty and thrust out her bottom while easing the waist band of her knickers down over her hips. Gradually, the smooth white skin of her bum was revealed. The knickers reached the top of her thighs and dropped to the floor just as the song reached its climax. Havana leapt in the air and twisted round as the final chord crashed from the speakers. The lights went out and the curtains closed just as Jasmine had a brief glimpse of Honey's huge, bouncing erect penis.

The music reverted to the original heavy rock and the lights came back up. 'Phew. That was some performance,' Greg shouted in Jasmine's ear. His hand landed on her knee again. 'She's got some tackle, that girl. Did you see it?'

Jasmine nodded, wondering how to get away and see Honey again. Greg's hand slid up her bare thigh. 'What about you, darling? What have you got between your legs? Did that performance make you hard? I am.'

Jasmine placed her hand over his, tried to push it back. He resisted. 'Come on,' he shouted in her face, his expression contorted in frustration and growing anger. 'You want it don't you? That's why you're here.'

Jasmine stiffened her arm as Greg struggled to push his hand into her groin. 'No, I don't want it. Leave me alone!'

His fingers gripped her thigh pressing into her flesh. If he'd had nails he would have pierced her skin. 'What are you then? You one of those trannies with a limp dick?'

Jasmine braced her feet against the floor and pushed back. Her chair slid back and toppled over as she stood up. Greg was pulled from his seat but his grip loosened and he fell forward. Jasmine grabbed her bag and fled before he had a chance to recover, reached the curtain and slipped through. She paused in the dark, catching her breath and hoping that Greg had not seen where she had gone. She felt her way to the door into the corridor and retraced her steps upstairs.

As she entered the top corridor, the door to room A opened and a figure emerged wearing a costume that seemed to consist solely of long, purple feathers. The figure pushed past her without a word and headed down the stairs. The next performer, Jasmine guessed.

She reached Honey's door, tapped, didn't wait for an answer, but entered immediately. Honey was lying on the couch wrapped in a towelling bathrobe with a whisky glass in one hand. The silver platform shoes were discarded on the floor and the blonde wig rested on her stomach like a contented cat. The silver dress was tossed over the back of the swivel chair.

'Oh, it's you again,' Honey drawled without moving. 'Get yourself a drink and pull up the chair.'

Jasmine crossed to the washbasin and found the glass she'd used earlier. She filled it with water.

'What did you think of it then?' Honey asked.

Jasmine rolled the chair over to the couch and sat down. 'Pretty powerful. You sing amazingly and you have, well, a presence.'

'Thanks. Anything else?'

Jasmine could see Honey's eyes searching her face for a reaction. 'I was expecting a drag show and I appreciate burlesque, but the strip – not my scene, I'm afraid.'

'You haven't seen the second half yet!'

'You're on again?'

'Yeah, after midnight. I do a brief résumé then carry on from where I left off with participation from certain... special members of the audience.'

'You mean you do a sex show?'

'You could call it that.'

'I thought you said you'd given up prostitution?'

Honey looked pained. She leaned forward wagging a finger 'This is performance art, darling. The crowd love it, I love it and the pay is good too.'

'I don't want to watch people writhing around on stage.'

'Hmm, aren't you prim and proper. Come on, you're trans. Don't you want a bit of cock action? Don't tell me you're a muff-muncher!'

Jasmine felt flustered, not sure how to respond. Her reactions to sexual imagery were confused and upsetting. She wasn't exactly sure what she fancied, but she certainly wasn't going to discuss it with a she-male. 'Look, I'm here to talk about Xristal.'

Honey sank back on the couch. 'OK. I was hoping my act might have had an effect on you, but there you go.' She took a swig of whisky, swallowed, 'What do you want to know?'

'All you know about Xristal. How you met - everything.'

Honey's vast chest heaved as she took a deep breath. 'I suppose it goes back further than that, to how I got started in this business.'

'OK. Go on.' Jasmine reached into her bag for her notebook and pen.

'I was in my teens, I suppose, and like every kid I was learning about sex. Like all boys, when I got hold of lads' mags and porn I wanked over the girls' tits. Didn't you?'

Jasmine scribbled "teen", "porn", "wanked". 'No. I was disgusted when I first got an erection.' The recollection of the first time it had happened was still burned in her memory.

'Hmm, I guess that proves you are TS then. Me, well, I loved it but the more I looked at pictures of girls I realised I wasn't lusting *after* them. I wanted to be *like* them. I wanted the smooth face, narrow waist and big tits. But I didn't want to lose my cock, no way.' She sipped her whisky. 'I looked after myself. Shaved carefully, my whole body, and moisturised. Let my hair grow. Started buying sexy girl-wear, but didn't let anyone see me. School was a bore but I just scraped in to university.'

'Where?'

'Reading. Not the posh one, the one that used to be the poly - TVU. I wasn't interested in the course much but I discovered the clubs, including one for gays and trannies where I could go dressed up. I discovered I wasn't the only one like me. There were other guys who liked dressing as girls who wanted sex with me, and there were blokes who fancied us.'

'Men who would pay?'

'Yeah. Easy money. I dropped out of uni, got a flat, started playing the market and began to do what I'd always wanted to do.'

'What was that?'

'Get my body altered so I looked more like those girls, except for the cock of course.'

'What did you have done?'

'At first? A nose job and my first boobs, then laser hair removal on my face.'

'That must have cost thousands.'

'Yeah, but I was making it. I wasn't on drugs and hardly drank back then, so all the money I earned went on clothes, make-up and cosmetic surgery. There were plenty of punters who wanted me.'

'And Xristal? Where does she fit in?'

'Later, over eight years ago I suppose. I was twenty two. One night at the club, she just appeared. She was young, attractive, but obviously had very little idea who or what she was or how to dress. I found out she'd slipped out of home, changed behind a bush somewhere and arrived in just about the only female clothes she possessed. Fashion-wise she was a mess, but, god, she was gorgeous.'

'Xristal was about fifteen then?'

'That's right. She was about the same height as you, slim, shoulders not too broad, long legs, and that shiny black hair down to her shoulders.'

'So, you seduced her?'

'No. No, that wasn't how it was. We talked.'

'Then you had sex?'

'No. It wasn't like that.'

'What was it like then?' Jasmine was convinced that Honey had led Xristal on. She continued to write in her notebook.

'We talked for a while. The next night she came again and we talked for longer. She was mixed up. She didn't understand these feelings she had about wanting to dress like a girl, to have the body of a girl.'

'So you persuaded her to be a she-male like you.'

'No, I didn't persuade her. I suppose me and my friends just assumed it. She talked about getting hard-ons and wanking off, so we just thought she was like us.'

'So you and your mates introduced her to she-male sex?'

'No,' Honey sat up and glared at Jasmine. 'I knew she was too young. We're not crazed sex-addicts always after a pull, well, most of us aren't. For a couple of years, she just hung out with us. Okay, she saw a few of the girls having it off with each other from time to time and she knew I was seeing guys regularly. She knew where the money for the ops was coming from. She was a bright girl and got even better-looking as she learned what to wear.'

'You groomed her until she was old enough to service your clients?'

Honey's face contorted in anger. 'Look, I'm getting pretty fed up with your accusations. I tell you, it wasn't like that.'

'It sounds a lot like it.'

'You fucking tee-esses. So holier than thou. You think there's just male and female and if you chop off your prick you'll change from a man to a woman!'

Jasmine felt her cheeks heat up. 'It's more than that. I AM a woman, but my body's wrong!'

'Oh yes, the old "woman trapped in a man's body" story!'

'It's true!'

'Well, perhaps it is for you. But male/female, gay/straight - it's more complicated than black and white.'

They both sat still, staring into each other's eyes, as if daring each other to claim the moral high ground. Jasmine recalled all the trans people she had known and met. Honey was right. Everyone had their own stories, their own feelings and position on the male-female spectrum. And it was a spectrum, not an either/or. She took a deep breath and sat back, folding her arms.

'OK. Tell me what it was like for you then.'

Honey held out her empty tumbler, 'Get me another whisky.'

Jasmine grabbed the glass and walked across the room, filled it and returned. Honey took it from her and gulped another mouthful.

'Well?' Jasmine asked.

'I fell in love,' Honey said softly.

'In love?' Jasmine could not keep the scepticism out of her voice.

'Yes. Is it so hard to believe? I was still pretty young. I thought I knew what I wanted – a body like a girl but still with working tackle – and I was easy about how I was earning the cash to achieve it. Xristal was beautiful, we got on and I thought she wanted the same as me.'

'And she fell in love with you too, I suppose?'

'Yes, I think so. We got on well, talked for hours, enjoyed doing things together.'

'And had sex.'

'Not straight away. I controlled myself. She kept urging me to let her make love to me, but I kept saying she was too young.'

'But you gave in.'

'Yes,' Honey sighed. 'Just after her seventeenth birthday. She was well over the age of consent.'

'OK, so it was legal.'

'She said she wanted to be with me. I said she should stay at school, go to university, get a career. She asked how she could save for her modifications if she had to pay her way through uni and start at the bottom of some fancy career. I tried to persuade her, and she did stay at school almost until her exams, but she said she couldn't go on. I let her come to live with me and she refused to have anything more to do with her parents.'

'So you embarked on a life together. What a lovely couple.'

'It was lovely. I paid for her to have her first pair of tits. We moved to London. I was picking up loads of clients. Xristal saw how it worked and asked to join in.'

'Simple, was it? Slipping into a life of prostitution.'

'Yeah. Well I looked after her. Made sure her customers were OK and that she took precautions. I agree I almost felt jealous of those guys who paid for her. She has, uh, had a super body and a gorgeous cock.'

'Just guys?'

'Well mainly guys and she-males. Occasionally we picked up some girls who liked to mix it up a bit.'

'And Xristal went along with all this?'

'Yeah, she loved it. At least I thought she did. We planned our next surgery. She went for vocal cord tightening to raise her voice pitch. I didn't want that, but I had hip and buttock implants which she didn't.'

'You lived your fantasy?'

'Yeah.'

'What about the BDSM? When did Xristal get into that?'

'I can't remember exactly when. I suppose we started playing around early on. I'm naturally a bit dom and Xristal was happy to play games. We began to use ropes and cuffs, picking up odd bits and pieces from time to time.'

'Just a bit of fun was it?'

'For me, yes, it was. But Xristal seem to take to it and started to introduce it into her services to clients. She found she could charge more if she allowed herself to be tied up.'

'Sounds risky to me.'

'That's what I thought. I warned her that someone might really hurt her if she was defenceless. She said she checked out her clients carefully, but I don't know how. She was a bit of a computer geek.'

'When was this?'

'We moved round quite a lot, making sure the fuzz didn't clock us. Sometimes we lived together, sometimes we had separate flats for appointments. Then a year ago we decided to move out of the city. We found the two flats in Kintbridge. That was when Xristal really started concentrating on the BDSM stuff.'

'What did you think of it?'

'It worried me and I realised that we weren't as close anymore. She was changing.'

'How?'

'I didn't really notice it at first. She was just less eager to use her tool. I thought it was because she was taking on too many clients, getting tired, you know.'

'I don't, but I can try to imagine.'

'Well, the thing was, I was changing too. I was getting bookings in small clubs all over the country, to do my act, so I was away a few nights a week.'

'Then you had a row?'

'No, we had a falling out. I had just got back from having my chin re-shaped and was off the circuit for a couple of weeks while the bruising went down. So I had more time in the flat with Xristal. Then I got the offer of the booking here, long term, nightly. That was when she told me she'd decided to have the full sex-change. I couldn't believe it.'

'I bet.'

'I asked her how she could think of getting rid of her gorgeous prick and balls.'

'What did she say?'

'She told me she'd been uncomfortable for a long time and had realised that she was "really a woman". She said she was just doing the BDSM thing to raise money for the op, in Thailand. She had it booked and the flights too.'

'You hadn't suspected anything?'

'No. Oh, I expect there were signs, like the voice pitch thing, but I missed them all. It was a complete surprise - and I suppose I reacted badly.'

'How?'

'I threw it all back at her. How we'd been a couple, looking out for each other. How much I'd done for her - all that crap. She walked out on me, went back up to her flat and wouldn't answer the door to me.'

'So that was it? You left and haven't been back?'

'Yes. I was due to start here the next day. I've barely been out of this room since except to perform.'

'Unless in fact you went back to Kintbridge, had another row and killed Xristal.'

'No,' Honey roared. She leapt from the couch, the wig dropping to the floor and her robe falling open to reveal her huge tits and flopping genitals.

'You didn't go back to try to change her mind? Have a fight, maybe?'

Honey grabbed Jasmine's arms and hauled her up. The notepad and pen flew across the floor. Honey shook her. Jasmine pushed her arms up between Honey's arms and levered them off her. She fell back into the chair and it rolled backwards until it hit the dressing table.

'You've got a temper, haven't you? Is that what happened with Xristal? All that male testosterone making you jealous that Xristal was leaving you to become the woman she really felt she was.'

Honey advanced towards Jasmine, fists clenched.

'You killed her, didn't you?' Jasmine went on, 'She had become disgusted at what you did and what you had made her do.'

Honey stopped and fell to her knees. She covered her face in her hands and sobbed.

'No, I didn't! I loved her! I didn't go back and see her.'

Jasmine wasn't listening. She was convinced that Honey had somehow got back to Kintbridge unseen and killed Xristal.

'Then you had to arrange her body to make it look as if one of her punters had killed her.'

The sobbing stopped. Honey looked up into Jasmine's eyes. She looked totally bemused. 'What do you mean? What did he do to her?'

'If you killed her you'd know.' But Jasmine could see that Honey had no knowledge of what she was talking about, that she had no idea that Xristal had been stretched out on the bed and set alight.

'I don't know! I didn't see her again! I told you.'

'If you really don't know I can't tell you. It's police information.'

'You've got to believe me!' Honey appealed. 'Don't tell the police I killed Xristal. I didn't.'

Jasmine chewed her thumbnail. Her gut instinct told her that Honey was telling the truth. There were none of the classic signs that she had come to recognise of a guilty person trying to pretend ignorance.

'Why didn't you go back to see Xristal? Didn't you think about her after you left?'

'Of course I thought about her, but I guessed she wouldn't want me anymore. She would go off and get the chop, take the hormones and that would be it. She'd be a different person.'

'OK. So if it wasn't you, who did kill her?'

Honey looked up at her, appealing. 'How should I know?'

'One of her clients?'

'Probably. I told you I was worried about Xristal letting them tie her up.'

'Why would one of them want to kill Xristal?'

'I don't know. Perhaps a scenario got out of hand and they didn't mean to kill her.'

'Was that likely with any of her customers?'

'I didn't know any of them. Xristal kept her arrangements to herself. Once or twice I saw someone arrive or leave, but I never met them.'

'And they were all blokes?'

'Men or she-males most likely. She did mention having a couple of dominatrixes practise on her, but I don't know who they were.'

'The police will find it difficult to believe that you didn't know who Xristal's clients were. Not if you were so close.'

'You can't put the cops on me!'

'I have to. You're the prime suspect.'

The pain on Honey's upturned face drove needles into Jasmine. 'You've got to tell them it wasn't me! I don't know who she was seeing. I told you we were going our separate ways. I hadn't realised it, but we were.'

'That's not very convincing. You'll need a rock-solid alibi.'

'I was here.'

'Are there people who will stand up in court and say that you were?'

'In court? Surely it won't come to that. You can persuade the police it wasn't me, can't you?' Honey's arms reached around Jasmine's legs, imploring her.

'What about the staff here?'

'They're not fond of the police. And they're not around during the day, especially Tuesdays and Wednesdays when the club doesn't open.'

'So you don't have an alibi?'

'You've got it in for me! That's what this is all about isn't it? You're a transsexual, I'm a she-male, but we both go to the surgeon to get the body we want. You have your cock and balls turned into a cunt and implants to enhance the little tits you grow yourself. You have had it done, haven't you?'

Jasmine was taken by surprise. 'No, not yet, I haven't.'

'You will though won't you. When?'

'Tomorrow.'

It was Honey's turn to look surprised and she sprawled back on the old, soiled carpet.

'Tomorrow? A sex-change?'

'Biorchidectomy.' Jasmine found herself blurting the word out.

Honey's face was wrinkled in thought. 'I know that. It means having your balls out.'

'Yes.'

'So you won't ever get an erection again?'

'That's right.'

'So you can be more like a woman.'

'One step closer...'

Honey shook her head, chuckling. 'And you look down your nose at what Xristal and I had done to fulfil our dreams, while you're planning your own changes? You and me, we'll both have bodies we've designed and planned and suffered for.'

'Yes, well, perhaps that's true.' Jasmine glanced at her watch. It was getting late. 'I've got an early start tomorrow at the hospital so it's about time I left.'

Honey got to her feet, drawing her robe around her and stood in front of the door, blocking Jasmine's exit.

'You can't leave here and get the police to come for me! You've got to tell them it was someone else that killed Xristal!'

'Well, you've got to tell me all you know. Apart from clients, who else could it have been?'

Honey looked pained. 'I don't know.'

'Tilly Jones?'

'Who?'

'The girl in the bottom flat.'

'Oh, her. Hardly got to know her. Sweet girl. I can't see any reason for her to kill Xristal.'

'What about the Taylors?'

'The landlords? Only met the husband once. A soft guy. She was hard though. A stick-like figure, nice tits though. Used to come to collect the rent. I paid in cash. She stayed pretty distant.'

'What about Xristal? Did she ever meet Marilyn Taylor?'

'Can't see why. Xristal paid by bank transfer. I didn't trust the banks to do that properly.'

Jasmine stepped towards Honey. 'That doesn't help much. You'll still be top of the list of suspects.'

Honey backed against the door, barring Jasmine's exit. 'Look, you've got to tell them it wasn't me. Don't they listen to you?'

Jasmine wondered how much notice Sloane would take of her gut instinct. 'Well, they've got no evidence that you were in Kintbridge on Wednesday. They may believe me if I say I don't think it was you. But you've got to speak to them. It would be best if you took yourself in for questioning.'

Honey slumped. Every part of her face and body, including her augmented breasts, seemed to sag. 'OK, but not yet.'

'Why not?'

'I've got a show tomorrow night,' Honey went on. 'Then I'm off for two days. I'll come to Kintbridge then.'

Jasmine reasoned that she herself wouldn't be back in Kintbridge till later the next day and then perhaps would not feel like meeting with Tom and Sloane until Tuesday. Would it be holding up the investigation if she didn't tell Tom about Honey till then? No. Especially if Honey was not the murderer. Besides, Tom would have his hands full tracing Xristal's clients for a day or two. He might even identify the murderer. 'OK. I'll keep it to myself until after I've had my op.'

Honey let out a relieved sigh and reached forward to clasp Jasmine's hands. 'Thank you, thank you.'

'But you've got to keep in touch with me,' Jasmine said, extracting her hands from Honey's grasp. She felt around in her bag until she found one of her business cards. She handed it to Honey. 'Here's my phone number.'

Honey read the card. '"See the full picture with Frame Investigations". A bit corny.'

'It does the trick,' Jasmine said, feeling mildly hurt, 'and it's not half as corny as "Havana Goodthyme".'

Honey gave her a lop-sided grin. 'A drag queen's name has got to have a pun in it.' She went to the dressing table, opened a drawer and pulled out a card. 'Here's my number.'

Jasmine took it from her and tucked it in her bag. Then she moved to the door. 'Sure you don't want to stay and see the second half?' Honey asked, making no attempt to stop Jasmine reaching the door.

'No thanks. I don't think I could stand the attention I would get from some of your admirers.'

'Was one of them coming on to you earlier?'

'Yes.'

'You don't dress like one of the girls, but I suppose some of the blokes just don't care as long as you've got big tits and a hard cock.'

'Well, I haven't got the former and after tomorrow I won't have the latter.' Jasmine couldn't believe how blasé she felt.

Honey winced. 'That's one cut I don't ever want.'

Jasmine shuddered at the mention of cutting.

'Hey, are you sure you're feeling all right about it?' Honey said.

'I want rid of the testosterone but I've got a phobia about knives and cutting.'

Honey nodded, 'I understand. I don't like anaesthetics. I don't like losing control and I'm always sick after an op, but I put up with it because it's the only way to get the body I want.'

'Yes, and I'll have to get over my phobia to get what I want.'

'We're not so different then, are we?'

'Oh, I'm not so sure about that,' Jasmine replied, catching a glimpse of Honey's penis through her undone robe. She opened the door. 'Remember, keep in touch or you'll find the police round here and dragging you off in handcuffs - and I don't mean for a bit of fun.'

'Okay, okay. I've got the message. Good luck tomorrow.' Honey was already sliding her arms out of the sleeves of the robe revealing more of her naked body. Jasmine didn't want to see any more and stepped into the corridor.

She hurried down the stairs, eager to get away from the club as quickly as possible, but the route through the small foyer to the side entrance was blocked by the hefty bouncer and three other characters whose appearance took Jasmine by surprise - despite the venue. One was wearing a parody of a maid's uniform in a shiny, stiff material, but was obviously a middle-aged man with a glossy, black wig and thick make-up. The second character was tall and slim with flame red hair above a short rubber dress of a similar colour. She had a good enough figure to be female, but Jasmine had her doubts. She was holding the end of dog lead attached to a collar around the third person's neck - a thin, bald-headed man in his twenties wearing a torn vest and a ragged pair of denim shorts held up only by a large safety pin through the flies.

Jasmine's appearance interrupted their conversation, and the tall, rubber-clad figure looked her up and down. 'Ooh, what do we have here? Do you want to join us, love?'

'Join you? Doing what?' Jasmine replied, feeling uncomfortable and confused.

'We're going to show Abigail how to be a pretty girl and teach her how to serve us,' she said, tugging on the lead, and Jasmine noticed the young man give a broad smile.

'What? No thanks.'

'Oh, come on. It'll be a laugh. You look as though you need some excitement in your life.'

'No. I'm leaving,' Jasmine was determined.

The tall woman pouted. 'Well, have it your way. Come on, Cynthia, let's get Abigail prepared.' She led the other two down the stairs into the basement.

'You've only got it for a couple of hours!' the bouncer called.

'That'll be plenty of time, love.'

'Where are they going?' Jasmine asked, not sure if she wanted to know.

'There's a fully-equipped dungeon down there,' he answered, 'available to members. But you're not a member, are you?'

'No, and I never will be,' Jasmine said, hurrying out of the door into the alleyway. It was a warm, humid night. Jasmine walked back up to the street and passed a queue of people waiting at the main entrance. They were a boisterous crowd, high on alcohol and other intoxicants, in a variety of extravagant and exotic outfits. She guessed that the majority were trannies of one description or another, but she noted a number of men amongst them. Havana Goodthyme's fans were obviously the same cross-section as her former clients.

Jasmine was relieved that the impatient and excited clubbers were more interested in each other than in her and she walked quickly away. She had spent more than enough time in the company of she-males and their acolytes for one night.

9

MONDAY

The hospital corridor was bright and had that typical hospital smell of cleaning fluid and other odours, the source of which she didn't want to think about. Jasmine sat in the straight-backed chair feeling uneasy. It wasn't that the chair itself was uncomfortable, but she felt exposed. Doctors, nurses, patients and their companions passed to and fro and she felt their eyes on her wondering what she was in for. She was also tired and anxious.

The journey back to the hotel had been slow with a long wait for the tube followed by a fraught trek through the unfamiliar streets. She had gone straight to bed, but despite it being so late had tossed and turned thinking about what Honey had told her, analysing her feelings about the club and its members, and becoming steadily more anxious about her appointment with the surgeon.

Now she tried to force herself to think about Honey's story instead of letting her nerves get the better of her. Nevertheless, her mind kept returning to the impending operation and in particular the image of the blade of the scalpel cutting into her skin. Really, she should have been feeling overjoyed as, aside from starting the course of drugs, this was the first medical step in her transition and the first stage of the transformation of her male body into a female one. She knew it was a massively important moment in her life. She was giving up being a man as far as sex was concerned and becoming, well, a nothing really. She wouldn't become a fully-functioning woman until she had the full gender reassignment surgery, god knows when. Despite her fears of the surgeon's scalpel, she was certain that this was what she wanted. The dangly bits between her legs weren't really part of her. They belonged to James Frame who was gone, departed. They were incongruous on Jasmine Frame, a proud, confident woman. She wouldn't regret this change, but she did wish they'd get it over with - she'd been sitting waiting for nearly an hour now, and that wasn't solely because she had arrived early.

She wondered if she should give Tom a call or perhaps just a text to see if there was any progress in tracking down Xristal's clients. Should she mention Honey? She had promised that she would not pass on Honey's whereabouts until Tuesday. Jasmine was pretty sure that Honey was not Xristal's murderer, but there was still doubt and a full statement from her was needed. She was thumbing the call button when a passing nurse glared and pointed to the "No Mobile Phones" sign. Jasmine hurriedly hit the off button and dropped the phone in her bag. She sank back into the chair feeling guilty.

At last a female nurse approached her. 'Jasmine Frame?' Jasmine nodded. 'Come with me please.'

Jasmine followed the nurse along a maze of corridors, towing her suitcase, before entering a small ward. Curtains were drawn around most of the beds. The nurse led Jasmine to the sole empty bed.

'Please undress and put the gown on.' The nurse indicated the hospital robe in thin, polka dotted material that lay folded on the mattress and she started to pull the curtains around the bed.

Jasmine began to undress, pulling her t-shirt over her head. She froze when the nurse peered around the end of the curtain. 'OK, there?'

'Um, yes. What do I do with my, uh, bits?' Jasmine was unwilling to refer to her breast enhancers directly.

'Oh, you can put your clothes and personal possessions in the cupboard by the bed.'

'Will they be safe?'

'We don't cover the loss of valuable items.'

'No? I haven't got anything valuable, just you know, credit cards, that sort of thing.'

'Oh, you should have left those with your companion.'

'I haven't got a companion.'

'How are you getting home?'

'A friend is coming to pick me up.'

'I see, well it should be safe to leave things here. This is only a day-case ward so there won't be many staff or visitors coming through.'

''I hope not.' Jasmine wanted to see as few people as possible while she was at the hospital and the possible theft of her bank cards was one worry she did not want.

'OK. I'll leave you for a few minutes. Lie on the bed when you're ready. One of the surgical team will be along soon.'

Jasmine carefully stripped and pulled the robe on. It was the usual backless variety but she was able to tie a bow in the two thin straps that held it together. It wasn't a particularly discreet garment but she was not too bothered, at least not while the curtains were drawn. She tucked her shoulder bag and her clothes into her case, put it by the bedside table, then lay on the bed and tried to relax.

It was difficult. She kept on seeing that familiar image of a blade slicing through skin, of blood oozing through the cut, the flesh parting. It was quite a shock when the curtain was suddenly tugged open and a bearded man in his mid-thirties leaned over her. He held a clipboard. 'Can you give me your name please?'

'Jasmine Frame.'

'And your date of birth and address.'

Jasmine recited the familiar facts. The surgeon, at least she presumed he was the surgeon, looked satisfied and shifted his gaze from the notes to look directly at her for the first time. 'So you're in for a biorchidectomy. You know what that means?'

'You're going to remove the testicles.' As she said it she realised she hadn't referred to them as hers. She didn't feel at all possessive of them even though they were attached to her.

'That's right. It's a simple, quick operation with very little risk of complications, but you do understand that it is not reversible?' He frowned at her to show how seriously he meant what he said.

'I know. It will mean the removal of my male characteristics.'

'Well, yes, I suppose that is true but we are not removing your penis and scrotum today. You will need that tissue for when you have the full gender reassignment surgery. I see you're down for that, but there's no date given.'

'That's why I'm having this done, so I don't have to keep taking the anti-androgens while I'm waiting.'

'Yes, I understand. You've had a bad reaction to them?'

'Yes.'

'Right, but we have to preserve as much skin as possible so that we have plenty to work with when we build your vagina. You'll have to exercise your penis.'

Jasmine had heard this before. 'Yes, I know. I have to stretch it now and again.'

'Daily. You won't be getting erections.'

'I know that,' Jasmine felt her irritation and embarrassment growing as the surgeon went on referring to matters she preferred not to think about.

'And we replace your testicles with silicone balls to fill out the sac.'

'Yes, I've been told that.'

'Well, I'm just checking. I have to make sure you understand the procedure.'

He was just doing his job, Jasmine reflected, trying to reply as calmly as she could. 'Yes, I do realise what this involves.'

'Good. You've opted for the medium-sized balls. Most people do that. They're like this.' He drew a white sphere the size of a squash ball from the pocket of his white coat. Jasmine hadn't seen one when Dr Gould had talked the operation over with her and she had just gone for the middle option. The ball looked a lot bigger than she imagined her testicles were, but she was not in the mood to argue.

'Yes, well, fine.'

'Good. One last thing – you haven't eaten anything in the last twelve hours and only drunk water?'

'Yes,' Jasmine was reminded of her empty stomach.

'We wouldn't want you throwing up on the operating table. Now, if you could sign the form we'll start getting you ready.'

He handed Jasmine a pen and she scribbled her name in the spaces he indicated.

'Thanks,' the surgeon smiled. 'It won't take long and you won't see or feel a thing apart from perhaps a little tugging when we stretch the sperm duct.' Jasmine swallowed, feeling a little unnerved, as he went on, 'A nurse will be along soon to prepare you, then we'll have you in and out in a few minutes.'

He stepped back letting the curtain fall back and left Jasmine alone again. This was it, she thought. She had signed her manhood away: the culmination of years of agonising and debating, both internally and with Angela, doctors and, just once, with her mother.

Jasmine was still thinking back to the fraught conversation she had had when she announced her decision to transition to her mother, when the curtain opened again. A male nurse appeared with a tray of instruments. 'Miss Frame?' Jasmine nodded. 'I've come to get you ready for your surgery.' He placed the tray on the table that stood at the end of the bed and pulled a pair of surgical gloves onto his hands. 'Could you pull the gown up to your waist please?'

Blood rushed to Jasmine's cheeks. He was asking her to reveal herself to him. She gripped the hem but didn't move it.

'Don't be embarrassed. I've got to get you ready for the local anaesthetic and then the surgeon can see to you.'

Which was most embarrassing? A man or a woman looking at her exposed genitals? She wasn't sure, but this went against all her instincts. She devoted a lot of time to making herself look like a woman, yet here she was revealing that she was, visually at least, a man. But he was a nurse. She overcame her resistance and pulled the gown slowly up to her waist while looking for a reaction in the man's face. There was none.

He gently took hold of her penis and testicles in his latex-covered hand. Jasmine's muscles stiffened and a memory flashed through her mind. Another man wearing surgical gloves had grabbed her genitals, a lot more roughly - the knife-wielding tranny-killer who she had been a decoy for and would have become a victim of if Tom Shepherd hadn't rescued her in time. That memory was still all too fresh after just a few months. She tried to push it from her mind.

Only one other person had ever touched her down there - Angela. It had been a pleasure to explore each other's bodies, but while they made love Jasmine had often imagined herself in Angela's position: the one who stroked the penis, the one with the breasts, the one who was penetrated. That had always seemed so much more pleasurable and satisfying than what she was actually doing.

'I'll have to give you a shave,' the nurse broke into Jasmine's brief reverie.

'What?'

'The surgeon won't want hairs getting in the way when he sews you up.'

'Oh, no, I suppose not.' Jasmine was beyond embarrassment now. Whatever was happening "down below" wasn't part of her. She didn't look as the nurse got busy with a safety razor, but she felt his skilled movements swiftly removing the hairs from her scrotum. He washed off the soap and patted her dry with a towel before wiping her whole groin area with a cold liquid.

'I'm just preparing you for the local anaesthetic now,' he said as the curtain parted again and they were joined by a young woman in scrubs. She also carried a tray and a clipboard which she laid on the table. She glanced at the notes then looked at Jasmine.

'Can you please confirm your name, address and date of birth before I give you the local anaesthetic?'

Jasmine recited the information and then lay her head flat on the pillow so that she couldn't see what was happening. Needles didn't bother her as much as knives, but she had no wish to watch the proceedings. She thought about Honey and Xristal. How many times had they each submitted to procedures like this when they had their numerous cosmetic alterations? Jasmine was forced to admit to herself that Honey was correct about one thing. Both she and Honey were both redesigning their own bodies to match their self-image. But there the similarities ended. For Jasmine this operation was essential if she was to live as the woman she believed herself to be. For Honey and Xristal it had been an option to achieve the appearance they desired.

There was a sudden, sharp pain as the needle entered, but it was soon over. The anaesthetist straightened up and pulled Jasmine's gown back down over her groin. 'Just lie still. You should find your lower abdomen becoming numb. We'll come and collect you in a few minutes.' She and the male nurse gathered up their instruments and left her in the seclusion of the curtained-off bed. There was the sound of movement and quiet conversation in the ward but Jasmine lay still, eyes closed, trying to take her mind off what was happening.

After what seemed like only a couple of minutes, the curtains were suddenly drawn back and she was surrounded by people. A trolley was pushed alongside her bed. 'Can you move onto the trolley please, Jasmine?' a voice said. 'We'll help you if the local has made it difficult for you.'

Jasmine used her arms and heels to push herself across the bed and onto the trolley. Her middle felt like a dead weight rather than part of her. She let herself flop down and lay flat.

'Good. Right, here we go, Jasmine. It'll soon be all over,' the same voice said. The trolley started to move and Jasmine watched the ceiling tiles and lights pass over her. They went through a number of doors until they entered a different room. The chandelier of operating lights hung over her. The bearded surgeon, now with a mask covering his mouth, looked down at her.

'Hello, Jasmine. Are you feeling OK?' Jasmine nodded unable to find her voice. 'Good. We'll make a start. You won't feel a thing and it'll be all over in a few minutes.'

He moved away leaving Jasmine staring at the ceiling, dark above the low hanging light. A sheet was laid over her and clipped to a frame placed across her abdomen so she couldn't see anything going on beyond. She felt her legs being moved apart, but the grip on her thighs was diffuse and leaden. The doctors and nurses mumbled to each other but Jasmine couldn't follow what was being said. It was as if the surgical team was operating on someone else and she just happened to be present as a bystander. She lay there with her mind surprisingly empty. Perhaps the anaesthetic was dulling her thoughts too.

Movements "down below" came to her as if from behind a door in an adjacent room and she didn't feel the scalpel. She wasn't even sure when the first cut was made. Then a gentle tug on a point somewhere below her navel brought her back to the moment. Was that what the surgeon had referred to – the cutting of a sperm duct? It hit her then. The moment she had longed for when she would cease to be a man - it was happening. A second tug. It was done. The process was not finished, she would not be a complete woman with vagina and breasts for perhaps years, but the symbol of the male, the erect phallus, no longer applied to her.

It wasn't much longer before she was being wheeled back along the corridors. She still felt an emptiness below her waist, the anaesthetic still doing its job. They reached the ward and her bed. 'We'll give you some help back onto the bed,' a voice said. There were hands under her shoulder and legs, lifting. She pushed against the trolley with her hands, guiding herself back to the mattress. She was laid down gently, sheets pulled over her, the curtains drawn.

'It will be a while before the anaesthetic wears off,' the voice said. Jasmine realised it was the male nurse speaking. 'Keep still if you can. There is quite a lot of dressing between your legs. It is important not to rupture the stitches. You don't want a ball dropping out do you?' The thought horrified Jasmine.

'If you start to feel pain, ask one of us for medication,' he continued. 'It will be sore for a few days. You must take things gently, particularly for the first twenty-four hours. No driving and stay sitting if you can.'

Jasmine had been hearing his voice without really listening. 'What about going to the loo?' she asked.

'That's OK. Go in your normal way. You still have a penis and the dressing won't be in the way.' Did he think she thought she had had the penis off too? Jasmine hoped she didn't look that daft. 'Just rest until the anaesthetic wears off. Then you can think about getting dressed, but there's no hurry.'

'Thanks.'

'When is your lift arriving?'

'I told him about midday.'

'Oh, plenty of time then. It's only just ten-thirty. Would you like a drink? Tea, coffee, water?'

Jasmine thought she should be hungry as she hadn't eaten for a long time, but the thought of eating or drinking didn't appeal. 'Just a water, please.'

'OK.' The nurse left, leaving Jasmine alone in her curtained space. She tried to work out what her emotions were. . The anxiety of the night before had drained away and now she just felt sleepy. Instead there was also relief and pleasure. Relief that the operation was behind her, for now at least, and pleasure that she had made the first step on her surgical journey. There was also pride that she had achieved a life's ambition, or part of it at least.

'Hello, Jasmine. Are you OK?'

Jasmine opened her eyes. Had she been asleep? The surgeon was looking down at her.

'Sorry, uh, I think I dropped off.'

'That's no problem. Make the most of the chance while you can. I was just passing and wanted to let you know that the biorchidectomy was carried out successfully. The synthetic replacements were fitted and I think we made a neat job of the sewing. How are you feeling?'

Jasmine had to think about her answer. Now she had woken up she felt thirsty and a bit hungry and she could feel her stomach and thighs again. And she was feeling sore. 'I think the anaesthetic has worn off,' she said.

'That's good. Do you have pain?'

'Some.'

'That's to be expected. I'll ask a nurse to give you some Paracetamol. You can have something stronger if you like.'

'No, Paracetamol will be fine, I hope.'

'Good. Have something to eat as well.'

He left, and a few minutes later the curtains were swept back again and the male nurse appeared holding a tray with a couple of tablets in a small dish and a tumbler of water on it.

'Here you are,' he said putting the tray on the cupboard beside her, 'and we'll let you see the rest of the world now.' He pulled the curtains open.

'Is Jasmine Frame here?' Jasmine recognised Viv's voice. She twisted to see where he was and felt a twinge of pain in her groin.

'Hi, I'm here,' she croaked.

Viv came into view, a look of concern on his face. He hurried across the ward to her bedside. 'Are you all right? Has it been done?'

Jasmine was surprised by the depth of emotion in his voice. She gave him a smile. 'I'm fine, I think. I've been dozing. I've had the op.'

'Don't forget your tablets,' the nurse said, leaving them to look after other patients.

'I won't, thanks.' Jasmine tried to reach to the cupboard for the pills and water but again felt a stab of pain in her groin. She let out a soft yelp.

'Oh, can I help?' Viv said, leaning forward.

'I'm a bit sore. Can you pass me the painkillers and the water please?'

Viv handed them to her and looked around for a chair while she popped the tablets into her mouth and washed them down. He sat down beside the bed. 'So? How did it go?'

'I didn't see anything of it and didn't feel much either, thank god.'

'That's good news. When can you leave?'

'As soon as I like, I suppose. I think they were waiting for you to come before booting me out.'

'Oh, am I late?' Viv looked worried.

'No, I told you midday and it must be that by now.'

'Just gone,' Viv said, glancing at his watch, 'I got a bit held up on the M4. Traffic, you know.'

'Yes, it's always bad.'

'Can I help you?'

'Well, I suppose I had better get dressed.' She rotated on her bottom so that her legs hung over the side of the bed and sat up feeling a little dizzy. 'Can you pass me my case please, Viv? I hope nothing's been nicked.'

Viv lifted the case onto the bed beside her. Jasmine flicked the lock and opened it up. Her clothes and handbag were all there. Jasmine looked in her handbag and checked her wallet and phone. 'It's all here,' she said, relieved. 'Can you pull the curtains round while I get dressed? It could take a while and I would prefer not to have an audience.'

Viv leapt up and dragged the curtains along their rails. Jasmine lifted the sheet off herself and pulled up the gown. The dressing in her groin was like an over-sized cod piece. 'I don't think I can get my knickers over that lot,' she said, catching Viv turning away after a sneak peek.

'Do you want me to go away?' he asked.

'No, stay, I may need some help,' Jasmine said, pulling her skirt on over her head and fastening it at her waist. She pulled the gown over her head then quickly put her bra around her when she realised that Viv could see her bare and almost flat chest. She saw him watching, but his eyes didn't show any signs of disgust or embarrassment. Once her enhancers were positioned in the cups, she pulled the T-shirt over her head. At last she felt respectable.

'There,' she said, 'I don't feel like a sad patient anymore.'

The male nurse's head appeared between the curtains. 'Are you leaving, Jasmine?' he asked when he saw that she was dressed.

'Yes, if I can get off this bed.'

Viv rushed to her side willingly giving her a helping hand.

'No, don't get onto your feet, just yet,' the nurse said, 'I'll find a wheelchair to get you to your car.' He disappeared again.

'I think I'm decent, now,' Jasmine said, 'you can pull the curtains back.'

Viv jumped to her orders and once again she was revealed to the ward.

'How are you feeling now?' he asked.

Jasmine examined herself. 'Tender between the legs, but okay. Hungry.'

'Oh, I don't suppose you had breakfast, did you?'

'No, and it's been a long time since dinner yesterday.'

'We'll pick up some sandwiches on the way out and I'll cook some real food when we get back home.'

'Thanks.' Jasmine was grateful for Viv's attention. It gave her a warm feeling like being wrapped in a cosy blanket.

The nurse returned pushing a wheelchair. He and Viv helped Jasmine off the bed and into the chair with a minimum of winces and groans. 'I feel like an old lady,' Jasmine said, wriggling her bottom until she felt comfortable.

'Not for long,' Viv said.

'Don't forget to take it easy for today,' the nurse said.

'I don't think I'll argue with that,' Jasmine replied, conscious of the soreness between her legs.

Viv began pushing her in the wheelchair, awkwardly dragging her case along as well. They went out of the ward, along the never-ending corridors, through a café where they stopped for Viv to pick up some sandwiches, and outside to the car which seemed to be a mile from the entrance.

'Here we are,' Viv said, as they stopped beside the Audi.

'I'm glad I didn't have to walk that distance,' Jasmine said. Viv opened the door and carefully helped her out of the chair and into the soft leather car-seat.

'This is much more comfortable than a wheelchair,' Jasmine said, relaxing.

'Well, you eat your sandwiches if you can, while I return the chair.'

He put Jasmine's case in the boot and then went off with the wheelchair. She devoured one sandwich and was contemplating a second during the few minutes that he was gone.

'Feeling OK?' he said, as he got into the driving seat.'

'Yes,' Jasmine said, nodding.

'Good. I don't want you being sick in my posh car,' Jasmine looked at him, suddenly worried that that might be exactly what could happen. She shouldn't have gobbled up the sandwich so greedily. But Viv was grinning and Jasmine realised he had been kidding.

'What will you do? Push me out onto the road?'

'Just joking. But seriously, do you feel up to the journey?'

'I'm fine. It was only a local anaesthetic, like having a tooth out.'

'Hmm. A bit more serious than that, I think.'

'Just two little lumps.'

'Stop, you're making me cringe.'

'OK, I won't say anything else. Just get us home.'

They were soon into the afternoon traffic and making their way to the M4. Jasmine was just allowing herself to drift off when she remembered she had turned off her phone. She hunted in her bag for it and switched it on. Moments later it gave an animated squawk.

'What's that?' Viv asked.

'It's telling me I've got lots of messages.'

'Who from?'

'Uh, Angela, by the look of it; nearly all of them.'

'What's she saying? Oh, sorry, I expect they're private.' Viv glanced across at her then resumed his concentration on the road.

'Not really, I'm just looking at them.'

<Where are you?>

<What are you doing?>

<Tom says you're in hospital>

<Why didn't you tell me?>

There were more with similar questions and demands for answers. Jasmine thought she could imagine what had happened. She rang Angela's number.

'Jasmine! Where are you?'

'Driving home.'

'What! You're driving? I thought…'

'No. Viv's driving.'

'Viv, who?'

'My neighbour, Viv. My friend, Viv.'

'Oh. Tom rang me asking how you were. He thought I was meeting you at the hospital.'

'That's what I guessed had happened.'

'He said you were having an op. The biorchidectomy. Well, he didn't call it that, couldn't remember the proper name.'

'That's it.'

'Why didn't you ask me to pick you up? Why didn't you tell me?'

'I was going to, Ange. In the pub on Friday.'

'You didn't. You dashed off. Luke said you had some business to attend to.'

'I left because Luke and I didn't get on.'

'What do you mean?'

'Luke said some things I don't want to repeat. I didn't want you to see me upset.'

There was a brief silence at the other end of the line, before Angela asked in a quiet voice, 'When will you be home, Jas?'

'We're almost at the motorway. Under an hour if there aren't any hold ups.'

'I'll be there.'

There were other messages too. A couple from Tom, first sending his best wishes then confessing that he may have put his foot in it with Angela. Jasmine rang his number but it went straight to voicemail. She left a short message and then looked at the last remaining text. It was from Honey who simply hoped that the operation went well. Jasmine was surprised and pleased. Surprised because she hadn't thought Honey would give her a second thought and pleased that someone else was wishing her well.

The comfortable leather seat and the quiet, smooth-running car lulled her into sleepiness. She dozed.

'We're back, Jasmine.'

Jasmine stirred and saw that they were indeed turning into the car park of their flats. Viv drew into his space. There was a car next to Jasmine's old Fiesta - Angela's.

Viv pulled on the handbrake, turned off the engine and got out of the car. He hurried around to the boot to get her case out and then to open Jasmine's door. Jasmine slowly swung herself round so that both feet were flat on the ground. Viv placed a hand under her armpit and steadied her as she pushed herself upright.

'Jas. Are you all right?'

Jasmine looked up to see Angela's concerned face. She was hopping from side to side around Viv trying to get a clear view.

'Hi, Ange. Yes, I'm fine thanks. This is Viv.' Jasmine placed her weight on Viv's arm a little as they took small steps towards the entrance to her flat. Angela grabbed the suitcase and towed it along behind Jasmine and Viv.

'Are you sure you're OK? Does it hurt?'

'Yes, I'm sure, Ange. It's a bit sore but no worse than I was told to expect. There's no need to fuss.'

They mounted the short flight of steps and arrived at the door side by side. Jasmine fumbled in her bag for her key.

'Let me do that.' Angela said, grabbing the bag from Jasmine's hands. She found the key and put it in the lock.

Angela pushed the door open and let Jasmine enter on Viv's arm. Jasmine lurched the few steps to her sofa and gingerly lowered herself onto it.

'I'll put the kettle on,' Viv said and moved into the kitchen.

'How long have you known him?' Angela whispered, carefully placing Jasmine's bag on the floor beside her and pushing the suitcase out of the way.

'A few days,' Jasmine replied. Was it really just that? It seemed like she knew Viv so well they must have been friends for months if not years. 'He's just moved into one of the flats, temporarily.'

'Why didn't you ask me to help you? I didn't even know you had the appointment.'

Jasmine wanted to pour it all out about what Luke had said to her, but stopped herself. 'I told you, Ange. I was going to when we went out for the evening. But Luke said a few things and I realised I don't have the right to expect you to leap to my assistance every time I ask.'

'Oh, don't be silly. Rights! We've been through a lot, me and you. OK, we're apart now, but I will always be there for you. Now, what did Luke say?'

Jasmine smiled. This was the Angela she knew and still loved - organised, eager, sympathetic. 'You'll have to ask Luke. It's not for me to say - not to you.'

Angela was silent. Jasmine almost counted the seconds before she spoke again, slowly, quietly. 'Luke's a bit of a hunk. Man's man type.'

Jasmine nodded.

'I think I had better have a few words with him.'

Viv appeared carrying a tray.

'Black coffee OK? Jasmine doesn't seem to do milk.'

'I'm sorry, I don't think I can stay,' Angela said, 'I need to speak to someone rather urgently. Bye, Jas. I'll come and see you again very soon.' She leaned down and kissed Jasmine on the cheek, then hurried out.

'What was that all about?' Viv asked, still standing holding

180

the tray.

'I think Luke is going to find himself under interrogation,' Jasmine said, 'I'd love a coffee, by the way.'

'Oh, yes, here,' Viv bent to lower the tray to Jasmine's level.

They drank their coffee and chatted for a while until Viv put his mug down on the table. 'I'm sure you could do with a bit of peace. I'll head back to my place, but I'll be back about six with dinner. Is that OK?'

'That's lovely, Viv. You're so kind,' Jasmine felt a tear of gratitude form in her eye and she wondered what she had done to deserve the support and friendship of such a nice guy. Viv leaned down like Angela had done and kissed her on the cheek. This was different though. Instead of the comfortable familiarity of Angela's lips, the touch of Viv's seemed to send a spark of electricity through Jasmine.

'Why, Viv?'

'Why what?'

'Why are you being so good to me? We hardly know each other.'

'That's true, but I hope we'll get to know each other a lot better. I like you Jas. You've had some difficult decisions to make and you go your own way. I like that and I want to help you.'

'Well, thanks.'

'I'll be back in a few hours. Take it easy.'

'I will. I promise.'

Viv left and pulled the door closed behind him. Jasmine sat quietly contemplating. Did her relationship with Viv have a future? She couldn't imagine him wanting someone who wasn't yet a fully-functioning woman, but he seemed prepared to wait and see how things went.

She felt drained. The lingering effects of the anaesthetic and a delayed response to the surgery made her feel as exhausted as if she'd done a 10K run. Content just to sit quietly, her thoughts turned once again to the identity of Xristal's murderer.

Who were the suspects? The list still seemed to include

Parfitt, Honey, the Taylors, the as yet un-named clients and perhaps persons of whom she had no knowledge at all. Parfitt seemed to be in the clear, and after her evening with Honey she felt that she too was an unlikely killer. How successful had Tom's search been, she wondered. She pulled her phone out of her bag and tried his number again. This time it was answered, but Tom's voice was accompanied by road and engine noise.

'Hi Jas, How are you? How did it go?'

'I'm fine. The op went well.'

'Good. Look I'm sorry if I said something wrong to Angela. I rang her to see how you were, thinking she'd be collecting you.'

'I'll explain it sometime.'

'OK, but how did you get back? I guess you are back home?'

'Yes, I'm home. Viv collected me.'

'Viv?'

'A friend.'

'Oh,'

'Look, I rang you to find out how the investigation's going. Where are you?'

'Between Brighton and Eastbourne. The last couple days have been a tour of southern England nicks.'

'Any result?'

'We've located and questioned a number of Xristal's clients.'

'And?'

'Well, once we got over their reluctance to talk about their experiences with a prostitute, a trans one with an interest in BDSM, they've been very keen to help.'

'But?'

'They all said what a fantastic person Xristal was and they couldn't imagine anyone wanting to hurt her as in really not make-believe hurt.'

'None of them a suspect then?'

'I suppose they're all technically still suspects, but their alibis hold up and even under hard questioning they've all stuck to the story that Xristal was a pretty special sort of whore who got to know her clients well before they got into the handcuffs and chains business. It seems she was very careful who she acted the submissive with. They all sounded very grateful for the experience she gave them and sorry she won't be around to do it again.'

'The perfect businesswoman.'

'Yeah, and she made enough from it too. Her fees were through the roof.'

'So, no dissatisfied customers, nobody wanting their money back or a free offer on the side?'

'Nothing like that.'

'That's not very helpful, Tom.'

'No, but it's the way it is. There are still quite a number to check out though. Xristal kept herself pretty busy in order to earn the money she needed. We're on the road tomorrow too, and Sloane's coming out as well. If we don't get any better leads from her clients it looks like Honey Potts is the prime suspect.'

'Hmm, perhaps.'

'We've got no lead on her yet, though.'

'No?' Jasmine almost blurted out what she knew about Honey, but she remembered her promise to keep it to herself until tomorrow.

'Anyway. You look after yourself. I'll fill you in when I get back tomorrow and let you know if we have any more leads.'

'OK, Tom. Take care.'

The phone went silent. Were Xristal's clients really all so highly satisfied with her, or was one hiding their guilt behind their effusive praise for her skills? Jasmine hoped one of them would let their cover slip and give them the vital lead to solve the crime, but she hoped it wouldn't be until she was running around again and could take a full part in the chase - perhaps in a couple of days' time.

She pushed herself out of her seat and turned on the TV. She'd watched a fair bit of daytime television when she hadn't been in demand as a private eye, but had thankfully lost the habit in the last couple of months when more business had come her way. She sat half-asleep, half-watching the afternoon soaps, an activity so tedious she almost wished she was back out in the car on surveillance duty. It must have been about five o'clock when the doorbell suddenly rang.

She clicked the TV off with the remote and again had to use her arms to lever herself from the sofa. Her groin was sore and ached. Perhaps it was time for some more painkillers? The bell rang again before she covered the few feet to the door. She opened it.

'Hello Jasmine. How are you?' It was Dr.Gould.

'Hi, Jilly, come in.' Jasmine turned and shuffled back to the sofa. Dr Gould followed her in and closed the door.

'I'm just off to the evening surgery but I thought I'd see how you were doing. How did it go?'

'Fine, so I'm told. I didn't see or feel a thing. A bit sore though.'

'Have you taken anything?'

'I think I'm due now.'

'Well, you take them. Let's have a look.' Jasmine lifted her skirt and Dr Gould peered at the thick dressing covering her genitalia. She pressed a pair of fingers to Jasmine's thighs and lower abdomen. 'Can you feel that?'

Jasmine reflected that more people had looked and poked at her groin area in the last twelve hours than at any time in her life. 'Yes. It feels normal.'

'Good. Well, I'm not going to take the dressing off to have a look at your scrotum. I've arranged for the District Nurse to come in tomorrow morning to change the dressing for you.'

'Thanks.'

'She'll probably be quite early, before she goes on her usual rounds.'

'That's OK.'

'You should feel better tomorrow, but be careful. It may seem like there's just two little incisions to heal, but there are all the blood vessels and things inside that have to close up too. You don't want to go straining the sutures.'

'No, I don't.'

'So how do you feel about it?'

'About what?'

'Losing your testicles.'

Jasmine realised that a few hours had passed since she last thought about it.

'I'm not sure. Pleased that it's over with. Proud that I've made a real start on my reassignment. Eager to see what the effects will be.'

'Good. I'm glad you don't have any regrets.'

'It would be a bit late for those, wouldn't it?'

'Indeed,' Jilly nodded.

'Anyway, it is something I've been looking forward to for a long time now, or at least part of what I've looked forward to – the rest is still to come.'

'That's right. At least you can stop taking those anti-androgens. You're not making testosterone anymore. We'll keep a check on things and see what dose of oestrogens you need, probably less now.'

'Good.'

'So you should now notice fewer side effects and a quicker change in your physical characteristics.'

'That's exactly what I want to hear.'

'I'm sorry I can't stay longer. Perhaps one day we can have that evening out we keep promising each other?'

Jasmine grinned. How often had they said that? 'Thanks for dropping in.'

'Well, you look after yourself. Don't get up, I can let myself out.' Jilly too leaned down and kissed her on the cheek before leaving.

Jasmine heaved herself up and went into the kitchen to take a couple of Paracetamol, then returned to the sofa. She felt happier now. Jilly's visit, though brief, had bucked her up. The aches and pains faded away as she thought about her future without testicles, her increasingly feminine appearance and, perhaps in the not too distant future, more surgery to provide her with a vagina. She was sexless at the moment, with neither male nor female genitalia - but determinedly female in her gender.

It wasn't long before the bell rang again and again Jasmine hauled herself upright. It was Viv bearing a tray laden with covered bowls. There was also a wine bottle tucked under his arm. Jasmine hurried as fast as her tightly-bound groin would let her to clear papers from the dining table. Viv bent to lower the tray to the table and extracted the bottle from his armpit.

'I've cooked Jamaican Curried Chicken – my father's recipe. You'll love it. It's really hot. And I've brought a bottle of bubbly to celebrate.'

'Celebrate?'

'Your successful de-manning!'

Jasmine laughed. 'Well, I'm very happy to celebrate that! I didn't expect anyone else to treat it as a joyful occasion though.'

'Anything that makes you happy makes me happy. I'll get some glasses and dishes. You sit down.'

Viv disappeared into the kitchen and Jasmine heard him crashing and banging in cupboards and drawers. Probably looking for my non-existent best china, Jasmine thought. He soon returned with bowls, wine glasses, knives and forks.

'These are all I could find.'

'I'm afraid they're all I've got,' Jasmine said, amused by the look of mock disgust on Viv's face. 'I don't entertain much.'

'Well, they'll have to do. Hold the glasses while I crack open the bottle.'

The cork came out of the bottle with a satisfying pop and bubbles gushed into and over the glasses. Jasmine giggled as she licked her fingers. 'Wow, this is such a treat.'

'Well, it's not a special cru, but it'll do.' He took a glass from Jasmine's hand. 'To you, Jasmine, and your future as a woman.'

'Thanks - and thank you for all your help today. You've been a total star.'

'My pleasure. Look, let's get stuck into the curry before it gets cold.'

Jasmine was just lifting the first forkful of curry to her mouth, the spicy aroma filling her with eager anticipation, when the door-bell rang again. She sighed and lowered her fork, contemplating heaving herself from the chair to answer it. Viv, however, was already on his feet, opening the door. Angela stumbled in. Jasmine was shocked by her appearance. Her eyes were a mess of smudged eyeshadow and mascara, and tears streaked her usually flawless cheeks.

'Oh, Jas, I'm sorry,' she sobbed, rushing to Jasmine and bending to hug her.

'What's the matter, Ange? Come and sit down. Join us. Viv's made a fantastic Jamaican curry.'

Angela stood up and looked around, apparently seeing Viv for the first time as he closed the door and returned to the dining table. 'I'm sorry. I'm disturbing your dinner,' she said.

'Stop saying you're sorry and come and join us.' Jasmine was not used to a flustered Angela.

'Here, take my seat,' Viv said, 'I'll go and see if Jas runs to another plate or dish.' He went out into the kitchen.

Angela sat at the table facing Jasmine. 'I've been such an idiot, Jas.'

'What do you mean? What's happened?'

'It's Luke. I hadn't realised what he was really like.'

'Oh.' Jasmine was able to guess a little of what had happened. 'You saw him, then?'

'Yes. I asked him what he'd said to you on Friday. He denied saying anything at first, but when I pressed him he got angry and then it all came out.'

'Did it? Oh, Ange,' Jasmine felt guilty now. She had come between Angela and her new boyfriend.

'I knew he was a bloke-ish sort of guy, but the vile things he came out with…'

'I can imagine,' Jasmine said quietly.

'I told him he mustn't say those things about you; that I still cared about you. That did it.'

'Really?'

'He said I had to choose between him and you. I couldn't have both. So I told him to get lost and that I didn't want to see him again.'

'Oh, Angela. I'm so sorry. I didn't want to come between you. I wanted you to have a good time.'

'I know, Jas. You've been so good encouraging me to meet someone.'

'Have I?' Jasmine could only recall her jealousy at hearing that Angela was seeing another man and probably having sex with him.

'I was enjoying it.'

'What?'

'The sex. It's been a while, Jas.'

'I know.'

'But I thought that we could all be friends. That I could still be there for you when you needed me – like today.' Angela let out a small croak of a sob.

'It's all right, Ange. Viv picked me up.'

Angela sniffed. 'Oh yes. Viv.'

'Look, Angela,' Jasmine took a deep breath. 'I'm so sorry that it hasn't worked out with Luke. We've discussed it a lot over the years. We agreed that we would have to part and perhaps find new partners. We'll always have the time we spent together and I hope we can always be friends. I owe you so much and I don't want to stand in your way of finding someone you can share a life with.' She became conscious of Viv standing by her side holding a plate.

'Perhaps I'd better go,' he said, 'leave you two to sort things out.'

'No, Viv. You cooked this meal for us and we're going to eat it together. Angela, would you like some?'

Angela got a tissue out of her handbag and wiped her eyes. She looked at the empty plate that Viv held out, then up at his face. 'No. Thank you, but I'll leave you both to finish your dinner.' She stood up, smoothed down her skirt and picked up her bag.

Jasmine pushed herself up, wincing as a stab of pain passed through her groin. 'Please don't go, Angela. There's plenty of food. I think Viv overestimated my appetite.'

'No, really, I don't want to disturb you. I'll give you a call tomorrow, Jas, to see how you're doing.'

She took the couple of steps to the door and pulled it open. She turned and gave Jasmine a thin smile and then was gone.

'Angela. I do love you still.' Jasmine murmured softly to the closing door. She felt a heaviness on her chest, an overwhelming feeling of regret, greater even than when she had moved out of their shared home, or even when the divorce had come through. Somehow, this parting seemed more final than any other. All their discussions and decision-making over the years hadn't prepared her for the realisation that at some point in her transition she would lose Angela; that the bond between them would be severed. Was that what had just happened in the last few minutes?

'Are you OK, Jasmine?' Viv's voice revealed his concern.

'Yes, thanks. I just feel that something has changed.'

'Angela has split up with her new boyfriend?'

'He was a macho, transphobic bully and probably a few other phobes as well, but Angela was getting on OK with him until he met me. I feel that I came between them.'

'It was always going to happen when she realised how bigoted he was and that would have come out sooner or later.'

'I suppose so.'

'She's a lovely lady.'

'Yes, she is.'

'I'm sure she'll find someone who can also get on with you, then you can all be friends.'

'I think you may be a bit over-optimistic, Viv. There are not many people who would be as accommodating as Angela was.' It occurred to Jas then that Viv himself was doing a pretty good impression of being accommodating.

'Well, you each have to go your own way. You can't be responsible for each other.'

'You're right. But it feels as if I've lost a good friend, as well as a wife and lover.'

'No. You'll still be friends, once you've both got over the emotion of today. Come on and eat – the curry *is* getting cold.'

10

TUESDAY

It had been a disturbed night, probably not helped by the bottle of champagne she had shared with Viv. No position had been totally comfortable and changing positions had also been a little painful. The nagging soreness in her groin was constant and she kept thinking about Angela. Last night's parting hurt so much. She couldn't imagine not having any contact with her, even if in the last few months they hadn't seen much of each other. Obviously she had fallen asleep at some point because now she was being woken by a loud ringing. It was the doorbell.

Jasmine opened her eyes and realised that the pain had lessened. The doorbell rang again.

'OK, I'm coming,' she shouted, hoping her voice would carry through the open door of her bedroom across the living room and through the front door. She pushed herself up and found it was easier to move than yesterday, but there was still a tenderness between her legs.

She had gone to bed in just a T-shirt, so she grabbed her dressing gown from behind the door and struggled to pull it on as she made her bowlegged way to the door. The bell sounded again as she turned the knob and pulled the door open. Standing in the entrance was a woman in a nurse's uniform carrying a plastic box.

'Jasmine Frame? I'm Nurse Arnold. I've come to change your dressing.'

Jasmine pulled the door further open feeling ashamed that she had not got herself up in time to greet the nurse properly.

'I'm so sorry, I was still asleep. What time is it?'

Nurse Arnold glanced at her watch. 'Seven-thirty. I know it's early, but I have my regulars to see to.'

'Of course, come in.' Now Jasmine felt guilty that she was adding to the woman's workload. She ushered Nurse Arnold into the living room.

'Shall we go into your bedroom, Jasmine? It will be easier to check everything if you are lying down.'

'Oh, yes, of course.' Jasmine led the nurse into her bedroom and eased herself down onto her bed.

'Can you open your dressing gown, please?'

Jasmine flushed, realising that the action requested of her would reveal her genitals. But that was what the nurse was here for. Stop being silly, Jasmine told herself. She loosened the belt and pulled the dressing gown open, staring fixedly at the ceiling to avoid seeing what was between her legs and to avoid making eye contact with the nurse. How would she react to her – a woman with a penis?

Nurse Arnold put her box down, leaned over and began to undo the dressing around her scrotum and groin. As far as Jasmine could tell she had not reacted at all to her transsexualism. There was a feeling of relief at that and pleasure that she didn't have to offer any explanations.

There were a few painful tugs as sticking plaster was unstuck that caused Jasmine to yelp, but the nurse was very gentle. She withdrew a wodge of lint and plaster, then peered even more closely. 'Ah yes, that looks fine.'

'Good,' Jasmine was relieved to hear it.

'You haven't had any trouble taking a pee?'

'No.'

'Good. I'll clean it up a bit down there and put a new dressing on. It won't need to be so bulky so you'll be able to move around a bit more easily.'

She worked quickly and efficiently and soon stood up to admire her handiwork. Jasmine still didn't look, she didn't want to be reminded about what she had between her legs.

'There. That should be fine for a couple of days. You can

wear loose knickers over the dressing but avoid anything tight.'

Loose knickers? That was something she didn't possess. All her pants were designed to hold her penis and testicles firmly out of sight.

'And don't exert yourself,' Nurse Arnold added. 'It's healing well, but don't put any strain on the sutures yet.' She was packing her bag almost before Jasmine had realised she had finished. She wrapped her gown around herself hurriedly, aware that she was still exposed.

Nurse Arnold stood up straight, grasping her box. 'Right. I'll be on my way. Carry on taking the painkillers if you need them, I expect you're still a bit sore. You'll have to go to the surgery to have the next dressing done. Give us a ring to book a time.' She bustled out of the bedroom and towards the front door. Jasmine struggled to her feet and followed her, feeling the odd twinge. Nurse Arnold opened the door, called out 'Goodbye' and was gone.

Jasmine pottered to the bathroom still reeling from Nurse Arnold's whirlwind visit, but already she could feel that the new dressing was less of an encumbrance and the soreness had retreated to a dull throb. Perhaps it would not be long before she could forget her surgery and also forget that she still had a penis and a scrotum between her legs. She sat on the loo still in a dreamlike state.

Shaving and washing woke her up a bit more. She slapped a damp flannel over her body taking care not to get the dressing wet. How long before she could have a shower, she wondered. As she towelled herself dry she heard her phone ringing. Running wasn't possible, but she hurried as much as she could into her bedroom and grabbed the phone from the bedside table. The identity of the caller surprised her.

'Hello, Honey,' she said

'Hi, Jasmine. I wanted to tell you, I'm on my way.'

'On your way? Here?'

'Yes. I know it's early for me but I couldn't sleep after last night's show. Actually the show itself was a bit of a disaster – I couldn't get it up.'

'Get what up? Oh, I see.'

'Sunday night, after you left, wasn't much better either.'

'Oh dear,' Jasmine wondered what Honey was getting at.

'I was thinking about what you said - and about Xristal.'

'Ah.'

'Yes. I realise I let her down. I should have looked out for her even though she was going her own way. I shouldn't have left her on her own so that one of her clients could harm her.'

'I don't think her death was your fault,' Jasmine said, wondering if that was indeed the case. Honey sounded convincing, but was still the one person who had both a possible motive and the opportunity to kill Xristal.

'I just wasn't there much for the last few weeks. I didn't know what Xristal was doing. I think she got to know the girl on the ground floor.'

'Tilly?'

'Yes, her.'

'She's a prostitute,' Jasmine almost added 'too' but stopped herself.

'I know. I'm going to call in and see her before I go to the police.'

'Oh. OK.' Jasmine wasn't sure it was a good idea. If there were still police officers hanging around Bredon Road they'd nab Honey before she got to see Tilly.

'How are you?'

Jasmine was surprised again that Honey was concerned about her surgery, but then again perhaps that was something they now had in common.

'Fine thanks. The soreness is easing and I've just had a new dressing put on.'

'Well, take it easy. I've always found that surgery takes a lot out of you, however minor it seems to be.'

'I will.'

'Perhaps we'll meet when I'm finished with the fuzz.'

'Yes.' That may not be as soon as you hope, Jasmine thought.

Honey could be questioned for a few days before they decided to let her go, and if they discovered sufficient evidence to pin the charge on her she wouldn't be out at all.

'Well, 'bye then.' The call ended.

Jasmine sat on her bed, the towel draped over her thighs,. So, Honey was on her way, but where were Tom and Sloane? Were they still picking up Xristal's clients? She thumbed Tom's contact on her phone but after a few seconds it went straight to voicemail. The feeling of being cut off from the case, immobile in her own home while Tom was off searching for suspects, frustrated her. Meanwhile, the suspect that she had tracked down was handing herself in. There didn't seem to be anything left for her to do. She was going to have to 'take it easy' as everyone, including Honey, had suggested. She didn't like it.

Her thoughts turned to what to wear. The top half was easy enough – bra and T-shirt. Dropping her enhancers into the cups stimulated the usual hope that her own breasts would develop soon. At least now with just the oestrogen in her bloodstream there might be more chance of that happening

With no loose knickers to pull on she decided she would have to go commando. Daring, perhaps - and she would need a long skirt for decency and to hide the bump of her genitals that were usually tucked away. She stared into her rather sparse wardrobe. There was only one ankle-length skirt, a stretchy striped one she'd picked up from Primark on a whim because it was cheap. She pulled it on, stood in front of her mirror and was appalled. The stretchiness was disastrous. The skirt clung to her hips and thighs and revealed the large bulge that looked like a codpiece. She tore it off in moments. What else could she wear that would cover her embarrassment? The only answer was a calf-length summer dress that had been in her wardrobe for a few years. She pulled off the T-shirt and dropped the flowery cotton dress over her head. Even if she achieved all that she wished for in the breast department, she would always have a manly shape – broad(ish) shoulders and narrow hips. The dress fitted her top half well and a real woman's proportions would have ensured a snug fit lower down but it fell loosely from her ribs.

She surveyed her image again. It would have to do: no visitors would notice her lack of panties or the protuberance between her legs. Her face needed attention though. She hadn't cared yesterday, but today she felt that she wanted to look herself even if there was nothing for her to do. She applied foundation and a little colour to her eyes and cheeks, and her favourite red to her lips. Now her appearance in the mirror went someway to satisfying her.

It was time for breakfast. A brief search in the fridge reminded her that she had given no thought to being housebound for a day or two. There was very little food in the flat. She cut the last remaining slice from a loaf that would surely soon be gaining a fuzz of mould.

She was munching her toast and sipping hot, black coffee when Viv called in. He was on his way to work and just checking she was OK. He promised to call in again on his return and then he was gone. Jasmine sat on the sofa thinking. How was she going to cope for even one or two days without being able to get out? Even sitting in the Fiesta on surveillance duty was preferable to being stuck in the flat with nothing to do. She checked her emails. That took all of a couple of minutes. At least there was a complimentary message from the Fraud Investigations office. It looked as though Parfitt would soon be in court and she would be getting further work chasing benefit cheats.

She opened up Xristal's website again and once more wondered what drove the young she-male to sell her body to clients, even if they were carefully selected. How difficult had it been for Xristal towards the end when she was anticipating giving it all up and becoming fully female? Perhaps that was the reason for her murder? Perhaps she had failed to satisfy one of her trusted clients and he - surely it was a he - had killed her in frustration.

She must have dozed on the sofa with the laptop on her knee.

She certainly had no idea of time passing, but she was jerked awake by her phone ringing by her side. It was Tom.

'Jas. Can't speak, but thought you'd want to know. There's been an incident in Bredon Road...'

'Bredon Road?'

'Yes, at the flats. The girl from the ground floor flat...'

'Tilly?'

'Yes. She's dead. Fell from the outside stairs.'

'No!'

'Can't talk. On my way back now. It may not have been an accident.' There was silence.

Surely it couldn't be a coincidence? Honey had spoken of meeting Tilly - and now she too was dead. Jasmine was perplexed. Why should Tilly die? She looked at her phone. The time was a few minutes after ten. Honey must have arrived in Kintbridge by now and had the time to get from the station to the flat. It was only a short walk.

As she stared at the screen of the phone it vibrated in her hand. Jasmine clamped it to her ear without looking to see who the caller was. The voice was breathless. 'Jasmine, it's me. It's terrible.'

'Honey, calm down. Where are you? What are you doing?'

There was the sound of puffing and panting before Honey spoke again. 'I've been running. Getting as far as I can from that place.'

'Right. Where are you now?'

'I'm by the canal, on the towpath.'

'Where? Which way are you going?'

'I don't know. I'm in the countryside. I've just gone under a high, wide bridge. I'm at one of those lock things.'

'You're heading west. You've just gone under the bypass.' Jasmine knew Honey's location exactly - she often went running out that way. 'Look, Honey stay put. You're not going anywhere. There's open country for miles ahead of you. Stop. Get your breath back. Tell me what happened.'

The panting slowed. Jasmine realised that Honey had

followed her advice and at least stopped her frantic flight from Kintbridge. Perhaps she had sat down on the grass beside the lock.

'I got to the flats,' Honey said, still gasping for breath. 'There was no reply at Tilly's front door so I wandered around to the back. I thought I'd have a look at Xristal's flat, see for myself what had happened in there. Then I saw her.'

'Tilly?'

'Yes. She was lying at the bottom of the metal steps, all twisted. There was blood, lots of blood. I could see she was dead. I just turned and ran.'

'Did anyone see you?'

'Yes. As I left the backyard one of the people from the flats next door saw me. They recognised me, called out, but I got away as fast as I could.'

'But why, Honey? You weren't responsible for Tilly's death.'

'You said the police think I murdered Xristal. They'll think I killed Tilly too.'

They certainly will now, Jasmine thought.

'Help me please, Jasmine!'

'Look, Honey, I want to help you. I will help you, but helping you run away won't do any good. If the police suspect you of being involved in Tilly's death they'll be hunting for you and they will find you.'

'They'll stitch me up if they get me. You know what the pigs think of people like you and me.'

I'm not like you, Jasmine thought, but perhaps in some people's eyes they were similar.

'They're not so bad. Sloane and Tom Shepherd are good cops. They won't pin anything on you without evidence.'

'I don't know Jasmine. I've had a few "meetings" with the police and transphobic doesn't even begin to cover it. Can't you be with me? I'll give myself up if you're there too.'

'I'm…' stuck here, Jasmine remembered.

'Oh God, I'm so fucking stupid! You're recovering from your op.'

Perhaps if she drove carefully, she'd be OK? She couldn't walk down the towpath though. 'No, Honey. I'm fine, it's a lot better today. I'll come and meet you in my car. But you'll have to walk back towards town.'

'Jasmine, are you sure?'

Jasmine closed her eyes visualising her jogs along the towpath. 'Yes, Honey I'm sure. Look, when you get back to the first houses on the edge of Kintbridge you'll see an alley that connects the towpath with a cul-de-sac. Wait there. I'll come and pick you up.'

'Thanks, Jasmine. I really appreciate it.'

'No problem.' Jasmine hung up. But there were problems. Would she be able to drive? Had she given Honey the correct directions? Was she doing the right thing or should she have just let Honey get hauled in by the Kintbridge police?

She stood up, found her bag and a pair of pumps to slip on her feet. She opened the door and stepped outside. It was overcast and damp although it felt warm. She took a deep breath and gingerly descended the short flight of steps to the car park. She felt the stitches in her groin stretching and flexing, but it didn't hurt. She eased herself into the driver's seat of her Fiesta and turned the engine over. It groaned into life. Pressing her feet on the pedals gave her a twinge between her legs, but it could hardly be described as painful.

She headed onto the main road. She had to travel in a big U in order to get across the river and canal, through the centre of Kintbridge and onto Salisbury Road that twisted and turned through the housing estates to the edge of the town. The houses changed from Edwardian to pre-war to sixties, and finally to recent new-builds, before she reached the cul-de-sac she was heading for. She pulled up. There was no sign of Honey. She opened her door and swung herself out, then used the door to haul herself up onto her feet. The light drizzle was cool on her head and arms.

The alley was a narrow gap between high hedges and just a few metres long. It emerged onto the narrow, rough-surfaced towpath. She looked westwards along the towpath and had a shock. A figure was coming towards her. It was Honey Potts - but not the confident diva she had met on Sunday evening. This was a bedraggled, limping, barefoot character, with her beehive wig sodden and drooping over her face. Her massive breasts had apparently burst out of her thin silk top. Her denim miniskirt had ridden up her thighs and her bare legs were streaked with mud and rainwater. Her toes were red, not because of her bright crimson nail varnish, but from blood oozing from scratches and blisters. In her hands Honey clutched a handbag and a pair of red shoes – stilettoes, of course. She finally reached Jasmine and leaned heavily on her shoulder.

Jasmine looked up at her. 'Come on, let's get you into the car.' She put an arm around Honey's waist and guided her along the alley. Honey puffed and groaned while Jasmine endured shafts of pain from her groin. Neither said a word until they were both in the car. Jasmine breathed out, relieved that now she was sitting again she felt comfortable down below.

Honey looked at her with a pathetically grateful expression. 'Thank you, Jasmine. I panicked.'

'It looks like it. You're a mess. Did you really choose that outfit to meet the police in?'

Honey looked down at herself uncomprehendingly. 'What do you mean?'

'Well, you could hardly look more like a whore if you tried.'

Jasmine put the car in gear, turned and headed back into town. She had intended to take Honey straight to the police station, but her bedraggled appearance suggested that some repairs were necessary first.

'I'm just being myself,' Honey declared, then groaned. 'Ow, my feet hurt.'

'Well, those shoes weren't exactly designed for a canalside walk.'

'I hadn't planned on going for a walk.'

'No, I don't suppose you had. I think I'd better take you home, get you cleaned up a bit and calmed down before you present yourself to the police.'

'Thanks. Do you still think it's a good idea for me to go to the police? If they are after me perhaps I could just wait until they pick me up?'

Jasmine sighed with exasperation. 'Look, I'm not having police cars turning up at my flat, sirens blaring, to arrest you, and it's always better if you hand yourself over. It gives a better impression, less guilty.'

'Hmm. If you say so.'

The mid-morning traffic was light, so it wasn't long before Jasmine pulled back into her parking place. She led Honey into her flat, sent her to the bathroom and went to the kitchen to put the kettle on.

She had made the coffee, taken it to the living room and sunk onto her sofa feeling tired, before Honey emerged. She had removed the wig and carried it over one hand. She had smoothed down her skirt and managed to fasten a few of her blouse buttons. Her pale, bald head was a stark contrast to her repaired foundation, eyeshadow and lipstick. She shook the wig. 'It'll dry soon,' she said confidently, 'and I found some plasters in your bathroom cabinet.' She looked down and Jasmine, following her gaze, saw her cleaned up legs and feet with plasters covering the scratches and blisters.

'There's a coffee for you,' Jasmine indicated the mug on the dining table. 'Now, tell me truthfully, why did you decide to go and see Tilly?'

'I told you. I was away a lot before I moved to London. Xristal and I became, how shall I say - distant? But I knew Tilly was there all that time, so I thought perhaps they had got to know each other. Perhaps Tilly knew which of her clients she was seeing.'

'I don't think you were on the right track there. When we interviewed Tilly she didn't seem to know much about Xristal at all and had nothing useful to tell us.'

'But she was on the ground floor. Her flat looks out on the parking area. She could see who was coming and going.'

'Her kitchen looks out on the back yard. I think Tilly spent a good deal of her time in her bedroom entertaining her clients.'

'Hmm. So Xristal was basically alone after I left?'

'Seems like it – except for her punters of course. We don't know how many she was seeing in those last few days. Her computer is missing.'

'Her laptop? She kept everything on that thing. All her client details, appointments, future plans, and loads of stuff on cosmetic and gender reassignment surgery. She showed it to me before we had that final, uh, parting.'

'Her murderer obviously knew that, which is why they removed it.'

'And the fact that I knew about it makes me the prime suspect?'

'Not necessarily. The police know all about you and Xristal; they don't need the computer to point them to you. No, it suggests a client. Someone who Xristal kept notes on, appointments, that sort of thing.'

'So, I'm in the clear?'

'Only if you can answer their questions fully and truthfully. You've got to be completely open about your relationship with Xristal.'

'I will be.'

'And there's Tilly, of course.'

'Oh yes. Tilly.'

'Running away was not a good idea.'

'I panicked! I told you.'

'That doesn't exactly remove you from the list of suspects.'

'I just saw her body. She was obviously dead. I had to get away.'

'OK, but it still leaves the question. Who would want to kill Tilly?'

There was silence until Honey muttered. 'I don't know.'

'Neither do I. Surely none of Xristal's clients had anything to do with Tilly?'

'Why do you say that?'

'Because Tilly and Xristal were catering for a very different clientele.'

'Oh, yes.'

'So what is the connection?'

'They just lived in the same block of flats?'

Jasmine shook her head. The answer eluded her. 'Come on. I'd better get you down the police station.'

'Are you sure?'

'Yes. The sooner you hand yourself in, the simpler things will be.'

Honey put down her empty mug and dragged the wig onto her head. There were still damp patches but the dome of hair had recovered its resilient shape. Honey pushed her feet into the red stilettoes, her winces evidence of the pain from her blisters and cuts.

Jasmine grabbed her bag and led the way, slowly, from the flat.

There was silence on the short drive to the Police HQ. Jasmine glanced once or twice at Honey and noticed the worry lines creasing her make-up. As they pulled to a stop, Honey turned to her. 'I know I let Xristal down by not supporting her sex-change but I did love her. You know that, Jasmine.'

'Yes.'

'I didn't kill her, or that other girl.'

'Just tell them that and answer all their questions.'

'You will tell them, won't you?'

'I'll give them a full report,' Jasmine said, getting out of the Fiesta.

Jasmine guided Honey up the steps to the main entrance to the police station. As they entered the main lobby, Jasmine saw DC Patel coming towards her. 'Hello, Jasmine,' Patel said and then her eyes widened as she turned to look at Honey. 'Is this...?'

'Honey Potts. She's come to answer your questions.'

'We'd just had a report that Potts had been seen down by the canal.'

'Well, she's here now.'

Patel turned to the desk officer.

'Can you get Miss Potts to an interview room, please? Now.' The middle-aged police officer looked surly and then moved into action. He emerged from the office and took hold of Honey's arm. 'You will tell them, Jasmine?' Honey appealed.

'Yes, Honey. Go on. Do as they say.' Honey allowed herself to be dragged away.

'How did she come to be with you?' Patel asked.

'It's a long story and I'll explain later, but she didn't do it.'

'What?'

'She didn't kill Xristal or Tilly.'

'The neighbour says he saw her running away, then he found the body.'

'Tom told me Tilly had fallen from the stairs.'

'That's what it looked like and Doctor Winslade says her head was smashed in by a fall.'

'Did the neighbour see Honey push her?'

'No.'

'So there's no evidence that Honey did it.'

'Did Potts have blood on her when you met her?'

'Yes, but only on her feet. It was her own. She'd tried running in high heels. She wasn't dressed for murder or a quick escape.'

'Hmm.'

'Did the neighbour see anything else?'

'No... well, yes, he said he saw a car leaving a good half hour earlier.'

'What type of car?'

'One of those new Jags.'

'A Jaguar?' That rang a bell with Jasmine, but she couldn't put her finger on why.

'Look, I'd better go and get Potts signed in and see what she has to say.'

'Yes, you go on. I'm supposed to be home, resting.'

'Oh, yes, Tom said you would be off for a few days. Are you sick?'

'No, just sore.'

Patel looked puzzled, but turned to hurry after Honey. She called over her shoulder. 'I'll give you a call to get your report about Potts.'

'Do that.'

Jasmine exited the building and walked slowly to her car. She got in but didn't start the engine straightaway. Two questions troubled her. What connections were there between Tilly and Xristal other than them both being prostitutes and living in the Taylors' rented property? Why did the mention of a Jag mean something?

Posing the two questions together did the trick. A broad smile spread across Jasmine's face and she dug into her bag for her phone. She dialled Tom's number. It went straight to voicemail.

'Tom, it's me, Jasmine. I've got it. It's Taylor, the landlord. I'm off there now.'

She terminated the call and started the engine. Soon she was following the familiar route to the Taylors' lavish residence.

The driveway in front of the bungalow was empty. No sign of the Jaguar. It had been parked here the first time she and Tom had called round. Perhaps it was in the double garage? Jasmine pulled up outside the front door and got out gingerly. She pressed the doorbell and waited. Nothing happened. There was no sound of anyone approaching the door, no shouted instructions. She pressed the bell again and waited, growing in impatience. She wanted answers and she wanted them now. Having to start a hunt for Kelvin Taylor would be an irritating delay to wrapping up the case. It had to be him. Middle-aged, flabby, rich, used to giving orders - he was the image of a typical client of someone like Xristal, and possibly Tilly too.

Had he seen her drive up and was hiding inside? She couldn't leave without taking a look. There was a wrought iron gate at the side of the house. Jasmine raised the latch. It opened. She pushed the gate wide and walked tentatively down a narrow path alongside the bungalow towards an expanse of lawn and flower beds.

'Mr Taylor! Are you in?' she called. Technically, she was trespassing. She didn't want to surprise him and perhaps provoke an instinctive violent reaction. She reached the back garden and turned to face a patio area and swimming pool. At the rear of the house was a huge expanse of glass covered with vertical blinds – presumably patio doors leading to the lounge. She put her face to the glass and peered between the slats of the blinds. What was that she could see? Something lying on the floor. A dog? No, it didn't have fur. It was naked skin. A body! The legs twitched. A live body!

Jasmine tugged at the handles of the patio doors. The body inside wriggled but didn't move. Was whoever it was injured? The doors were locked. She contemplated breaking the glass, but how? The double-glazed French windows were probably toughened glass. There had to be another way in. She returned to the side of the house. There was a side door, half-glazed. She looked around for a tool or some other implement, but nothing suitable had been left carelessly lying around for the opportunistic burglar. Then she noticed a small ornamental heron in one of the flower beds. She leaned over to pick it up – good, it was satisfyingly heavy, made of concrete not resin. She gripped it firmly with both hands and rammed it against the glazed door pane. There was a loud thud but the glass only cracked. She tried again. This time the outer pane shattered and shards of glass fell to the ground. She tried a third time. The inner glass disintegrated. She knocked out the jagged remnants of the window then reached in. Relief. She wouldn't have to do any athletic clambering – the key was in the lock. She twisted the key, pressed on the door handle and pushed the door open. She was inside.

She hurried through the kitchen and hallway and into the lounge. Sprawled face down on the luxurious cream carpet, looking like a beached whale, was a totally naked Kelvin Taylor. His pasty skin was almost the same colour as the carpet and rolls of fat from his paunch spread out either side of his hips. His arms were behind his back, legs bent at the knee, both wrists and ankles bound by stiff leather cuffs joined by short chains to an X-shaped stainless steel bar. There was a leather strap around his face holding a red ball in his mouth. He wriggled and his flabby buttocks wobbled but he was unable to change his position. Strange gurgling noises came from his throat.

Jasmine knelt beside him and examined the gag. It was fastened by a buckle at the back of his head. She undid it and tugged. The ball popped out of his mouth. He sucked in air with a noisy gasp. Jasmine wondered if he was choking, but then he breathed out and took another deep breath.

'Are you all right?' she asked. He nodded still breathing in deep, open-mouthed gulps. Jasmine looked more closely at the cuffs around his wrists and ankles. There were locks with keyholes. He wriggled and tried to turn himself over, but only succeeded in rocking from side to side. He gave up trying to shift his position and rested his forehead back on the floor with his arms and ankles firmly hog-tied. She tried pulling on the thick, heavy leather bands, but they were securely locked. 'Where are the keys?'

'She's got them,' Taylor grunted, 'She's gone. Taken them with her.'

'Why? Is it because you killed Xristal and Tilly?'

His head shook violently from side to side against the carpet. 'You've got to stop her! I don't know what she's going to do!'

'She discovered you are a murderer so she trussed you up? Gave you a taste of your own medicine?'

'No!' Taylor groaned, 'It wasn't me! It was her!'

'You're denying killing those two women?'

'Yes! Look you've got to catch her,' he gasped. 'She's the dom. I'm her sub. Have been since we met.'

Marilyn Taylor the murderer? Jasmine called her image to mind. Tall, slim, leather trousers...haughty, imperious, domineering. What else? Narrow hips, wider shoulders, firm breasts…she suddenly understood… 'Marilyn is trans!'

'What are you talking about?' Taylor groaned, straining against his bonds, 'She's my wife!'

'When did you get married?'

'2007.' He twisted his head from side to side.

'How long have you two been into BDSM?'

'From the start. It's how we met. I like being a sub. She's a sought-after dominatrix.'

'Really? You didn't know she was a trans-woman?'

'What do you mean?'

'She couldn't have children?'

'Neither of us were interested in children. We were passed all that. I had two kids with my first wife.'

'Does your ex-wife know Marilyn? Surely she would have guessed, even if you didn't.'

'We divorced ten years ago. Audrey took the kids to Australia. She's never met Marilyn. Look, I don't understand. We got married. Marilyn had a birth certificate, well a new copy of it.'

'Of course she did,' Jasmine nodded. It was after the Gender Recognition Act had been passed. Marilyn would have got a new birth certificate showing her changed gender.

'Look, you've got to stop her! I think she's going to kill herself!' There was pain in Taylor's voice.

Jasmine was shaken out of her thoughts. 'Why?'

'She told me she'd killed those girls. She knew she would be caught soon. She said she couldn't bear to be put away for the rest of her life. She preferred to end it now.'

'Why didn't you stop her?'

Taylor grunted pathetically. 'Stop Marilyn? You don't know her. I tried to persuade her. She wouldn't listen. I've always obeyed her, but I did try to stop her leaving.'

'You didn't do much.'

'How could I?'

'I don't know. Hold her, tie her up, something.'

'I couldn't, could I?'

'Why not?'

'Because she'd already left me like this when she went out earlier.'

Jasmine gasped. 'She locked you into this, uh, thing, before she went out to kill Tilly?'

'If that's what happened, yes. Look, it wasn't unusual. We do this sort of thing all the time. Sometimes I spend all day bound while she, uh, does things. But she didn't gag me.'

'So she came back?'

'Yes, she was in a right state. Raving about two girls being dead, that she'd be banged up for the rest of her life, that she couldn't take it, wouldn't let it happen.'

'And you spoke to her?'

'Yes. I wanted her to explain. She wouldn't. She just went on about ending it all. I tried to talk her out of it, but she just told me to shut up. Marilyn often did that. When I went on she got the gag and made sure I kept quiet.'

Jasmine realised she'd been mistaken about Kelvin Taylor. She'd thought he was a domineering inadequate using young women to get his satisfaction. Instead, he was a middle-aged masochist who enjoyed being the butt of his wife's domination.

'Look. Can I get you out of that thing?'

'No, you can't,' he groaned again, 'this is a top quality hog-tie. The locks are foolproof and Marilyn put all the keys in her bag when she left. You'll need a hacksaw which will take ages or a bolt cutter.'

'OK. What about making you more comfortable? Turning you over?'

'There is no comfortable position. That's the point.'

'Well, I could cover you up.'

'Forget me. Find Marilyn!'

'How? Where has she gone?'

'I don't know.' Kelvin seemed to sag. His head hit the carpet and but for his arms and legs being held in their forced positions it seemed that his body would have subsided into a puddle of misery.

'Think! Where would she be likely to go?'

'I don't … wait. There is one place.'

'Where?'

'It's a flat we bought recently, a basement. Marilyn wanted a dungeon. She's been fitting it out. Wouldn't let me see it till it was ready.'

'Where is it?'

'Wantage Road, number four, on the left just up from the roundabout. Do you know it?'

'Yes.'

'Well, go then! Don't let her kill herself! She'd be quite capable of it, but I don't want her to die, whatever she's done. I love her.'

The emotion in his voice was obvious. Jasmine realised that though their relationship was unusual Kelvin Taylor obviously liked what Marilyn did to him. 'What about you?'

'I'm fine. I can take this for a lot longer.' His voice carried a note of strain which wasn't entirely convincing. He rested his head on the floor again.

'OK, I'll go.' Jasmine picked up her bag and eased herself to her feet. She couldn't imagine what the strain of his position was doing to the muscles in Taylor's arms and legs and she couldn't see how it could ever be pleasurable.

She left by the door by which she had broken in, stepping gingerly over the fragments of glass. A few moments later, she was racing back into Kintbridge with her foot pressing the accelerator flat against the floor. How on earth had she missed the signs? It now seemed blindingly obvious to Jasmine that Marilyn Taylor was not only trans, but also a dominating and controlling sadist. She could see it now, of course, in both her appearance and her manner. But what was her attraction to Xristal, who couldn't be more different to Kelvin as a subject for her pleasure? And why kill Xristal and then go back for Tilly? There were still more questions than she had answers for except for the most important one – she now knew who the killer was.

She sped past a speed camera and noticed the flash in her mirror. She turned left at the roundabout with tyres screaming and skidded to a halt outside the first pair of large, Victorian semi-detached houses. Jasmine turned into the gateway and drove onto a large gravelled area that could easily accommodate half a dozen cars. A new black Jaguar was the sole occupant. Marilyn's here, Jasmine thought, or at least nearby. She pulled her Fiesta up alongside the Jaguar, got out and stood looking and listening. Apart from the rumble of the traffic on the main road there was silence. Tall trees guarded the house, putting it in shadow. It was a large house with two floors and rooms in the attic in addition to the basement. Stone steps led up to a tiled porch and an imposing painted front door flanked by stained glass windows. It wasn't the ground floor she needed. Was there a separate entrance to the basement flat? The tops of the basement windows were just visible at ground level. Jasmine stepped forward and looked down into a narrow vaulted area. From what she could see of the windows it looked like they were shuttered on the inside.

She went to the side of the building. The car park area merged into a scruffy lawn which extended down the side of the house and sloped into the back garden. The pit between the building and the garden became wider and shallower. Steps led down into it midway along the side of the house. Jasmine walked slowly towards them scanning the side of the building for any sign of occupancy or that her arrival had been noticed. There were a couple of small side windows, but they too seemed to be sealed and shuttered. She reached the steps. They were steep and narrow but led down to a doorway. Her ears straining to catch any sound, Jasmine stepped gingerly down - one, two, three, four steps, wincing slightly at each. The basement door looked old and in need of renovation. There was an old brass knob - she turned it. The door swung inwards. Jasmine stepped inside onto a rush doormat.

'Mrs Taylor! I'm Jasmine Frame, detective,' she called,

'We've met a couple of times. We need to talk.'

Jasmine braced herself, half expecting Marilyn Taylor to come running at her with a knife or some other weapon in her hand. She dropped her shoulder bag to the floor so that she could move her arms freely.

There was no reply. Not a sound. She found herself standing in a dark hallway that extended in front of her with three doors off to her right and one halfway along the wall to her left. The only light came from the doorway in which she stood. She took two steps forward, placing her feet very deliberately on the thick pile of the carpet so that she felt balanced, prepared. She reached the first door on the right and pushed it. It swung open revealing a large, dark room. Thin strips of daylight around the shutters provided just enough light to show it was a bedroom. There was a large metal-framed bed not unlike the one in Xristal's flat, but otherwise the room was empty.

She moved on, reached the second door and pushed it open. A bathroom. Spacious, dark but with the usual fittings. A few more steps across the hall took her to the single door on the other side. It was different to the others - new. She placed her hand against it. It didn't move. There was a handle. She pressed it down and pushed. The door unsealed itself with a sigh and squeak of rubber and moved slowly open due to its great weight and thickness. Light flooded out, banishing the darkness of the hallway. Jasmine stared.

Marilyn Taylor was standing in her red stilettoes on a low, wooden stool in the middle of the room. Her legs were covered to mid-thigh with fishnet stockings held up by suspenders attached to a black leather corset studded with steel points. Her bare upper thighs and groin were smooth white but for an inverted triangle of meticulously trimmed black pubic hair, and her breasts rested on the rigid quarter cups with her dark nipples pointing towards Jasmine. Her hair was drawn up in a tight bun. Behind her, the windows were covered by shutters that let no light through at all. The room was illuminated by small LED spotlights arranged in a rectangle in the centre of the ceiling right above where Marilyn Taylor was standing. Some were directed at the walls and others towards the centre of the room. Each lamp produced a narrow cone of light, but in between there was shadow. In fact, Jasmine realised, the lights only emphasised the darkness of the vast room which took up almost half the basement. Marilyn herself seemed to be suspended in light in the centre of the room - the centre of her universe.

'You!' she screeched, 'I thought it would be the other one. The man.'

Jasmine took a step forward into the room. The floor felt different under her feet. She glanced down. The carpet was confined to the hallway. Here, in Marilyn's dungeon, the floor was stone. From the way that light reflected off it, it looked like black marble or polished granite.

'Stop! Don't come any closer.'

Jasmine looked up again at Marilyn and saw that she was holding a chain. It was connected to a steel beam that ran the length of the room. She noticed that the chain was wound around Marilyn's neck with very little slack. 'If you take another step I'll jump off the stool,' she said, her voice steely. 'I'm going to do it anyway.'

'Now Mrs Taylor, Marilyn, can I call you that?'

'Marilyn or Mistress. Don't you dare call me by *his* name!'

'OK, Marilyn. You know why I'm here. I've been to your house. I've spoken to Mr Taylor, Kelvin.'

'That weak, snivelling sack!'

'He told me you had accepted responsibility for the death of Xristal Newman and Tilly Jones.'

'The Jones girl was an accident, the stupid bitch,' Marilyn spoke defiantly. 'Xristal...' her voice faltered, 'Xristal was different. I didn't want to kill her, but I had to.'

'That's good, Marilyn. You've admitted it. We can move on.' Jasmine stepped forward.

'I said, don't move!' The stool wobbled. Marilyn gripped the chain above her head. 'I won't go to prison!'

'OK, Marilyn. You've admitted you were responsible for Xristal's death. Come down. Let's get you out of here and get things sorted out.'

'I won't go to prison!' Marilyn shouted. 'All those women. I can't spend my life surrounded by women. I'm going to end it, now.' She bent her knees as if preparing to jump, the chain pulling taut on her neck.

Shit, she's really going to do it, Jasmine thought, I've got to stop her.

'OK, Marilyn, I'm staying here.' Jasmine put her feet together, hands by her side, hoping desperately that Tom would arrive soon. Then she remembered. She had forgotten to phone him and tell her where she was going. He would go to the Taylors' house first and have to get the address from Kelvin. Her phone was in her bag which she had dropped by the entrance. She would have to keep Marilyn talking, take her mind off killing herself.

'Talk to me, Marilyn. You said Tilly's death was an accident. Tell me about it.'

'She fell, banged her head. Pathetic little whore.'

'How, Marilyn? Why were you there?' Jasmine tentatively took a step forward.

'I went to tell her she was going to be evicted.'

'Why?'

'You told us she was living as a common prostitute. We couldn't have that.'

So it was my fault, Jasmine thought.

'What was her reaction?'

'She totally flipped. Started yelling at me. I went up to look at the top floor flat - Xristal's flat. She followed me up the stairs. She grabbed me. I pushed her off. She slipped, rolled down the stairs. I heard her head hit a step. She reached the ground in a heap and just stayed there.. It was obvious she was dead. So I left.'

'Did she say anything about Xristal? About you and Xristal?'

'No. She didn't know a thing, the little fuckwit.'

Jasmine took another step forward.

'Don't move!' Marilyn ordered, 'I said if you wanted my story you'd have to keep away from me. Go back to the door – now!' She tensed as if again preparing to jump.

'OK, Marilyn, I'm backing off,' Jasmine backed a couple of paces until she felt the wall behind her. 'Tell me about yourself, about you and Kelvin. He seems to love you.'

'Fat pig. He was no use as a sub.'

'A sub? You mean submissive? He was your sex slave?'

'Huh. He was no use for sex with his shrivelled little prick - he could barely get it up. Binding him, beating him, humiliating him gave me some pleasure, but I only married him for his money.'

So, the idolisation was all one-sided. Jasmine couldn't understand how a man could be successful in his career as Kelvin Taylor had been, and yet desire to be trampled on by his mistress.

'So, he didn't know you were a trans-woman?'

'No, not that it would have mattered to him. He wanted to be dominated and used – and to flaunt an attractive woman on his arm. I gave him what he wanted, but he couldn't satisfy me.'

'What do you want, Marilyn?'

'Cock!'

Jasmine almost fell back against the wall at the force of Marilyn's answer. The tiny ceiling lights dazzled her; she leaned forward to avoid the beam, searching Marilyn's face.

'I suppose you want to know my story?' Marilyn continued, calmer now. 'Well, I'll tell you before I end it all.'

'That's right, Marilyn. Tell me everything,' Jasmine said, praying that Tom or Patel or Sloane would arrive in time to help her stop Marilyn Taylor killing herself.

Marilyn straightened up on her stool. 'It was all about Xristal, you see. I loved her because she reminded me of myself. I was like her once, you see - a sexy girl with a big cock.'

She paused, as if waiting for Jasmine to react.

'Tell me about it,' Jasmine said, and took a half pace forward.

'I was a pretty boy with long hair who liked to dress as a girl. I kept it to myself until I was seventeen when my father found me dressed up. I was wearing my sexiest miniskirt and T-shirt with a bra stuffed out with tights. He slapped me round the face a few times and threw me out. He told me he never wanted to see me again. That suited me fine. I hitchhiked to London and wandered around until I found an address I'd come across in a porn mag. It was a club for trannies and other weirdoes. It was there I met my mistress.'

'You were a sub?' Another half step forward...

'Of course. You don't learn to be a Dom without being a sub first. My mistress taught me all I needed to know to become a Dom myself. She gave me lovely girls' clothes to wear when I was out and paid for me to get my tits done.'

'And you didn't mind what she did to you? The S & M?' One more step...

'Mind it? I loved it - the loss of control, the lack of responsibility - but I also knew that I would like to be in charge, to decide for myself when I would come and how I'd use my cock. You see, I found I enjoyed fucking both girls and boys.' She smiled.

'What did you do?' Another few inches...

'I left and went into business myself. I called myself Miss Adventure. I did well. The people who wanted to be subs, men and women, loved what I did to them, loved that I looked like a young sexy woman but had a stonking erection between my legs.'

'But that changed?' A discreet shuffle...

'Everything does, doesn't it? I was successful, but it's an expensive business. You need the right property, good equipment, new attractions all the time, payments to people who need to be kept happy, a few slaves to keep the place tidy and service the guests. My subs paid well, but I was never rich. It began to become a chore just keeping up.' She sounded as though she were running a corner shop.

'But you didn't give up being a dominatrix?'

'Oh, no. I couldn't give up being the one in charge. I decided to look for a partner with the finance. Someone who had the money to keep me in the style I wanted and who would appreciate my talents.'

'That sounds an unlikely mix.' Half a step...

'You'd be surprised. There are many powerful men who like to be subjugated from time to time. I wanted a man – a man that would marry me.'

'Wouldn't a civil partnership do?' Another creep forward...

'Not for the men I was after. They weren't gay. They needed a woman at their side, to give the outward impression of normality - whatever else they wanted to get up to in private.'

Marilyn seemed so absorbed in telling her life story that Jasmine felt able to take further small, slow steps forward.

'So, you had to become a woman?' With the Gender Recognition Act becoming law in 2004 Jasmine realised that Marilyn must have been able to complete her plan once she had a gender certificate. No-one would have suspected she had been a man as she would have had a new birth certificate.

'I already was in every way, except for my cock.'

'But you said you enjoyed using that. Surely you didn't want to have surgery?'

'I thought I was ready. I was approaching forty. Sex was less of a novelty and, in any case, I enjoyed being penetrated so long as I was in charge. I weighed up the options and took the decision. I had the chop.'

'And what happened then?'

'I realised I'd made a huge mistake.'

'But you married Kelvin. That was your plan, wasn't it?'

'Oh yes, that part went perfectly. I went back to work and soon had a number of clients who were marriage prospects. I chose Kelvin because he was the richest and had no family here - just the ex-wife and kids in Australia. He was older too, not very fit. I hoped he might die fairly quickly and leave me his money.'

'What went wrong?'

'He was boring - and he didn't die. My treatment of him gave him just enough exercise to keep him from eating and drinking himself to death. But he couldn't give me any satisfaction with his miniscule prick.'

'You couldn't get an orgasm? Is that what you mean?' Jasmine hoped that wasn't too sensitive a question.

Marilyn sighed. 'That was it.'

Jasmine was anticipating that sex-change surgery would leave her, like most trans-women, with the ability to reach orgasm, but it didn't work with everyone. Marilyn was obviously one of the unlucky ones.

'I was perpetually on the edge but never got there.' The frustration was evident in Marilyn's voice.

Jasmine was closer now, able to examine Marilyn's face and see the pain and anguish that was revealed there. She seemed totally wrapped up in telling her story.

'What did you do?'

'The only thing I knew how. I looked for other subs to fill the void that Kelvin left. I picked up men and women here and there who wanted an experience of domination, but it wasn't the same without my cock or the testosterone.'

'What about Xristal?'

'Ah, Xristal.' Marilyn's face took on an expression of ecstasy and she swayed slightly. Jasmine readied herself to leap forward and grab her. 'She was everything I had been. Together we were as I had been with my mistress. She took me back. When she was inside me it felt like the reverse and as if I had my penis back and was fucking this beautiful, submissive young girl.'

'But then?' Now Jasmine was just a pace from Marilyn.

'She told me she wanted to go away to have the chop, to become a full woman. She wanted to lose that wonderful tool she had. I couldn't bear it. She was going to make the same mistake I had made. I would lose her, lose the pleasure she gave me!' Marilyn cried and rocked from side to side, the stool wobbling and the chain tightening around her throat.

'I pleaded, but she wouldn't listen. I couldn't let her do it! I couldn't let her go away!'

'So, you killed her?' As Jasmine spoke she knew it was the wrong thing to say. She should have chosen her words more carefully.

Marilyn's eyes opened wide and she appeared to become aware of Jasmine standing less than a metre from her. 'You disobeyed me!' Her eyes bored into Jasmine. 'You're a fake, aren't you? You're no more a real woman than me. You may have had yours off - but you're still pretending to be a woman.'

'No, I'm still waiting.' Jasmine was taken aback that Marilyn had turned on her.

'Oh, you've still got it, have you? But it's not good for anything, is it? You're sexless, a eunuch.' Her cheeks were flushed, and drool was running down her chin. 'I didn't give you permission to approach me!' she screamed. 'Get back!'

Marilyn suddenly lashed out with her pointed-toe stiletto. The kick expressed all the regret, frustration and anger that her story had revealed. The sharp, leather-capped toe connected with Jasmine's groin. An electric shock, a lightning bolt, a grenade, all at once, speared up through her bowels and exploded in her head. She fell backwards, cracking her head on the stone floor. Darkness started to cloud her eyes, but through the roaring in her ears she heard other noises – a thud as something quite heavy fell to the floor, a brief cry and groan. Then there was silence.

Her head felt full of lead, her eyes wouldn't focus and it felt as if there was a red hot poker between her legs. There was liquid flowing down her legs. It couldn't be blood, surely blood wouldn't flow as fast. She didn't have that much blood in her – did she?

Jasmine rolled onto her front, the pain making her gasp. She pushed herself to her knees, crawled. Her knee slipped on slick liquid. Her blood? Her legs collapsed and she fell forward. She tried again but her body seemed to have stretched, her limbs had become distant and floppy. Somehow she dragged herself a few inches feeling as if she was swimming through crude oil. Her identity was dissolving, parts of her splitting off and floating away. Her head - it was only her head she had left - spun. She was tired, exhausted. Where did she want to go? What was she doing? Wouldn't it be nice to just sleep? Sleep...

11

TUESDAY EVENING

A knife slashing, cutting. Her windpipe blocked. No air to breathe. Tightly bound.

No, that was in the past. A recurring nightmare stored deep in her psyche. Now there was the recent memory of agony. She remembered pain in her groin. And blood, her blood, pouring from her.

There was no pain now, just a dull discomfort between her legs and a tiredness in her limbs. Then Jasmine remembered...the operation...Marilyn Taylor's story...her savage kick... the pain and blood. All memories now, like that thud on the stone floor and the brief cry. What had that been?

There was light beyond her eyelids. She half-opened them, fearing a bright light. A pale wall in front of her, daylight from her left. She knew this place. She had been here or somewhere similar before.

'Jasmine? Are you awake?' Angela's voice. Angela?

She opened her eyes, turned her head to the right. Angela was leaning over her.

'Oh, you *are* awake. Are you comfortable?'

Jasmine nodded her head almost imperceptibly, still trying to summon the energy to speak. She started to push against the mattress with her hands and feet. Something was impeding her left arm.

'No, don't try to move, Jasmine. You're hooked up to the machine.'

Jasmine looked to the left and saw her arm encumbered with tubes.

'You lost a lot of blood, Jas,' Angela went on.

'Hospital?' Jasmine could only manage the one word, her mouth was so dry and she felt so tired.

'Yes.'

'Again?'

'Yes, Jas. You need to learn to look after yourself.'

'Tom?'

'Yes. Tom saved you – again. He found you bleeding to death.'

'Marilyn?'

'What?'

'Marilyn Taylor?'

'The woman in the basement?'

Jasmine nodded.

'Um. I don't know.'

Angela sounded uncertain. Did she really not know? What had happened after Marilyn delivered her kick.

'Would you like a drink?'

Jasmine nodded again. Angela held a cup to her lips, and carefully tipped it. Some water trickled down her neck but most went into her mouth. Her tongue became unstuck from the roof of her mouth. She swallowed. That felt better, almost normal.

'You came.' The remembered strain of their last parting was like a heavy weight on her chest.

'Tom rang me as soon as they got you in the ambulance. He thought it looked pretty serious.'

Jasmine had no recollection of Tom finding her or of an ambulance or of arriving at the hospital. There was nothing after the kick that Marilyn Taylor delivered. I must have been completely out, she thought. Perhaps it was pretty serious. She felt OK now though; no pain. Her mind seemed to be clearing. She was just so tired. Why? She hadn't done anything energetic. Was it loss of blood?

'They've given you a lot of blood, Jas, but you're going to be fine. Go to sleep. It'll be dark soon.'

Dark soon? Was it evening? Jasmine wondered how long

she'd been out. But already her eyes were feeling heavy and it didn't seem worth the bother to make any more conversation.

Had she slept? It didn't seem like more than a few moments since she had closed her eyes. She opened them again. She saw the same wall as she had seen the last time she awoke. Now though there was bright sunshine streaming in from the window on the left.

'Morning, Jasmine.' For some reason she had expected Angela's voice, but this was a man. A man with a Birmingham accent. Viv. She turned her head and saw his dark face grinning down at her.

'You're awake. That's great.'

'Angela? She was here,' Jasmine muttered, but finding her voice becoming stronger.

'She was. She was here all night. She's just gone off to have a shower and freshen up.'

'And you?'

'I just got here. I got a bit frantic to tell you the truth. I got back yesterday afternoon to find you weren't in and your car gone. You weren't supposed to be out and about.'

'I got a call.'

'So I heard. When you didn't turn up, I guessed something had cropped up so I phoned the police station. They didn't want to tell me, but it was obvious that there'd been something going off. I finally persuaded them to give my number to that ex-colleague of yours, Shepherd. He rang me last night and told me you were in here.'

'Thanks for coming.'

'I came last night. Angela was here. Said you were going to be all right. You were asleep.'

'Oh, I see.' Jasmine struggled to imagine Angela and Viv sitting beside her bed while she slept, oblivious.

'Shepherd looked in as well. We had a bit of a chat about you. Angela said she was going to stay. So I've had a night's sleep and now had better get off to work. Glad I've seen you awake, though. You're looking better than you did last night.'

Jasmine saw that the tubes had been removed from her except for the thin leads to sensors stuck to her chest. She felt almost normal this morning, except for a constriction around her groin. She felt carefully. There was a thick dressing between her legs and around her thighs. Obviously, she wasn't completely right then.

'Thanks, Viv. It's lovely to see you. Thank you for being concerned.'

'I was. We all were.'

'Seeing Angela here surprised me.'

'I told you she was a great girl.'

'But when she went…' When was it? Monday. It was only Wednesday today wasn't it?

'I said you'd get back together.'

'But we can't. She needs a man. I can't give her what she wants anymore.' Tears clouded Jasmine's eyes.

'Of course not. But you can be friends. Close friends. Women friends.'

'I'll get in the way.'

'No, you won't. That Luke twat was a bigoted fool, but Angela will find a guy who can accommodate her friendship with you. She's an intelligent woman. She'll work it out. Just give her time. But she'll always be there for you. You've shared so much.'

'You seem to know a lot, Viv.'

'We had quite a chat last night, Jas.'

'Oh.'

The door opened and a doctor entered, followed by a nurse.

'Good morning, Miss Frame,' the doctor said. She was young, slim, with short brown hair and a broad smile. 'We need to check you over.'

'Oh, I'll be going then,' Viv said, getting to his feet. 'I'll drop by later. See how you're doing.' He bent down and planted a kiss on Jasmine's forehead before leaving.

'Your boyfriend?' the doctor asked.

Boyfriend? Jasmine had only ever considered the idea in her fantasies. Was Viv really a boyfriend? They'd visited each other, been out on a date, he'd kissed her a couple of times. But - boyfriend?

'A close friend,' she said.

'Ah,' the doctor said approaching the side of the bed and peering at the monitor. She turned to face her. Jasmine noticed her name badge which read Dr Katie Armitage. 'You seem to be back to normal, Miss Frame, but we are going to keep you in for a day or two. Perhaps you don't realise what happened to you yesterday?'

Jasmine shook her head.

'You ruptured the sutures in your scrotum and haemorrhaged severely. We've sewn you up, but we need to keep an eye on you to make sure you don't tear them again. Obviously we had to replace the blood you lost. Oh, and we replaced the false testicle which was missing.'

Jasmine could only remember the pain and the gushing blood after Marilyn had kicked out at her. She hadn't felt one of the balls drop out.

'So we're going to keep you quiet until you are really healing. Then, no more chasing after criminals. Not for a few weeks anyway.'

Dr Armitage seemed to know the full story, perhaps more than Jasmine herself knew. She nodded and resigned herself to days of boredom.

'Nurse Grainger will check your dressing and I'll look in on you later to see that you're feeling OK.'

'Thanks, doctor.' Despite not relishing lying in bed for an extended period, Jasmine wanted to express her gratitude as she did feel truly thankful. These people had saved her when she was possibly bleeding to death. 'Thank you for looking after me,' she added with more feeling.

'My pleasure.' The doctor left and the nurse pulled down the sheets covering Jasmine. She lifted the hem of the hospital gown to examine the mound of dressing that protected her genitalia.

Jasmine experienced her usual feeling of shame at being looked at. She hoped that would disappear when she "looked right" down there.

'It looks fine. If you need to go to the loo, we'll fix it for you. Just try not to move too much.'

She covered her up again and then left, leaving Jasmine alone with her thoughts for the first time since she had come round. What had happened when Marilyn kicked her? Had it damaged her chances of having the full gender reassignment? She would have to ask Dr Armitage when she returned. Lying with her head on the pillow, she wondered how long she would have to stay like this. Surely she'd soon be allowed to sit up, get up and move about, even if they might have to monitor her to prevent her damaging herself again.

The door opened and Angela came in, followed by the towering figure of Tom Shepherd.

'Viv said you had woken up, Jas,' Angela said, hurrying to her side and planting a kiss on her cheek. She sat in the chair that Viv had vacated. Tom loomed over her.

'Find a chair, Tom. You're straining my neck.'

'I see you've recovered then,' Tom said as he went to collect a chair from the other side of the room. He carried it over and sat down next to Angela.

'How are you feeling this morning?' Angela asked.

'I feel fine. A bit tender down below.'

'I'm not surprised. You wouldn't believe how much blood there was when I found you.' Tom said.

'I was out of it by then,' Jasmine said.

'I know. I thought you'd gone. You hardly had a pulse but the paramedic was there in no time, and the ambulance. They got you back, I'm glad to say. But you are an idiot. What were you doing haring off to the Taylors' when you were supposed to be recuperating?'

'I didn't stop to think,' Jasmine admitted, 'When I dropped off Honey Potts, DC Patel mentioned a Jaguar at the Bredon Road flats and it suddenly came to me where I'd seen one before.'

'So you rushed off to check it out?'

'Yes. I did send you a message.'

'Just as well you did. You didn't when you went off to find Marilyn Taylor.'

'No. Sorry. I was too keen to get some answers.'

'Well, I hope you got them.'

'Why? Hasn't Marilyn given a statement?'

'She can't. She's dead.'

Tom's answer hit Jasmine like a punch in the stomach. The moment she was kicked replayed in her mind - the thud of something hitting the stone floor, the cry that was cut off abruptly. 'So, she hanged herself?'

'Yes. When we got there you were unconscious in a pool of blood and Marilyn Taylor was dangling by her neck with a stool on its side a couple of feet away.'

'I found her with the chains wound round her neck and she was standing on the stool. I thought she was about to do it then, but she was keen to talk. I got close,' Jasmine recited, 'She kicked out at me and caught me, uh, where I'd had the surgery. She must have lost her balance and knocked the stool over.'

'That sounds like it. She broke her neck.'

'It was my fault. I'd tried to get close enough to grab her to stop her jumping off that stool, but when she kicked me I collapsed on the floor. She died because I couldn't help her.'

'Oh, Jasmine. It's not your fault,' Angela said.

To Jasmine it felt very much as if it was. A police officer's job is to protect people – from themselves as well as others. If she hadn't gone dashing off on her own, if she'd let Tom or Patel or Hopkins - or even Sloane himself - follow up the lead, perhaps Marilyn Taylor would still be alive and able to tell her story in court.

'She probably would have done it anyway,' Tom said, 'She had enough chain wound around her neck.'

'She said she was going to.'

'Well, there you are.'

'But I wasn't sure she really meant it.'

'From what Taylor told us she seemed pretty twisted. Don't beat yourself up about her.'

'You closed the case,' Angela said.

'With three deaths not just the one,' Jasmine sighed.

'But Marilyn Taylor talked to you?' Tom asked.

'Oh, yes,' Jasmine nodded, 'she told me the whole story about herself, her relationship with Xristal and why Tilly died.' Another death she was responsible for.

'Tilly is my fault too,' Jasmine added.

'Why?' Tom and Angela asked together.

'Because I told the Taylors that she was working as a prostitute at the flat and Marilyn went to tell her she was being evicted.'

'That's just an excuse,' Tom said, 'Taylor has told us that they knew what Tilly was up to before *we* – that's you and me - mentioned it. Marilyn Taylor was just trying to pass her guilt on to you.'

'There you see, Jas. It's not your fault and that woman was to blame for all the deaths, including her own,' Angela took Jasmine's hand in hers and squeezed it.

'Thanks, Ange,' Jasmine said sadly, 'I know you're right, but there's still the feeling that three people are dead who shouldn't be.'

'You're a detective, Jas, not someone who can magically manage people's lives.'

'Hmm, some detective. Thrashing around getting nowhere and then getting the answers when it's too late.'

'Well, at least we have solved this case,' Tom said. 'Look, I'm sorry Jas, but we'll have to get a detailed statement from you as soon as you feel you're up to it so we can close the file on this one. You know what Sloane is like for wrapping things up.'

'And what am I like, Shepherd?'

Tom leapt to his feet as Jasmine looked up to see the grey-suited bulk of Chief Inspector Sloane filling the doorway. 'Glad to see you back with us, Frame,' he said in his deep growl of a voice.

What the hell's he here for? Jasmine wondered. Surely not to enquire after her health. She couldn't think what to say to him.

'Have my seat, sir,' Tom said gesturing to the chair he had vacated.

'No, I won't sit. Just called to see how Frame was and make sure you got back to work, Shepherd.'

'Yes, sir.' Although Tom was a few inches taller than his boss he suddenly seemed like a schoolboy bunking off from lessons.

'Now then, Frame. I believe you have quite a story to tell us. Not just about this Taylor woman, but also about how that Potts character came to hand herself in while Shepherd and I were scurrying around the country looking for the dead girl's clients.'

Jasmine noticed Tom looking at her accusingly. 'That's right, Jas. You didn't tell us you had located Honey Potts.'

'I'll explain it all,' Jasmine said. How angry was Sloane? He was not likely to approve of the manner in which she had pursued her side of the investigation while keeping the rest of the team in the dark.

'I should hope so,' Sloane said, 'I'll send someone to take your statement. Not immediately, but as soon as you've recovered a little.'

'Thank you,' Jasmine found herself saying.

'Come on then, Shepherd. You have a report to write.' Sloane turned away.

'Yes, sir.' Tom started to follow obediently, but paused and turned back to Jasmine. 'I'll look in later. See how you're doing. By the way, when we searched that basement flat we found a laptop and handbag.'

'You mean Xristal's?'

'Yes. Her phone was in the bag along with the tickets for her return flight to Bangkok'

'So she did have it all arranged?' Jasmine said.

'Seems like it.' Tom put a hand in his jacket pocket. 'Oh, and we found this when we searched the flat. We think it may be yours.' He lobbed something into Jasmine's lap. She grabbed hold of it and picked it up to examine it. It was a hard, white plastic ball. Tom hurried after his departing boss.

'What is it?' Angela asked.

'Um,' Jasmine hesitated, 'I lost it when Marilyn kicked me. It fell out.'

'Oh!' Angela giggled, 'Is it a false testicle?'

'Yes,' Jasmine said, feeling the colour rise up her cheeks.

'Well, you can keep it as a spare or as a souvenir,' Angela said grinning. Jasmine felt her cheeks burning.

'I hope I won't need a spare and I don't think I will need much reminding of this case.' She closed her hand around the hard plastic sphere, hiding it from view. Her other hand rested on the mound in the bedclothes covering her padded groin.

'I'll see if I can get some breakfast for you. You must be hungry.' Angela said, rising from her seat.

Jasmine was barely aware of Angela leaving the room as she was absorbed in her thoughts. She rolled the ball around in her hand. It was certainly a memento of what she'd been through - not that she wanted any more reminders. Perhaps she wouldn't have to keep the inanimate objects between her legs for long. How she wished she could complete her gender reassignment and fulfil her wish to be a woman at last. That was what Xristal had wanted and what Marilyn had succeeded in achieving - except that in her case it had not turned out to be all that she had hoped for.

Jasmine lay on her bed, idly flicking the pages of a magazine Angela had bought her. She had only been awake a few hours but she was already bored. At least she was wearing a proper nightie now - another purchase by Angela – and her dressing had been redone so that she could go for a pee herself. She still felt unsteady on her feet and walked like a penguin with the thick padding between her legs, but she felt much better. The excitement of breakfast and lunch had passed and Angela had gone home for a while so she was left to entertain herself, which was something she had never been good at if there was no work to do.

The sound of the door opening drew her eyes from a not very informative article about female sexuality.

'Hello, Jasmine,' DC Patel said, pausing in the doorway

'Oh, hi.' Jasmine said, tossing the magazine to the side of the bed. 'Come and have a seat.   Are you here to take my statement?' She felt a burst of excitement. Relating her part in the investigation would be far more interesting than any magazine article.

'Yes, but I'm going to get a coffee first. Would you like one?'

'Yes, please. Black no sugar.'

'Right. Oh, there's someone else here to see you.'   Patel backed through the door. Jasmine wondered who else could possibly wish to see her. She gasped and giggled when she got the answer. Honey Potts bustled in wearing the same outfit she had been in the previous morning. Her denim skirt and blue silk blouse looked creased and stained as she minced in on her stiletto heels, but at least she looked cool and calm today. Jasmine winced when she saw the shoes as they were the same red colour and similar style to those worn by Marilyn Taylor.

'Hello, Honey. This is a surprise. Come and have a seat.'

Honey wobbled across the room and sat down heavily on the chair beside the bed, her large breasts bouncing up and down independently.

'Are you OK?' Honey asked. There seemed to be genuine concern on her face.

'Yes, I'm fine,' Jasmine replied.

'Really. And your tackle? They told me you ruptured and lost a lot of blood.'

'Yeah. They've stitched me back up and now they're making sure I don't do anything to tear them again.'

'Good. So you're OK for your vaginoplasty?'

'The doctor says I'm OK. I've still got to wait till my number comes up.'   Doctor Armitage had indeed reassured Jasmine when she had called in during the afternoon, but an appointment for the surgery to provide her with a vagina was still a distant dream.

'Good. The police officer, what's her name, Patel, told me what had happened to you.'

'When did they release you?'

'A half hour ago. I've been sitting in a cell since yesterday evening waiting for them to let me go. At least they loaned me a razor so I didn't have to leave with a day's growth.'

'Did they question you?'

'Oh yes. After you dropped me off at the station. That other detective, Hopkins, gave me a grilling first. I don't think he likes people like me – or you.'

Jasmine recalled the frosty, almost phobic, response she had had from DC Hopkins. 'I don't think his diversity training took that well.'

Honey chortled 'Perhaps he needs to meet a few more of us. Anyway, after a while they all got called away. When they came back their mood was different, as if I was just filling in a few gaps for them.'

'That would have been after we found out that Marilyn Taylor was responsible for the deaths.'

'Xristal and Tilly?'

'Yes.' Jasmine told Honey what Marilyn had said.

'So, Marilyn Taylor had been like me and Xristal?'

'Yes, except that she took to domination as her way of getting her kicks and making a living.'

'Don't fancy it myself, though they do a bit at the club.'

'I saw.'

'But she had the full change done like Xristal wanted. Like you want?'

'Yes, but then discovered it wasn't what she wanted after all. Perhaps because the surgery didn't work properly so she couldn't have an orgasm.'

'I don't have any sympathy for her because of what she did to Xristal, but I can imagine her frustration.'

'It was no excuse.' Jasmine said. But she may still be alive if I'd let the police know where she was, she thought.

'She sounds like a mad bitch. I'm just so angry and sorry that Xristal got mixed up with her.' Honey's eyes blazed. 'If only I'd kept more of an eye on her clients. If only I'd understood what she wanted.'

'You've got a couple of "if onlys" to go with a few of my own.'

Honey gave Jasmine a questioning look. 'I know. But it's too late to have regrets.'

'So what are you going to do now?' Jasmine asked.

Honey was thoughtful for a moment. 'Head back to London, I suppose. On with the show, as they say.'

'I expect that's what Xristal would have wanted you to do.'

'Yeah. I'm sorry she won't be there. We could have been a great double act... stupid me. There I go again. Thinking everyone wants to be like me. It wasn't what she wanted in the end. She wanted to be woman, like you.'

'Apparently. Be yourself. Isn't that what everyone says?'

'Yeah.' Honey smiled.

'So, do you have any plans for yourself?

'Plans?'

'Cosmetic.'

'Oh, I see what you mean. There's always a list; a nip and a tuck here and there. I have to watch the ageing now. I need to keep my good looks, don't I?' Honey sat up straight, thrusting out her breasts, tousling her long blonde hair and fluttering her long false eyelashes.

Jasmine laughed so hard that she felt a twinge in her groin. 'Stop or they'll have to take me into surgery again!' she cried.

'What's so funny?' Honey grinned. 'Don't you have plans for yourself, too?'

That made Jasmine think. She was one more step along her path to womanhood but there were many more to come.

'Well, I hope that now my body will react to the hormones and make me more feminine, but most of all I hope I don't have to wait too long for the gender reassignment. But I might still need electrolysis, breast augmentation, larynx surgery.'

'Sounds like quite a list.'

Perhaps it was. Were they all necessary to give her the female body she desired? Maybe.

'I just want to be me.'

'Don't we all,' Honey said nodding, 'but some of us have to work extra hard to get the body we have designs on.'

The End.

ACKNOWLEDGEMENTS

Jasmine Frame was introduced in my first crime novel, *Painted Ladies*. In that story she was at an early stage in her transition from male to female. It is a difficult process that can take many years. *Bodies By Design* picks up Jasmine's story a little later and there are other novels in the pipeline that follow Jasmine through the later stages of the change. There are also prequels revealing Jasmine's formative years both as a transsexual and a detective.

For the background to these stories I would like to thank the many trans-people I know or have heard or read about that have gone through the process and who each contribute a little to Jasmine and the other trans men and women who appear in the stories. While I have some idea of what they have gone through I have not experienced it all myself.

In the production of this book I would first like to thank my agent, Sara Keane for knocking my draft into shape; Peter and Alison at Alnpete PrePress for their work in preparing the manuscript for printing, including answering my many no doubt naïve questions; Scott Wood for the cover design and Barbara Addyman for the final proofreading.

Finally, as ever I would like to thank Lou for her support, not least in encouraging the expenditure on getting BBD into print and online, but for being my first and best critic.

To everyone who purchased *Painted Ladies* and this novel – thank you. I hope you enjoy this volume just as much and that you look forward to acquiring the other Jasmine Frame stories. To those of you discovering Jasmine for the first time I hope you too will go on to read the other novels and novellas in the series.

P R Ellis

LOOK OUT FOR

The Brides' Club Murder
The 3rd Jasmine Frame novel

It is November, a few months after the events of *Bodies by Design*. DS Tom Shepherd, Jasmine Frame's former buddy and colleague, has been called to an incident at the Ashmore Lodge Hotel on the outskirts of Kintbridge, where the participants are assembling for a convention.

… Tom arrived at the suite at a gallop, panting just a little having ascended the stairs three steps at a time. He scudded to a halt as he entered the lounge. DC Patel and Sarah Winslade were standing in the middle of the room dominated by the grey-suited bulk of DCI Sloane.

'Ah, Shepherd. There you are,' Sloane said as soon as Tom entered the room. 'Dr Winslade tells me we have a murder rather clumsily disguised as suicide.'

'That's my suggestion,' Sarah Winslade said gently, 'I'll be more certain when I've got the body back to the lab.'

'I gather that there is some kind of convention going on here of which the victim was a member,' Sloane continued.

'Yes, Sir,' Tom answered. 'It's a weekend for transgender people.'

Sloane appeared mystified, then his top lip curled. 'You mean it's a gathering of transvestites? People like Frame?'

'Well, I think some are transsexual like Jasmine, Sir, but most of them are men who like to dress up as women.'

'Some have their wives or partners with them,' DC Patel added.

'But I gather this Vokins fellow belonged to a group called the Wedding Belles. Is that right, Shepherd?'

'So I'm told, Sir.'

'Are they part of the entertainment or something?'

'No, Sir, they are men who wear wedding dresses.' Tom observed Sloane's neck take on a shade of pink. 'I don't fully understand it, Sir,' Tom added quickly.

'Hmph. Well I suggest you do so very quickly if you're going to solve this crime, Shepherd. How do you propose to organise the investigation?'

'Me, Sir.'

'Yes, you, Shepherd. You're the investigating officer. I have other tasks to attend to. So let me have your plan. I presume you are going to lock down the hotel.'

Tom felt a quiver of nervousness pass through him. 'Actually Sir, I think it would be best to let the convention go ahead so that we keep all the potential suspects and witnesses close. We'll let them think we are just investigating the suicide while we question them.'

Sloane nodded slowly. 'I understand Shepherd. You are hoping the killer is going to hide amongst the crowd thinking that his or her subterfuge has been successful and at some point will drop his guard and reveal himself.'

'Er, something like that Sir.' Sloane's agreement gave Tom some confidence.

'A suicide investigation will require a lower key style of interrogation,' Sloane continued.

'Yes, Sir.'

'And fewer officers.'

'Yes Sir.'

'But you have limited time. I presume this "weekend" you refer to is just that.'

'Yes, Sir.'

'You need someone on the inside, a person who will talk to these transvestites as one of themselves and so perhaps overhear a clue to the perpetrator's identity.'

Tom wondered where the DCI was headed. 'Umm, I think I follow, Sir.'

'Get on to Frame,' Sloane said firmly. 'Get her here as one of the participants, a Wedding Belle. She can get to know the people closest to the victim.'

PAINTED LADIES

A JASMINE FRAME STORY

P.R.ELLIS

Read the first novel in the Jasmine Frame series.

Painted Ladies

A Jasmine Frame Story

Jasmine Frame was scared of knives when she was a policeman. Now she finds herself on the trail of a knife killer, but it's not just her skin that is in danger. Her identity as a woman is under threat.

Praise for *Painted Ladies*

…Jasmine is a very engaging character, well written and believable. Her emotions and feelings are central to the book and, I hope, will shed light on a situation that cannot be easy to accept and live with in face of everyday prejudice. However, this is a crime novel and stands on its own as such. I found it a page-turner and really enjoyed reading it…

Susan White, Eurocrime

…*Painted Ladies* is the first literary examination, that we have seen, of the trans community in the role of both detective and victim, a rare and exquisite treat…

Jake Basford, So So Gay Magazine

Purchase *Painted Ladies* paperback for £8.99 inc. postage and packing by ordering from:

paintedladiesnovel@btinternet.com

Painted Ladies is also available as an e-book.

Find out more about Jasmine Frame at:

www.ellifont.wordpress.com

DISCOVERING
JASMINE

A JASMINE FRAME STORY

7'0"
6'0"
5'0"
4'0"
3'0"
2'0"
1'0"

P R ELLIS

Discovering Jasmine
A Jasmine Frame story

James Frame is seventeen and enjoying his last summer holiday while at school. That means using the absence of his parents and his older sister, Holly, to dress up as girl and call himself Jasmine. He is discovering the power of his urge to be female and wondering whether it is just dressing up or whether he is transsexual. But discovery comes in other forms and venturing out he finds himself drawn into a case that tests his character as well as his need to be Jasmine.

Discovering Jasmine is available as an e-book on kindle and other platforms, or in pdf to download for free from ellifont:

www.ellifont.wordpress.com

or order from:

paintedladiesnovel@btinternet.com

Each week there is a new episode in the current Jasmine Frame prequel (all the action takes place before the events of *Painted Ladies*).

Stories serialised so far:

Blueprint

James Frame has just begun working for DCI Sloane in the Violent and Serious Crime Unit based at Kintbridge Police Station in Berkshire and spends his spare time dressed as Jasmine. When James is called to investigate a suicide he suspects there is more to the death than is immediately apparent. He finds that Jasmine is needed to investigate the case, which means he must reveal his double life to his colleague DC Tom Shepherd and DCI Sloane. The trail leads from Kintbridge to Manchester and James/Jasmine faces decisions about his future as a man or woman.

Self-portraits

Jasmine Frame is on leave from the police service as she starts her transition to full time life as a woman. While out jogging she comes across a teenage boy being attacked by a gang. Befriending the boy draws her into a murder mystery that means she must disobey her boss DCI Sloane and antagonise her colleagues in the Violent and Serious Crime Unit.

Read more Jasmine Frame stories at:
www.ellifont.wordpress.com

Each week there is a new episode in the current Jasmine Frame prequel (all the action takes place before the events of *Painted Ladies*).

Stories serialised so far:

Discovering Jasmine

James Frame is seventeen and enjoying his last summer holiday while at school. That means using the absence of his parents and his older sister, Holly, to dress up as girl and call himself Jasmine. He is discovering the power of his urge to be female and wondering whether it is just dressing up or whether he is transsexual. But discovery comes in other forms and venturing out he finds himself drawn into a case that tests his character as well as his need to be Jasmine.

Discovering Jasmine is now available as an e-book and pdf.

Close-up

Jasmine is back on duty having started her transition and finding that her colleagues in the Violent and Serious Crime Unit are sidelining her for the interesting jobs. Nevertheless when a child is snatched in Kintbridge High Street Jasmine's investigations show that the case is not as straightforward as it appears. She comes up against DS Denise Palmerston, DCI Sloane's new deputy, who does not want Jasmine working on the case. Nevertheless Jasmine makes some startling discoveries.

Read more Jasmine Frame stories at:
www.ellifont.wordpress.com

Each week there is a new episode in the current Jasmine Frame prequel (all the action takes place before the events of *Painted Ladies*).

Stories serialised so far:

Soft Focus

James Frame is in his first term at Bristol University and wondering whether the freedom of student life means he can reveal the female side of his character. A friend in the LGBT society persuades Jasmine to venture out and meet other students. He meets Angela who finds James/Jasmine dual nature fascinating. When one of his new acquaintances dies, James/Jasmine feels (s)he must investigate – with Angela by his/her side.

Split Mirror

Jasmine has finally split up from Angela but is distracted from the task of unpacking in her flat by the report of a missing person. DS Palmerston does not think it is a case for the Violent and Serious Crime Unit but Jasmine investigates nevertheless. The trail leads her to sordid activities at a layby some miles outside Kintbridge and to discoveries that mean she must fight for her place in the Unit.

Volume 1 of Evil Above the Stars

Seventh Child

Peter R. Ellis

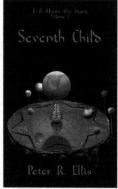

September Weekes is accustomed to facing teasing and bullying because of her white hair, tubby figure and silly name, but the discovery of a clear, smooth stone at her home casts her into a struggle between good and evil that will present her with sterner challenges.

The stone takes her to *Gwlad*, the Land, where the people hail her as the *Cludydd o Maengolauseren*, the bearer of the starstone, with the power to defend them against the evil known as the Malevolence. September meets the people's leader, the *Mordeyrn Aurddolen*, and the bearers of the seven metals linked to the seven 'planets'. Each metal gives the bearer specialised powers to resist the manifestations of the Malevolence, formed from the four elements of earth, air, fire and water, such as the comets known as *Draig tân*, fire dragons.

She returns to her home, but is drawn back to the Land a fortnight later to find that two years have passed and the villagers have experienced more destructive attacks by manifestations. September must now help defend *Gwlad* against the Malevolence.

Seventh Child is the first volume in the thrilling fantasy series, *Evil Above the Stars*, by Peter R. Ellis, that appeals to readers, of all ages, of fantasy or science fiction, especially fans of JRR Tolkien and Stephen Donaldson. If old theories are correct until a new idea comes along, does the universe change with our perception of it? Were the ideas embodied in alchemy ever right? What realities were the basis of Celtic mythology?

ISBN: 9781908168702 (epub, kindle)
ISBN: 9781908168603 (256pp paperback)

Visit bit.ly/EvilAbove

Volume 2 of Evil Above the Stars

The Power of Seven
Peter R. Ellis

September Weekes found a smooth stone which took her to *Gwlad*, the Land, where the people hailed her as the *Cludydd o Maengolauseren*, the bearer of the starstone, with the power to defend them against the evil known as the Malevolence. Now, having reached Arsyllfa she is re-united with the *Mordeyrn Aurddolen* with whom, together with the other senior metal bearers that make up the Council of *Gwlad*, she must plan the defence of the Land.

The time of the next Conjunction will soon be at hand. The planets, the Sun and the Moon will all be together in the sky. At that point the protection of the heavenly bodies will be at its weakest and *Gwlad* will be more dependent than ever on September. But now it seems that she must defeat Malice, the guiding force behind the Malevolence, if she is to save the Land and all its people. Will she be strong enough; and, if not, to whom can she turn for help?

The Power of Seven is the second volume in the thrilling fantasy series, *Evil Above the Stars*, by Peter R. Ellis, that appeals to readers, of all ages, of fantasy or science fiction, especially fans of JRR Tolkien and Stephen Donaldson. If old theories are correct until a new idea comes along, does the universe change with our perception of it? Were the ideas embodied in alchemy ever right? What realities were the basis of Celtic mythology?

ISBN: 9781908168719 (epub, kindle)
ISBN: 9781908168610 (288pp paperback)

Visit bit.ly/EvilAbove

Volume 3 of Evil Above the Stars

Unity of Seven
Peter R. Ellis

September is back home and it is still the night of her birthday, despite her having spent over three months in *Gwlad* battling the Malevolence at the seventh conjunction of the planets. She no longer has the *Maengolauseren* nor the powers it gave her. It is back to facing the bullies at school and her struggles with her weight and studies, but she worries about how well the people of *Gwlad* have recovered from the terror of the Malevolence. She is also unsure what happened to Malice/Mairwen as the *Cemegwr* said that *Toddfa penbaladr*, the universal solvent, would join the twins together. Is Malice inside her? Could she turn to evil?

She must discover a way to return to the universe of *Gwlad* and the answer seems to lie in her family history. The five *Cludydds* before September and her mother were her ancestors. The clues take her on a journey in time and space which reveals that while in great danger she is also the key to the survival of all the universes. September must overcome her own fears, accept an extraordinary future and, once again, face the evil above the stars.

Unity of Seven is the third volume in the thrilling fantasy series, *Evil Above the Stars*, by Peter R. Ellis, that appeals to readers, of all ages, of fantasy or science fiction, especially fans of JRR Tolkien and Stephen Donaldson. If old theories are correct until a new idea comes along, does the universe change with our perception of it? Were the ideas embodied in alchemy ever right? What realities were the basis of Celtic mythology?

Unity of Seven will be available in digital and print editions in 2016

Visit bit.ly/EvilAbove

About the Author

P R Ellis was supposed to be a mysterious figure, an author whose gender was not readily apparent. That ended with the publicity for *Painted Ladies*. Now it can be revealed that it is Penny or Peter Ellis. That's right two names because I live in two/both genders. I was born Peter and have lived my life largely male, happily married to Lou and for 35 years a chemistry teacher. Now retired I live in Leominster and spend most of my time writing fiction although still enjoying science and chemistry. During my life I discovered an urge to be female and revealed this to Lou in 2000. Since then I have developed as Penny and now spend some of my time in female mode. Changes in society and being retired means that I can reveal my dual nature, although I feel I am one person. Jasmine is transsexual and wishes to transition permanently. My feelings are not the same hence Jasmine is not me and the stories are not autobiographical although some of her opinions are mine and some of the situations she finds herself in have happened to other trans people.

. . . .

Finally, if the reader has been affected by the issues associated with transgenderism, as described in this story, there are a number of organisations that can give advice and support, particularly the Beaumont Society. See the website www.beaumontsociety.org.uk or phone the information line 01582 412220.